ARKHAM HORROR

It is the height of the Roaring Twenties – a fresh enthusiasm for the arts, science, and exploration of the past have opened doors to a wider world, and beyond...

And yet, a dark shadow grows over the town of Arkham. Alien entities known as Ancient Ones lurk in the emptiness beyond space and time, writhing at the thresholds between worlds.

Occult rituals must be stopped and alien creatures destroyed before the Ancient Ones make our world their ruined dominion.

Only a handful of brave souls with inquisitive minds and the will to act stand against the horrors threatening to tear this world apart.

Will they prevail?

ALSO AVAILABLE IN ARKHAM HORROR

ARKHAM HORROR™

The RAVENING DEEP

TIM PRATT

ACONYTE

First published by Aconyte Books in 2023

ISBN 978 1 83908 241 2

Ebook ISBN 978 1 83908 249 2

Cover art by John Coulthart

Distributed in North America by Simon & Schuster Inc, New York, USA

Printed in the United States of America

9 8 7 6 5 4 3 2 1

ACONYTE BOOKS

An imprint of Asmodee Entertainment Ltd

Mercury House, Shipstones Business Centre

North Gate, Nottingham NG7 7FN, UK

aconytebooks.com // twitter.com/aconytebooks

*For the Wayne County Public Library,
where as a teenager I first read
Lovecraft and Chambers
and Leiber and Bloch*

BOOK ONE

PROPHET, HUNTRESS, THIEF

CHAPTER ONE
The Prophet

There was a time when Abel Davenport looked at the sea and felt wonder. Now, as he stood on the rocking deck of his beat-up trawler, the *Hydra*, and watched a storm flick fingers of lightning toward him from the southwest, he felt only a sense of impending doom… but even that was mingled with relief. When the doom came, at last, you were finally finished. You didn't have to keep fighting anymore. When the ship at last went down, it would stay down, and all would be quiet.

A huge swell lifted the boat high and tipped it hard to one side, but Abel kept his feet. He'd been working on fishing boats since he was a boy, first going out with his father, who'd fished these same cold New England waters, and as an adult he'd made his entire living on the water.

He just hadn't expected to finish living before he turned thirty-five.

For years Abel had run the *Hydra* with a crew of four, but that was before his mother's medical bills and funeral expenses, before the engine failures and shipworm, before the termites ate half the house and the bank ate the rest. Before that terrible month this season when every haul brought in fish that were inexplicably rotting, or had too many eyes, or too few.

He shuddered at the memory of a monstrous four-foot-long monkfish with vestigial arms tipped by weakly gripping hands. He'd kept that one, overcoming his revulsion, hoping to sell it to some college professor or maybe to a sideshow, but it turned into unidentifiable slime and bones before the ship was halfway back to port.

Abel had to let the other men go, one at a time, reluctantly, when he could no longer cover their wages, not even by cutting his own. You couldn't really make a living on a boat like this by yourself, but what choice did he have? He was sleeping on the *Hydra* these days, and only the kindness of the dockmaster, who'd known him for years, allowed him to get away with that. He was eating the fish he caught to stay alive, and selling just enough to buy bootleg whiskey and pay his dock fees, but he could see the way things were going. Down, down, down.

When the storm warning came, and the other fisherman cursed about a lost day of work, Abel had unmoored the *Hydra* and set off across the eerily still waters, toward that massing wall of lead-gray clouds. His old friends, who mostly avoided him now, shouted at him to come back, it was too dangerous, but he ignored them. He told himself he couldn't afford to miss a day's work, nor'easter or not, but now that he watched the oncoming storm, he wondered if on some level he'd been hoping for a final disaster to end his dissolution.

Still, he made the *Hydra* as ready for rough weather as he could, pulling up the nets, readying the storm sails, battening the hatches. He could try to run out of the path of the storm.

Another swell picked up the boat, this time lifting it so high and dropping it so abruptly that Abel was sure the *Hydra* had hung suspended in the air for a moment. He crashed to the deck, heart pounding, and he suddenly *very much* wanted to live. Amazing how the closeness of death could clarify that!

Abel crawled toward the mast as the first wave of cold rain passed over him, stinging pellets peppering the back of his neck and his hands, and instantly soaking his clothes. The ship groaned and pitched, and he rolled across the deck, unable to find his feet. The clouds were right above him now, the rain and flashes of lightning all around, the storm moving with fiendish speed.

He crawled forward, reached a coil of rope, and began to tie himself to the mast. Abel had never received much formal education, but his mother had been a voracious reader, and she'd told him stories about the gods and heroes of the ancient world. Abel had named his boat after the sea monster Hercules killed, the serpent with nine heads, because he liked how that beast kept getting up again, growing two new heads for every one that Hercules cut away. Abel liked to think he would be similarly indomitable in the face of adversity (if, he hoped, ultimately more successful).

Now, though, he thought of the seafaring hero Ulysses, lashing himself to his ship's mast so he wouldn't be able to follow the beguiling song of the Sirens to his death. Abel tied the rope around his waist, crisscrossed it over his chest, and finished the makeshift harness with a sturdy knot. His fate was literally tied to the *Hydra* now. If the boat made it through, so would he. If not... well. There were worse ways for a life like his to finish up, though he didn't much like the idea of sinking down into the depths, not since he'd glimpsed some of the unnatural things that dwelled there.

Lightning flashed around him – and then, to Abel's wonder, bluish-purple light flickered along the railings of the boat, casting the scene in dreamlike illumination. He tilted his head back and watched a ball of coruscating light slowly roll along the yardarm. St Elmo's Fire, the old sailors called it, but Abel had never seen the phenomenon himself before. He'd heard this fire, which burned but did not consume, could be a good omen or a bad one, depending–

A wave struck the boat, spun it, and the back of Abel's head cracked so hard against the mast behind him that he first saw black stars, and then only the blackness.

Abel woke with a groan. There was something rough, irregular, and sharp underneath him, cutting into his shoulders as he shifted. Had he fallen asleep on top of a pile of oyster shells or something?

He struggled upright, memory slowly returning. The storm!

He opened his eyes and looked up into a clear blue sky wisped with shreds of cloud, the sun casting its light nearly sideways, close to the western horizon. The storm had passed. The storm had passed him *over*. He was alive!

He laughed aloud, but only for a moment, because his

throat was sore, and his lips were cracked and salty. His head hurt, his right cheek stung from a cut, his whole body ached, and there were scrapes and abrasions all over his arms and hands. He was going to turn into one big all-over bruise in a day or two.

Abel looked down, expecting to find himself on the deck of his boat, but he was sitting on a shelf of rock, or… a coral reef? There *was* coral in these cold Atlantic waters, northern star coral he thought it was called, but that was found on the bottom of the ocean, and didn't build elaborate surface-breaking reefs like this. Abel's late uncle Jericho, a Navy man, had served in Hawaii, and had described the weird beauty of such formations. He'd brought young Abel a chunk of coral as a souvenir, and this rock was sharp and porous and looked strangely organic, just like that. Abel still had that piece of coral in his makeshift bedroom belowdecks on the *Hydra*–

His boat! Abel struggled to his feet, untangling the wet rope that hung loosely about him. He looked at the water surrounding this strange island, and there was no sign of the *Hydra*… but there was flotsam there, a few weathered gray boards, a stretch of torn net, a length of canvas, and a mangled life preserver.

He sank to his knees and stared at the bobbing fragments of his meager livelihood, then looked up and scanned the horizon to the west, shading his eyes from the sun. He couldn't make out so much as a dark smudge to indicate the possibility of land. He took slow breaths, fighting against a rising tide of panic. People knew he'd gone out into the storm, and when he didn't come back, they'd send out rescue boats… but would they find him? How far off his usual routes had the storm carried him? He didn't have food or fresh water or shelter…

Abel got off his knees. Nearly dying had restored his desire to live, and living in this situation was going to require effort. He'd better take stock of what he *did* have, and what he could use.

He explored his surroundings, such as they were. The rocky outcropping he'd somehow miraculously washed up on didn't merit the name "island." He was on a stony sort of platform that rose barely a foot above the surface of the sea, a space just big enough for him to lie down on, if he curled up a bit and didn't mind being poked with sharp edges.

An irregular tower of stone rose up beside that flat section, easily thirty feet high, pointing at the sky like a misshapen and accusing finger. He couldn't see around the tower or guess at its diameter, but there was a small outcropping like a ledge off to his left, disappearing around the side of the spire, and ample footholds and handholds. Maybe there was more space on the far side of the tower, if he could work his way around. If nothing else, moving would keep him warm, and loosen up his tightened muscles.

Abel climbed up the tower slowly, testing each foothold carefully, pressing his chest against the rock even though its hard ridges poked through his shirt, finding handholds with questing fingers, inching himself around the rocky pillar. It was easier once he reached that ledge, and could shuffle along with surer footing.

There *was* more space on the other side of the spire, an expanse of stone easily a dozen square feet, like a front courtyard before the tower. A deep tide pool stood in the center of the courtyard, suggesting this rock was sometimes submerged, which meant he should climb higher, if he could. Abel dropped exhausted to his knees and looked into the pool, stomach already rumbling. The water was full of starfish in brilliant colors, bright yellow and deep blue and blushing pink. There were no fish there, though, no crabs, no mollusks, nothing he could *eat*. Well, he'd heard you could technically eat the arms of starfish, or anyway they wouldn't kill you, but he wasn't *that* hungry yet. He suspected he'd die of thirst before he had a chance to starve – wait. The *rain*. The storm had passed, but not that long ago.

He rose and staggered toward the tower, which on this side was covered in little buttresses and outcroppings and ridges, looking for puddles – and, yes, there were a few deep depressions, high above sea level and full of water. He sniffed, grinned, and scooped the rainwater up with his hands. Every mouthful was gritty and sun-warmed, but it was drinkable, and though the water stung his salt-dried lips, he lapped until he was full.

Refreshed, Abel looked up at the spire. It was larger than he would have imagined, bigger around than the biggest tree he'd ever seen, the size of an *actual* tower. Maybe he could climb up to the top and rig some sort of a flag or banner from the netting and rope and sail that floated around him. If he could create something clearly man-made, something that had a *chance* of being spotted from a distance, it might improve his chances.

Or it might be pointless busywork, but even that would spare him a little longer from despair.

Abel began to climb, even more carefully, since he was

going higher now. There were ample hand and footholds, but this side of the tower was full of sharp edges that wanted his blood. He made his way slowly, working himself up and around the tower, following the easiest path. The seas were liberally dotted with uncharted desert islands and heaps of unnoticed rocks, but still, the formation was remarkable – the ocean here must be deep, which meant this was just the visible tip of some much vaster foundation that rose up from the distant sea floor. The towerlike structure was memorable, too, but he'd never heard anyone mention sighting something like this, even from a distance. How far from his home waters *was* he? Too far to be found?

He was about two-thirds of the way to the top of the tower when he found the cave.

The mouth was roughly oval, and big, about five feet high and three feet wide, with a small ledge in front. He knelt on that ledge and peered into the hole, then gasped. There was *light* inside, and at first he imagined some sort of mad sea hermit burning a driftwood fire, but then realized there must be holes in the top of the tower, letting the late rays of sunlight shine through. Except this light had a peculiar, greenish-yellow cast. Reflecting off scummy water, perhaps?

Abel crawled inside the cave. The floor was still rough, but nowhere near as sharp as the outside, as if it had been worn smooth somehow. A few steps inside, the ceiling of the cavern sloped upward, and soon it was high enough for him to stand comfortably, even at six-foot-one.

He followed the tunnel a short distance to a large central chamber, as big as the main room at the old homestead, and

Abel frowned, taking in the space. The tower got *narrower* as it rose, so how was there so much space inside? He must have misjudged the spire's diameter, but then, it wasn't like he ever got a look at the whole structure at once – maybe there was a section that bulged out on one side.

Abel stepped into the chamber and looked up, expecting to see holes and sky, but instead, the ceiling was covered in irregular blotches of some glowing substance, shining yellow-green. Upon closer inspection, the growths looked like starfish, ranging in size from smaller than his palm to bigger than his chest, but he thought they must really be some kind of luminescent algae.

As his eyes adjusted to the dimness, more strange details revealed themselves. There was a big hole in the center of the chamber, about four feet across – lucky he hadn't stepped in *that* – but he couldn't see how deep it went. He was more interested in the back of the cave anyway.

What he'd taken for a rock formation now looked like something more intentional: a smooth, dark stone table, or maybe an altar, big enough for a person to lie down on, projecting from the back wall. Even in the low light, Abel could clearly see the bas-relief carving above the table. It depicted an immense seven-pointed starfish, as wide across as Abel's outstretched arms. There was a circle cut into the center of the starfish's body, the inside of its curve carved with rows of inward-pointing triangles that reminded Abel of the teeth of a lamprey. Starfish had mouths on their undersides, he knew, but not mouths like *that*. He shuddered, revulsion crawling up and down his skin. Who would dream up such a thing?

There were other tiny drawings carved near the bottom of the starfish, a few on either side – they looked like crude human figures, kneeling, their arms reaching up. Abel frowned. If those were supposed to be *people*, then that starfish would be the size of… well. They didn't make starfish as big as whales, now did they? He shook his head. What strange and ancient seafaring people had come here, and decorated this place? What forgotten god had they venerated?

There was a long depression in the altar, and it was full of water, briny and dark. Abel leaned forward and thought he saw something glitter in the water, catching the barest hint of that eerie light. Abel plunged a hand into the water, surprised at how deep it went, his arm disappearing into the shocking cold up to his elbow. His questing fingers closed on something that felt like a thick chain.

He pulled a necklace out of the water, its links made of gold, and his mouth went dry. That chain was *heavy*. If it was really gold, and if he could get it back home, that length of bright metal would solve most of his problems. He might even be able to get his home back, or at least make a start on it.

A large, silver-and-black medallion dangled from the end of the chain: a seven-armed starfish, with a mouth of triangle teeth in the center, just like the carving on the wall, but in miniature. The amulet wasn't gold, unfortunately – it felt like carved stone, and he considered snapping the thing off and tossing it aside, but maybe it had value as an artifact. There were college professors and the like who'd pay for such things, maybe at Miskatonic University up in Arkham.

Abel's home village of Strossport was an easy day trip from there by car.

He held the amulet up and watched it lazily turn in the eerie light. If he ever made it off this rock, at least he'd have some treasure to show for it. Necklaces were easy to transport, too. Abel dropped the chain over his head, letting the medallion rest against his chest–

The chamber filled with water, rising around him with impossible speed, and he sucked in a breath as he was submerged. He spun, but there was no exit anymore, just smooth walls on all sides, carved with the sigil of the starfish god in every size from miniature to vast, except they weren't carvings, they couldn't be, because their arms were *reaching*.

Abel opened his mouth to scream, too terrified even to fear drowning, but then the walls and the starfish vanished, and he saw:

Chanting multitudes in long, dripping-wet robes, walking on a stony shore beside black water.

A man rising from a pool of water, gasping, and reaching out his hands toward an identical man, or at least, a mirror image, who pulled him out and embraced him.

Horrid creatures, like people with the faces of deep-sea fish, swimming through lightless depths, spears clutched in their webbed hands.

Great gouts and clouds of blood in the water.

Huge chunks of pebbled flesh floating on the surface of the ocean like rotting whale blubber.

A distorted view of a dark-paneled room, as if seen through a thick sheet of curved glass, with a gray-haired, dark-eyed man in a neat suit entering through an unseen door and picking up a carved stone object from a shelf, then going back out again.

Abel moaned, back in his body, or so it seemed, but now he was in a cavern surrounded by heaps of pearls and the soft glow of gold coins, firelight flickering from torches on the walls, with unseen figures in the shadows all around, chanting, and the chant echoed and reverberated and filled the air:

"RESTORE ME
AND BE RESTORED"

He blinked, and found himself suspended in a watery void. Below him stretched a great seven-pointed starfish, and as he watched, its arms grew, and lengthened, and stretched, until they seemed so long that they might wrap around the whole of the world. He couldn't tell if the starfish had become immense, or if Abel had become very small; his sense of scale and proportion were baffled, and both space itself and his own mind seemed as pliable as saltwater taffy. In the center of that starfish, whose reaching limbs now stretched on all sides to all horizons, a horrible, squirming mouth opened, and the thing inhaled, pulling water into its maw, and pulling Abel down with it.

Abel woke again, this time on gritty sand. He winced preemptively, expecting spikes of pain, since that was what happened *last* time he woke up… but he felt fine. Better than fine. He felt *wonderful*: no agonies in his body, and no clamor in his mind, as if he'd rested well on a soft bed at the end of a day without worries, instead of on a shore after a shipwreck.

He sat up on the beach and looked east, toward the ocean and the rising sun. He turned his head to look along the shore, where he saw a familiar pier, and the tiny dots of distant figures going about their morning business. He knew this place. He was just down the beach from the docks in Strossport, where he'd spent most of his days for two decades.

Abel was home. He had no real memory of the night before, apart from swimming. He'd somehow made his way across countless miles of open ocean in the dark, despite hunger and dehydration and pain. There was no pain now. His arms and legs felt strong, ready for a day of good, honest work.

He wasn't confused. He wasn't frightened. He understood. His luck had turned. He'd been blessed. He'd been *chosen*. Plans and purpose unfolded within him, stretching out to the horizons of his mind.

Restore me, a voice whispered in his mind – his suddenly crowded mind. He knew so much, now, new truths bobbing to the surface of his mind with every passing moment. He knew about ancient depths, and forgotten temples, and bloody wars fought in a lightless abyss. He knew about the power, and the priesthood he now held. He knew the thousand names of his god, his savior, the most holy of which were:

Asterias.

That Which When Divided, Multiplies.

The Ravening Deep.

Abel's clothes were in tatters, and one of his boots was missing. The cuts and scrapes on his hands and arms were gone, though, and he knew no bruises would surface on his body. That was the gift of his god. He took off the boot, removed the lace, and then tenderly lifted the gold necklace off his neck. The necklace didn't matter: it was merely a resource. The medallion was all he needed, the source of his revelation, a gift from his god, a holy relic. He removed the medallion from the heavy chain and strung it on the bootlace, then put it back around his neck, under his shirt, against his skin.

He rose, gold chain in hand. He would nod and smile at any acquaintances he passed – they were used to seeing him damp and shabby, and no one would notice his interior transformation. He would go to the pawnbroker – who was well acquainted with Abel, especially in recent months – and drive the hardest bargain he could. He would make the broker throw in a sharp knife as part of the deal. He would rent a room, one near the water… one with a big bathtub.

And then, in blood and salt, Abel would begin his ministry, and gather his congregation.

CHAPTER TWO
The Huntress

Six months later.

Diana sat in the small office in the back of her clothing shop, going over the books, and trying not to think of those *other* books – the ones in the Seeker's library at the Silver Twilight Lodge. The ones in languages she couldn't read, but with letters that somehow squirmed in her mind's eye anyway.

Diana had only been running her business for two years, since selling the family farm and moving to Arkham in 1924. She'd used the money from her father's estate to buy a dusty old place called Emmie's Boutique, and transformed it into the most successful women's shop in town.

She'd always been interested in fashion, and the way the right clothes could change the way the world looked at you – and the way you looked at *yourself*. She'd renamed the shop Huntress Fashions in honor of her mythological namesake, and cultivated a wealthy clientele. She'd been savvy about building her reputation, joining the Chamber of Commerce, the Women's League, and the Historical Society, and using them as opportunities to make connections. The people she met, and the good impression she made with her impeccable sense of style, led to success after success.

The only downside was that she had to dodge well-meaning people who wanted to set her up with their sons or cousins or nephews. She politely told them she had to focus on building her business, and once she was more established, she would have time to think about such things. In truth, she didn't know if she ever would think of them; she felt complete in herself, and took pride in her self-reliance. When she did think of sharing her life with someone, she didn't usually think about men, and while her ambitions were many, they didn't include motherhood. Maybe that would change, but for now, she had a plan, and she was going to follow it, and she was *not* going to fail.

Or anyway, she'd *had* a plan. Now she had doubts, questions, and bad dreams.

Things had started to turn for her when local luminary Carl Sanford invited her to join the Silver Twilight Lodge. Diana's father had been a lifelong Mason, and she'd assumed the Lodge was a fraternal order like that, albeit one open to women members. The only other order she'd heard of that allowed women to join was the International Organization of Good Templars, and Diana enjoyed an occasional drink too much to join a temperance group.

The Silver Twilight Lodge wasn't devoted to temperance, though – back then she wasn't sure *what* it was devoted to, and when she asked, she got vague answers about heritage, and history, and "ancient lore", the same sort of things her father's Mason brothers talked about when they had too many drinks. So when Sanford asked her to join last year, she'd said yes with enthusiasm. The Lodge was an important and exclusive part of Arkham society, and as a member she'd meet rich women who wanted the latest fashions, and their rich husbands who needed to buy them gifts (and gifts for their mistresses, too). Her business would grow, and she would build a secure future, one free from the constant uncertainty her father had suffered at the farm.

Or so she'd assumed. Instead, after a few months at the Lodge, she'd been given more responsibilities, and seen incredible, terrible things. The nature of reality had shifted beneath her, and everything she thought she understood about life and reality was thrown into question. Horrors she'd never imagined teemed at the edges of her understanding.

The question was: what would she do about it?

Diana rose from the desk and stretched, groaning as her aching back unkinked. How long had she been sitting there? She'd closed up shop at five, and a glimpse at the windows showed it was fully dark now – the days were getting shorter as autumn crept on. She'd always had a gift for disappearing into numbers and projections and possibilities – she'd done the books for her father's farm from the time she was thirteen. She liked numbers. They always added up the same way, and if they didn't, it was because *you'd* made a mistake, not because suddenly two plus two equaled five. Diana had always prided herself on being a hardheaded New Englander who only believed in those things she could see with her own eyes.

The problem was, she'd seen things that no reasonable person could believe.

She trudged up the back stairs to her small apartment above the shop. She was saving up to buy a house, maybe one of the cute Victorians with cupolas and widow's walks. That had been the plan, anyway. But how could she stay in Arkham now, knowing about the rot at its heart, presided over by charming Carl Sanford? Maybe it wasn't just Arkham. Maybe the whole world was like this: a thin patina of normality covering up the filth and horror underneath. She couldn't take responsibility for the whole world, though. She could only take responsibility for her own life... and the things she'd done.

Or the things she hadn't stopped *others* from doing. Those things followed her into dreams.

Diana sat in the threadbare armchair that was the only piece of furniture she'd brought from the farm. The upholstery still smelled faintly of her father's pipe smoke, and though the seat was shaped to his body from long years of occupation, it suited her well enough, and was gradually shaping itself to fit her, too.

She liked the space she'd made for herself in Arkham. The shop below was chic, sleek, and elegant, all draped silks and shining mirrors, with dresses arranged on mannequins as smooth and pale as ancient marble statues. But upstairs, her living area was cluttered and cozy, with patterned rugs and overstuffed bookshelves and end tables showing off her antique-shop finds, all lit by lamps with tasseled shades.

She poured herself a glass of sherry – one of her wealthy customers had amassed a vast private cellar in the years before Prohibition, and her client brought over the occasional bottle in exchange for getting first look at the new designs from Paris. Diana sipped, and sighed, and settled back in the lamplight, gazing at the dark window that overlooked the rear of the shop.

Until two months ago, on the night of the ritual below French Hill, she'd felt so *comfortable* here. That was all she'd wanted. To find a place where she was beholden only to herself, and could make a life to suit her. She'd managed it, too, until Carl Sanford decided she was ready to advance in the Order.

She twisted her mouth, half rueful smile, half frown. It was her own fault. She'd been so *eager*. She could have stayed on the fringes of the Lodge, enjoying the private dining room and bar, mingling with the other new members and hangers-on. But she'd never lacked for ambition, and once she knew there were *levels* she could progress through in the Order, greater ranks she could attain, she was seized with a fervor to rise through those ranks.

She thought that joining the higher levels would give her access to more rarefied company, more powerful people, and more opportunities to improve her position. And while that was true, she could admit now that she'd also wanted to rise for her own sake. *Some* was good, after all, but *more* was always better. On the farm, she'd worn patched dresses and secondhand shoes, they'd often eaten no better than the pigs, and life had been a constant struggle of mending and making-do. She'd dreamed of a better life, and the Lodge seemed to promise that. A new world, where she could excel, and be seen, and respected, and appreciated.

She'd heard the names of the various ranks of the Order whispered: Initiate, Seeker, Brother of the Dark, Knight of the Stars, Keeper of the Red Stone, Guardian of the Black Stone, and many more with titles an Initiate as lowly as Diana was not permitted to know. Some said there were sixty-one distinct ranks, with the highest being held only by Carl Sanford himself.

Diana had expressed her desire to rise and learn the sacred mysteries after just a few months in the order, and though Carl Sanford had seemed amused by her enthusiasm, he had given her certain texts to read, later quizzing her on the information.

Her mind was always adept at patterns and organization, and she'd easily retained the names of ancient gods and places and relics from across the world. She'd assumed it was all just set-dressing and play-acting, pretense at a storied lineage to make the members feel important, like the Masons with their secret handshakes and claims to ancient knowledge. She'd memorized stories about wars among incomprehensible entities, which she assumed were complex allegories, like the symbolic stories in the alchemy books she also studied. Sanford taught her phrases she was ordered to remember though she could not understand them, drawn from extinct languages whose origins were unknown to her: Akkadian, and Aklo, and Bactrian, and Senzar. At first, her ceaseless intellectual curiosity was what drove her, but in time she began to believe there might be *real* secrets here. Sanford, after all, was a wildly successful man who seemed to understand the world on a level Diana could only guess at, and she wanted that understanding for herself.

Finally, after Sanford deemed her sufficiently suffused

with esoteric knowledge, she was invited to a ceremony in a room of the lodge building she'd never seen before, one with red curtains on the walls and a red-and-white marble floor. She wore a dark hooded robe, and she was nervous, but did her best to keep her head high and hide her trembling. This was the first step on a long road to the top, to the *inside*, that theoretical place where people like Sanford dwelled, free from want and worry, directing their own destinies, and the destinies of others. The place she wanted to be.

Diana knelt on the stones, sipped something murky (wine, she thought, but thickened) from a stone cup, and murmured an oath in Aklo. The air seemed charged, as if a thunderstorm were approaching, and her senses were strangely heightened. She could feel the hard marble beneath her knees, the cool air on her face, and every hair standing up on her arms. She was on the edge of something.

Sanford, also robed and surrounded by other members of the Lodge, said, "Do you pledge to faithfully pursue hidden knowledge, to aid your brothers and sisters in the Order, and to make ours that which has been forbidden?"

"I will," she murmured.

Sanford touched her on each shoulder with a gnarled cane of black wood. "I now pronounce you Seeker."

Then the lights came up, and the hoods came down, and everyone congratulated her and clapped her on the back. She wasn't at the top, but she was no longer on the bottom, either; she had her foot in the door.

The new rank of Seeker gave her access to new parts of the Lodge, including the Seeker's library, where those of her rank with a more scholarly bent were translating books Sanford or his agents had acquired. She'd idly flipped through them from time to time, finding most incomprehensible and the readable ones dull, until she'd opened a tome with a blank cover of greasy black leather and found her eyes assaulted by sigils in crusty red ink that *still* squirmed in her vision when she closed her eyes some nights. She'd avoided the library after that.

Her new rank came not just with privileges but with responsibilities. Sanford or his trusted Lodge members often gave her tasks, and she spent months going on errands she did not understand, accompanying higher-ranking Lodge members and serving as a set of watchful eyes and useful hands. She was not permitted to ask questions on those errands, and so many of the things they did were *baffling*.

Once she'd sat in the stern of a rowboat while a bald man with a scarred face worked the oars and took them to the center of a perfectly circular pond in the Massachusetts countryside, where she was instructed to empty a small velvet pouch of what looked alarmingly like finger bones and teeth over the side. The fragments sank without causing any ripples, and they'd rowed silently back to shore and departed without incident.

A month later, she'd joined two women in black hooded robes in a grove of thorny trees, who handed her a shovel with a silver blade. Diana dug a hole in the dirt until her shoulders screamed from the effort while they smoked cigarettes and shared a flask and chuckled, speaking in a language Diana didn't recognize. She'd finally struck a white root, as thick as her arm but slick and wormlike, and the women told her to climb out of the pit. They'd gone into the hole themselves then, carrying a stone jug, and poured what she hoped was wine but suspected was diluted blood all over the root. After they made her refill the hole, they all left, the women chatting with her amiably about how her shop was doing, as if none of it had happened.

She'd been sent to a burned farmhouse in western Massachusetts with a hawk-nosed man who wore a bandana on his head like a storybook pirate. They'd sorted through the rubble until they found a hatch that led to a cellar, and he'd descended. She waited above for half an hour, and then ruby light shone through the ash-streaked floorboards, and a droning sound that made her teeth ache emerged from below, before abruptly cutting off. The man emerged, sweaty and covered in dust and cobwebs, carrying a bulbous earthenware jar tucked under one arm. His bandana had slipped awry, and Diana stared at the hint of intricate red lines tattooed on his scalp until he snarled at her to get the car started and sent her scurrying away. By the time he joined her, he'd adjusted the bandana, and hidden the jar away in a valise, and said only that their excursion had been successful, and the master would be pleased. Looking back, Diana was appalled at her own naivete. She'd found those missions exciting, and sometimes scary, but even the latter had tantalized her with the promise of secret knowledge. Now she wondered what dark designs she'd played a part in.

Even the strangest of those excursions were nothing compared to what she saw in the tunnels beneath the Silver Twilight Lodge itself, after Carl Sanford decided she could be trusted with–

Diana jumped at the sound of shattering glass. She

looked down through the window but didn't see anything in the alley behind the shop. Except... was that a flicker of movement?

If there was someone down there breaking things, they were too close to the wall for her to see them, given the angle of her vantage. What if someone was breaking *in* to the shop? She could call the police... but her telephone was downstairs, because she used it for business. She couldn't count on neighbors to notice a disturbance and call the authorities for her, either. This part of Arkham kept firmly to business hours, and she was the only shopkeeper who lived on the premises, at least on this block.

The sensible choice would be to lock and secure the door at the top of the stairs and wait things out. Confronting a potential burglar was a dangerous proposition. But after the horrors Diana had witnessed – the things she'd had a hand in bringing into this world, unwittingly or not – she was no longer inclined to be sensible. She felt helpless in the matter of the Silver Twilight Lodge, and would not accept helplessness in her shop as well.

Diana went to the corner and picked up an ebony walking stick, topped with a tarnished silver sphere. She'd found the stick among the jumble of items the former owner of Emmie's Boutique had left behind when they fled town ahead of foreclosure. The heavy cane felt good in her hand, and she gave it a couple of experimental swings, satisfied that it would give any housebreaker pause. Then Diana opened the door and listened from the top of the stairs. She didn't hear more breakage, but was that... someone singing?

She moved down the stairs, which led to the back room of

the shop, where her supplies and extra inventory were stored neatly on racks and shelves. A curtained archway separated this area from the front of the shop, but she didn't need to go out there. The noise had come from the alleyway out back.

There were two windows in the back wall, far smaller than the great plate glass display windows out front, but still large enough for an intruder to crawl through. They were curtained for privacy, and quite dirty on the outside too... and neither window was broken. Not a burglary, then. She listened at the window and heard a hoarse voice crooning: "...we will steer. We'll make them valleys ring, my boys, a-drinking of strong beer..." Then a sort of coughing sob.

Diana sighed. Not a burglar at all. Just some drunk, maybe a fisherman, since he was singing an old whaling song. She turned on the lights, then unbolted the back door and eased it open so she could tell him to move along. The moon shone down, bright and nearly full, illuminating the alley and turning the shattered whiskey bottle on the pavement into a glittering strew of diamonds. That explained the noise she'd heard. There was no reek of whiskey, which meant the bottle had been empty when her unwelcome visitor broke it. That was probably *why* he'd broken it.

The man sat with his back to the wall of her shop and his legs extended straight out before him. He wore stained trousers with ragged hems at the ankles, a shirt with missing buttons, and a brown jacket with one sleeve dangling by threads. His left hand was wrapped in a handkerchief like it was injured. He looked up at her, face ragged with stubble, eyes squinting, and she was surprised to see that he was relatively young, probably just in his thirties.

"An angel," he said. "You're radiant."

Diana frowned, then realized the light from inside the shop must have surrounded her with a backlit glow. "You're drunk, and you're breaking things outside my shop. You should leave."

"I have nowhere to go." He looked down at his bandaged hand.

She felt sympathy for the poor man, but she had problems of her own. "Nowhere is a big place, and you can choose to occupy some part of it that isn't right next to my back door."

"If they find me… I made them, but they hate me…" He struggled to his feet, leaning heavily against the wall. "I think… they can *sense* me… but when I drink it makes me blurry, changes the shape of me, so maybe they can't…" Diana started to go inside, content that he was about to move on, until she heard him say, "But I can't risk going to the Lodge, not if they can find me."

"What Lodge?" Diana said. He couldn't possibly mean *her* Lodge, could he? Sanford would never give the time of day to a man like this. But maybe he hadn't always been *like this*. Maybe he'd seen things that had *reduced* him to this. She shivered at the thought.

He looked at her, blinking, then shrugged. "Silver. Silver Twilight Lodge. It's… they have… it's there. What's left of it. All that's left. And if my comets find it…" He shook his head. "That which when divided multiplies."

His words were all but incomprehensible… but tantalizing. What did this ruined man know about the Silver Twilight Lodge? Could it be something of use to her? She wanted to stop Sanford from performing his horrible rituals, from using the vulnerable for his own ends, but she had no idea how to go about that. Might this man know something to break the logjam in her mind, and show her a path to action?

"Who are you?" Diana said.

"Who am I?" He chuckled, a sound that was all fishhooks and bilge pumps. "Abel. Davenport. High priest. Laid low." He shook his head, blinked at her, and frowned. "Who are *you*?"

"Diana Stanley. This is my shop."

"Diana," Abel said, and his smile was radiant. "The goddess of the hunt." Then he closed his eyes and swayed, and only the fact that he swayed into the wall instead of away from it kept him upright.

"Perhaps you'd better come inside," Diana decided.

CHAPTER THREE
The Thief

Ruby Standish was in a place she wasn't supposed to be, and she was about to take something that didn't belong to her. There was nowhere else she'd rather be, and nothing else she'd rather be doing.

The secret panel was just where her client had promised, hidden in the back of a walk-in closet behind a row of hanging suits. Her client didn't know the trick to *opening* the hidden door, so Ruby slipped a narrow-bladed knife from the sheath at her belt and slid it into the crack beside the panel, moving it slowly up and down until she hit an obstruction. There was the latch... She grinned as she wiggled the blade, applying pressure, until there was a soft *click*, and the wall panel swung inward.

She pushed it open all the way, half-wincing in fear of an alarm. The old-timer she'd learned her craft from, Thorley, complained bitterly about the emergence of such devices in recent decades, especially the hidden switches that set off clanging bells. When Ruby set out to become a thief, she made a point of only learning from the *successful* ones. Thorley had never seen the inside of a jail cell, and that was one of Ruby's principal ambitions. Of course, one of Thorley's secrets was he stole mainly from people who wouldn't *bother* calling the law on you; they'd try to find you themselves instead. Dangerous people were, well, dangerous, but they also tended to get killed themselves, and then they'd stop looking, while the law was relentless.

Ruby still exchanged the odd letter with Thorley, full of empty chatter and coded queries – one such letter had allowed him to connect Ruby with her current client. Thorley knew a lot of people who dabbled in the occult, and Ruby had gradually and almost accidentally eased into that realm as her area of expertise.

There were a shocking number of rich collectors obsessed with paraphernalia from ancient civilizations, often rumored to possess impossible properties. Ruby thought most of the artifacts in circulation were fakes... but she knew some were real, or at least, really *strange*. She still had the twisted scar around her left ankle to remind her there were things in the world she never particularly wanted to understand.

No bells clanged, which meant her target trusted the building's security and the secrecy of his hiding space to protect his treasures. To be fair, most of the time they would have been ample defense. Getting in through the lobby of an exclusive building like this, let alone up to the private penthouse that sprawled over the whole top floor, would have been tricky, though with the right outfit and attitude, Ruby might have managed it. She'd smiled and charmed and batted her eyelashes into even better defended locations.

The problem with that kind of approach, though, was that she'd be remembered by the doorman and security people, and with a target like *this*, you didn't want to give them any leads to pursue. Sometimes Ruby could be very memorable; sometimes she could be a ghost. This was a ghost job.

So she hadn't entered through the lobby. She'd come up the side of the building, dressed in black, a shadow on the wall, using pipes, ledges, crenellations, and all the other ornamental foofaraw the architects had kindly provided for her use. She had a slim metal tool for unfastening latches, but few people bothered to lock their windows when they were six stories high. Her target didn't even lock the French doors leading to his private terrace. A swift climb and an easy entry, just the way she liked it.

The space beyond the secret panel was dark, and the beam from her small flashlight was just bright enough to fill the space with tantalizing glitters. Her client said there were lights in the hidden room, and with the closet door shut she could turn those on safely without illuminating the apartment windows. She felt around on the wall beyond the panel until she found the button and pushed it in.

A chandelier dripping crystal teardrops began to glow in the ceiling overhead, illuminating the prettiest little secret showroom Ruby had ever seen. The space was small, only about six feet square, with a plush armchair in the center, arranged to offer a perfect view of the treasures arrayed on tables and shelves on the opposite wall.

There were a couple of grotesque little statues carved of ebony and onyx, and she shuddered just glimpsing them. Things like that could be valuable to the right collector, but she'd cut her hand on a similar statue last year. *It bit you,* a stubborn voice whispered in the back of her mind. Her hand had swelled up like a hot water bottle, and she'd had a fever for two days afterward, full of nasty visions. She didn't *like* those little idols, and the pickings here were rich enough that she could afford to be superstitious.

She passed over a gold scroll-case that was too big to fit in the bag slung over her shoulder, but there was a necklace of black pearls that would fit easily, and she also took a crude flute made from a length of scrimshawed bone, and a stone jar made of lapis lazuli, smaller than her dainty fist. Her client hadn't mentioned those items, but he might want them anyway, and if not, there were always other interested parties.

The last thing she picked up was the object of her commission, and the centerpiece of the collection, standing on its own custom stand of dark wood: a red jewel almost big enough to cover her palm. The tiny, intricate facets cut across its face reminded her of the scales of a snake or a fish. The gem was nestled in a dark metal setting shaped a bit like a medieval shield. There was a loop to hang the jewel from, but no chain; too bad. Gold necklaces were easily negotiable.

"The Ruby of R'lyeh," she murmured, and then smirked. "A ruby for Ruby." Her client might have been amused by that coincidence – he was a former professor of ancient literature and languages at Miskatonic University, now an antiquities dealer – but, of course, he didn't know her real name. It was better not to use *that* name when she was doing business with someone in Arkham. Not since everything that happened with the Silver Twilight Lodge. She tried to avoid Arkham entirely, but he was paying her well enough to overcome her hesitancy.

Ruby tucked the jewel away with the rest of her spoils, made sure the bag was closed, then adjusted the strap until everything hung comfortably on her back. The things she'd stolen didn't weigh much, so she wasn't worried about her balance being thrown off on the descent. Going down was easier in some respects than going up, and harder in others. You couldn't see your path as well, but gravity did some of the work for you. You had to be careful, though, because if you weren't, gravity would do *all* the work for you, and offer you a far speedier descent than you'd prefer.

She turned off the light, slipped out of the vault, closed the panel, adjusted the suits until they appeared undisturbed, and went to the door of the closet, already planning her next moves. She'd slip out of the bedroom, down the hall, into the living room, through the French doors to the terrace, over the railing on the right, onto the ledge, shimmy over to the gargoyle, clamber down to that nice fat drain pipe–

She heard a metallic rattle and froze. The private elevator was arriving! The doors would open right in the living room: the privileges of wealth. She flattened herself against the wall next to the bedroom door and swore under her breath. Her client had *assured* her the ruby's owner was going to be at the symphony, and then out getting drinks, until at least one in the morning – that he *never* came home earlier than that on a Saturday night – but it wasn't even midnight yet. That's what she got for trusting someone else's intel instead of doing her own. She sidled closer to the door and peered through the crack, down the hallway, which afforded her a glimpse of the living room.

There was the owner of the gem, dressed in black tie, all broad shoulders and silver hair and the kind of jaw you could hang a campaign poster on. He wasn't a politician, though. He was a prominent attorney here in Boston, and rumored to have close ties to organized crime. He wasn't alone, either: he had two men with him, and they didn't look like symphony lovers.

One was big, maybe six-four, with a face like a side of beef somebody had used for a punching bag, and the other was lean as a knife, and dressed more elegantly than the lawyer. A bruno and a button-man, if she had to guess: fists and a pistol. She wondered if they were the lawyer's bodyguards... or his minders. Being the attorney for a gangster had to be a delicate position, and fraught with danger, though maybe not quite as fraught as Ruby's current situation.

She went to the windows in the bedroom. They were big, and would swing wide enough for her to get out, if there was anyplace to get *to*. There was a ledge under the windows, narrower than she liked, but she'd dealt with worse. All those years of ballet practice Mummy had insisted on were still paying dividends in terms of gracefulness and balance. She stuck her head out the window and looked both ways. The closest corner of the building was off to the left, and it was encrusted with ornamental handholds. She was pretty sure she could make her way to the ground that way, though it was more exposed than the drainpipe, which was hidden in shadow. That was why she'd picked that route in the first place. The streets of Boston's Back Bay weren't bustling at the moment, though, so it would probably be safe enough–

"What in heaven's name?" a voice made for the courtroom boomed at her.

Ruby didn't bother to look back: she knew what she would see. The lawyer, probably tugging his bow tie off and kicking loose his shoes. Seventeen rooms in this penthouse, and he had to come in *here*? He couldn't pour himself a brandy or go to the bathroom first? She scrambled out the window, ignoring his startled yelp and cry of "Stop, thief!" Speed was the whole thing now.

The higher up Ruby climbed, the windier it got. She wondered why. Maybe when she was at the university she'd ask a scientist. She pressed herself to the wall, cheek on stone, and shuffle-stepped along the ledge toward the corner of the building. She was looking back at the window, so she had a nice clear view when the lawyer and the goon and the button-man all stuck their heads out, one after another, and looked at her, identically wide-eyed and gaping. She almost giggled: they reminded her of a vaudeville act she'd seen on a date, Ted Healy and His Stooges, where the performers had stuck their heads out of the curtain like that, one on top of the other.

Then the button-man reached out an arm and pointed a pistol at her, and it wasn't so funny anymore.

"Don't shoot her!" the lawyer boomed.

Ruby winced. She was dressed in black trousers, loose enough for easy movement and cinched at the ankles so she wouldn't trip over the hems, and a black tunic, with a scarf tied over her blonde hair. She was rather hoping they'd assume she was a man, as most thieves were, but the lawyer had gotten too good a look at her. Well, if he was reluctant to kill a woman, she wouldn't complain–

"The ruby might survive the fall, but she got the urn, too, and my flute," he boomed. "They'll shatter!"

Ah. Yes. That explained his reluctance better.

The button-man glared at her, but she didn't care: her reaching hand touched the building's corner. There were clamshells and seahorses and such carved all over it, providing a dozen places for her to grab and step, and she swung out. The wind blew sharply around the corner, and yanked the scarf right off her head, sending the scrap of silk billowing into the night. Her hair whipped into her eyes, because of course it did. She'd noticed that when your luck turned, it tended to turn all at once, and hard.

She made it around the corner to the other side of the building, though, out of sight of the lawyer and his friends, and protected a little from the wind. She looked down. No sign of the goon and the shooter down on the sidewalk yet… but they'd be in the elevator right now, ready to take her when she hit the pavement. She didn't highly rate her chances of seeing the sunrise. Even seeing midnight was looking unlikely.

She couldn't go down.

That left up.

It wasn't much of a climb at all, really: the penthouse was already on the top floor, so she just had to climb the one story. The roof was sloping and tiled, very pretty really, and a nightmare to scramble up, but Ruby moved low and slow, testing each tile before trusting it with her grip. At the top, there was a flat area surrounded by a low wall, enclosing a big skylight and a few chimneys and a lot of soot and dirt. She'd curl up against the little wall, lie low, wait for the thugs to assume she'd somehow escaped, and then in a couple of hours, she actually *would* escape.

There was a small structure in one corner, like a tiny fishing shack with a door in it: roof access for maintenance, likely not even reachable from the penthouse, but it was a worry. There were three men looking for her, after all: easy enough for one or two to cover the ground, and one to check the roof, just in case. She looked around, chewed her lip, and then rummaged in her bag and made some hasty preparations.

She'd just finished when the door eased open and the button-man slipped out. She tried to crouch against the low wall where the roof turned to sloping tile, thinking, *I am a shadow*, but the treacherous moon picked that moment to come out of the clouds and shine down on her and her blonde hair. The killer strolled around the skylight, pointing his pistol at her almost casually.

"A cat burglar who's a dame," he said. "You're a regular Robert Delaney, ain't you? Roberta Delaney! Ha." He didn't even laugh – he just said "Ha."

Ruby rose to her feet. She was an inch or so taller than the man. "The difference between Delaney and me is, Scotland Yard caught Delaney, and no one has ever caught me."

"Until tonight. *I* caught you. My friend downstairs wants I should bring you in alive. Seems like only a few people knew about his little hidey-hole – I sure didn't – and he wants to know who's been talking… and who hired you."

He wasn't going to shoot her immediately, then. That was

good. He was moving too slowly, though. She needed him to *rush*. "Sorry, must go," she said, and started to clamber up onto the sloping tiles.

"Hold it!" he yelled, and, as she'd hoped, sprinted toward her.

Which meant sprinting right into the trip-line she'd strung up from the corner of the skylight to one of the chimneys. Like the infamous British cat burglar Robert Delaney, Ruby carried black silk rope, and the button-man hit a taut length of it at speed. He fell on his face, the pistol flying from his grip. That was the most dangerous part of the whole situation: the gun might have gone off, and her luck was bad enough tonight that she didn't like her odds of avoiding a stray bullet. Fortunately, the pistol just clattered on the roof, and Ruby was on it like a shot. She didn't carry guns herself – they were just asking for trouble – but she knew how to use one.

She wasn't *going* to, though, or at least, not the way the pistol was intended. She hadn't killed anyone yet in the course of her work, and she didn't want to start tonight. She was a burglar, not a robber. She preferred to do her stealing when nobody else was around, to minimize opportunities for violence or capture.

The button-man got to his hands and knees, but she didn't let him get any farther. Ruby reversed the gun in her hand and brought the butt down hard on the back of the killer's head. He crumpled, and she winced. Hitting people over the head didn't work the way writers pretended it did in the crime stories in *Black Mask*. Getting knocked out wasn't the same as going to sleep, and you didn't always wake up in two hours with just a little headache. Bash somebody in the back of the head, and you could kill them by accident, or mess them up for life. But she had to prioritize her *own* life, didn't she? He'd chosen his business, and this was a pretty foreseeable sort of consequence.

Ruby didn't have time for moral qualms. She took another length of cord and hog-tied the button-man, in case he was feigning. The moon had gone back behind a cloud, so she couldn't see if there was blood coming from his ears, but she checked his pulse at the throat, and it was strong and steady. Good enough.

She crawled on her belly to the edge of the roof and looked down. The goon and the lawyer were down there, gesticulating, walking back and forth. The lawyer pointed and waved his arms and then went back into the building, doubtless to come up and check on his pet killer. The goon stood out front, crossed his arms, and turned his head back and forth, back and forth, like he was watching an invisible tennis match.

Ruby clambered down to the lawyer's balcony, climbed over the railing to the ledge, found her shadowed drainpipe – on the far side of the building from the goon's guard post – and shimmied the seventy feet or so down to the ground. She snagged the sack she'd hidden in the shrubs and pulled out the dress she'd stashed, a little *la garçonne* number with a darling fringed hem.

Once she'd pulled the dress over her head, the pants came off, and she shoved them in the sack. She put on a cloche hat and slipped on a pair of shoes with a clunky Cuban heel. A beaded handbag would hold her climbing shoes and all her treasures, though she had to wedge the bone flute in there a bit to make it fit. She wasn't wearing makeup, which didn't quite match the sort of girl she was pretending to be, but it was dark, and the wind probably made her cheeks look rosy anyway.

Now transformed into what she quite often actually was – a fashionable young woman out on the town – Ruby went the long way around the block to avoid passing by the goon. She had one ear cocked for the sound of pursuit, but she didn't expect any, and she wasn't disappointed. Two streets over, she reached a more lively part of the neighborhood, and caught a Checker cab to her hotel.

She relaxed into the back seat of the cab and let the driver's chatter stream past her. In the morning, she'd take the train to Arkham, deliver the Ruby of R'lyeh, and collect her pay. She'd be in and out before Carl Sanford could even get a hint that she was back in his territory. *The hard part of the job is over*, she thought.

CHAPTER FOUR
Comets

Abel woke with a groan, a pounding head, and a mouth dry as sand. That was the only way he woke, these days, and he supposed he was lucky to wake at all.

He'd taken a beating weeks ago, ordered by the new prophet of his god, the one calling himself "Cain". To think, Abel had once thought the creatures he called comets were a *miracle*, the greatest demonstration of his god's power, but now he knew they were monsters.

The assault had left Abel with a couple of cracked ribs and deep bruises, but he'd stopped seeing blood in his urine a while ago, and most of his injuries were mended, apart from a little stiffness in his right leg... and, of course, the trouble with his left hand. No, the beating was no longer the main source of his troubles. These days, he was in pain from the drink, which, ironically, he'd turned to in the first place in order to *dull* his pain. His theory that being drunk made it harder for the comets to sense his location was mostly rationalization, he feared. Still, he'd best go in search of the next bottle...

Wait. Where was he? He squinted around the unfamiliar room. At this point, *any* room was unfamiliar. He'd run out of money even for dockside flophouses last week, and he couldn't get more cash easily, since Cain had emptied his bank accounts. Abel had expected to wake up in an alley, a day closer to some ignoble death, but there was a roof over his head, and a pillow under it, smelling of lavender. Was this heaven? If so, he'd take it, though he didn't know how he'd slipped in, given his brief tenure as the earthly emissary of an evil god.

Abel sat up, swung his legs over the edge of the bed, and blinked at the strangeness. It was daytime, sunlight slanting in a window, but whether it was morning or afternoon he couldn't say without knowing which way the room was facing. He was in a lady's bedroom, judging by the vanity table against the wall, and by all the hats. He could see himself in the vanity mirror, a gaunt, hollow-eyed wretch, and he rubbed his cheek, which had gone from rough stubble to the beginnings of a beard. He hadn't looked at himself in a while, and if he hadn't felt so defeated and hollowed out, the sight would have filled him with horror. Healthy, prosperous Cain was wearing Abel's real face, and Abel looked like the monster.

"Hello?" he called, tentatively. He couldn't think of a good reason he'd be in a place like this, and only a few bad ones.

A woman appeared in the doorway. She was a few years younger than him, late twenties, and pretty, wearing a simple shift dress, her long auburn hair pulled back from her face. She was holding a steaming mug. Probably morning, then, though not early.

"You're awake," she said. "Do you want coffee?"

"I'd be grateful." His voice was a croak, and he cleared his throat. "Water first, maybe?"

"I put a pitcher by the bed. I had a feeling you'd need it this morning. There's a tin of aspirin too. Take a couple. I don't have much in the way of clothes in your size, but the people who lived here before left some things behind, including a couple of old shirts." She nodded toward folded clothes on a chair by the vanity. "The washroom is through that door. Come out to the kitchen when you're put together a little more." She departed.

Brave woman, to let a strange man sleep in her room, Abel thought, and then laughed like a rusty gate hinge. He supposed he didn't present much of a threat. He'd been strong, once, from his years on the fishing boat, but months of easy living had softened him, and weeks of recovery from his injuries, and the generous application of bootleg liquor, had ruined him further. He was only a danger to himself these days. He went through the clothes she'd left, several shirts and two pairs of pants and even a hat. He changed, glad to be out of the rags, the secondhand clothes fitting well enough on his slighter-than-usual frame. Then he poured a glass of water with a shaking hand, took two of the aspirin from the tin, went to the washroom to do the necessary and splash water on his face, and then made his hesitant way to the door.

The woman's apartment was small but comfortable. The bedroom led onto a living room, and a long counter separated that from the kitchen. His benefactor was standing by the stove, and a steaming cup of coffee waited for him on the tiled counter, next to a piece of dry toast, which he thought he could just about stomach. He slid onto a stool on his side of the counter and picked up the mug, inhaling the steam. "I am grateful to you."

She crossed her arms and looked at him, expression serious, voice mild. "You can repay me with information."

Abel took a sip, then shrugged. "I can't imagine what I know that would do *you* any good, but I'm pleased to help if I can."

"Last night, you mentioned the Silver Twilight Lodge."

He jolted and looked around, as if expecting hooded cultists to appear from the shadows... and maybe that was *exactly* what he expected. "I, I don't know what you're talking about, ma'am – miss?"

"Diana," she said, without further clarification, but Abel saw no sign that a man lived here, and there was no ring on her finger.

He couldn't help but smile, thinking of his mother's stories of gods and heroes again. "Like the huntress. I'm Abel Davenport."

"Like the unlucky brother." She sighed. "You don't remember anything you said last night?"

"I... don't, but, whatever it was, you must have misunderstood me." He didn't want to jeopardize this good fortune; new clothes, a roof, and hot coffee were pleasures he hadn't experienced in a while, and he was loath to give them up. But he didn't know what to make of this strange woman and her stranger questions. Was she an agent of Cain? No, that was paranoia talking. Cain wouldn't bother with subterfuge. He didn't respect Abel enough for that. But then, who was she, and what danger did she represent? "What kind of lodge, did you say?"

"Don't do that." Her voice was sharp. "I helped you, so the least you can do is help me. You said there's something in the Silver Twilight Lodge. Something dangerous, I gather, and you know people who want it, or you want it yourself. I need to know what you're talking about."

He saw there was no use in trying to play ignorant, but that wasn't the only option available to him. Abel shook his head. "You'd never believe me. And even if you did, you don't want to get mixed up in all this. It's far too dangerous for–"

She drew herself taller. "I am a Seeker in the Order of the Silver Twilight. I am *already* mixed up in this. I am aware there's danger. I've... I may have... contributed to that danger, though I didn't know what I was doing at the time. I didn't understand what the Lodge was. Now I do, and I'm horrified by it. I want to stop them."

"You're a Seeker?" Maybe he *should* have run. "That's... more advanced than an Initiate, but..." His mind whirled with possibilities, and too many questions to ask. She was part of the Lodge, but she opposed it? Someone in her position could be a real help to him. Hope in a hopeless world. But why–

"What rank are you?" she said.

He frowned. "Me? No, I'm not... I'm not a member of the Lodge. Never was." He smiled, and it made his face hurt, because he hadn't done so in a long time. "I was part of what you might call a... rival organization... though not anymore. My brothers expelled me for insufficient zeal. But if you're a Seeker... then that means you have access to parts of the Lodge that are closed off to the rank-and-file...

not *everything*, nowhere near, but you do have access to the people who *can* get into those places." He'd researched the Lodge extensively, though probably not as extensively as Cain had since their falling out.

"I suppose I do," she said. "What good would that kind of access do for you?"

"I... it's a long story, miss. Diana."

"It's Sunday. My shop is closed anyway. I have plenty of time for a long story."

Abel took a sip of coffee, and a bite of toast, and tried to order his disordered mind. Should he tell her? What harm could it do? Even if she was lying, and she handed him over the Lodge, that might be something he could turn to his advantage. This was the first glimmer of a way forward he'd seen in weeks. He cleared his throat.

"My fishing boat was caught in a storm, and wrecked, and I washed up on a rocky island..."

After Abel woke up on the beach in his hometown, he had gone into town and sold the golden chain. The pawnbroker had wanted to cheat him, Abel was sure, but something about his eyes and his smile made the man turn halfway honest, and Abel walked out with more money than he'd ever seen in his life.

He'd convinced the man to throw in a knife from his glass case with the deal, too, but it wasn't a fisherman's working knife; it was a fancy thing, with a sharkskin handle and a pearl at the base of the hilt, its moon-colored blade razor sharp on both sides.

He went to a clothing shop and showed them the color of

his money before they could throw him out, thinking him a vagrant. Once he was outfitted in better style, he got a shave and a haircut, so he looked presentable when he headed over to the jewelry store. His pockets were filled with pearls – where they'd come from, and how they'd stayed put in his pockets during his long swim, was a mystery, but he was comfortable with mysteries now. He was anointed by a god, and the god would provide. The jeweler drove a harder bargain than the pawnbroker, but the pearls were good quality, and between those and the necklace, Abel made enough to live on for months.

His next stop was the bank. He'd had an account there for years, though there'd been precious little money it these past few years, drained by his misfortunes. The banker, Mr Eustermann, pumped Abel's hand for half a minute and congratulated him on the obvious uptick in his good fortunes. "If there's *anything* we can do for you," he said.

Abel replied, "You foreclosed on my mother's house."

The banker nodded his head, eyes sorrowful. "A terrible necessity indeed–"

"It's still standing empty, isn't it? The foreclosure auction didn't have any takers because it's in rough shape."

"Another regrettable truth," the banker said.

"I can't afford to buy the house back outright, not yet, but I'd like you to rent it to me, and in a few months, I'll be able to pay in full."

Eustermann shifted and pulled at his collar. Abel's direct stare was clearly making him uncomfortable. "Rent you the house? We are not in the business of property management here, Mr Davenport…"

Abel put an arm over the man's shoulder and moved in close. "I'm sure we can make an arrangement, Mr Eustermann. Perhaps something unofficial…"

Eustermann was greedy, and Abel was relentless, so they struck a deal. Abel hired a car to give him a ride out to the home where he'd grown up, a saltbox house nestled on an unhospitable stretch of shoreline on an unlovely curve of the bay. For the next part of the work, he needed solitude, and easy access to sea water. Going back home for both made the whole situation sweeter.

Abel didn't bother to clear out the cobwebs in the house. He found an old tin bucket in the shed and walked down to the water, scooping it full, and walked it back inside, to the big tub on the ground floor. He went back and forth until the shadows grew long, until the tub was full of salt water, deep enough to immerse himself in. He took his clothes off, folded them neatly, and then lowered himself into the water. It was frigid, but he didn't mind: the cold invigorated him, and lit up his mind. The amulet still hung on its bootlace around his neck and pressed against his breastbone. He lay back in the water, let it close over his face… and then allowed himself to breathe. The water wouldn't hurt him now. The amulet would make sure of that.

Abel opened his eyes, and he did not see the water-stained ceiling he'd looked at so many times throughout his childhood. Instead he saw a cavern, lit by glowing clusters of star-shaped fungi, and figures in robes moving with inhuman gaits. One of the figures brandished a knife, a crude thing with a blade made from a sharpened oyster shell. When it moved, Abel saw the amulet sway on a golden chain around the creature's throat: the last high priest, before Abel discovered the temple and took up the role.

The priest placed one of its hands on a stone altar, and in one swift motion, sliced off one of its fingers. The other worshippers chanted as the figure stood up and tossed the severed digit into a pool of water ringed by triangular stones that pointed inward like teeth. The chanting rose, and then the voices sped up, and the lights flickered rapidly, and Abel understood that time was passing in his vision, though how much time, he could not have said.

Time slowed to normal again, and something crawled out of the water.

Abel sat up in the tub with a gasp. He knew what he had to do. He knew why he needed a knife, and that salt water was good for so much more than strengthening his visions.

Still naked and dripping, Abel went to his old bedroom, with its sagging abandoned mattress, and picked up the knife from the dresser. He returned to the bathroom, leaving wet footprints on the dusty floor. He had no altar stone, but the edge of the tub would do well enough. He pressed his hand against the tub and, before he could talk himself out of this course of action, pressed down with the knife.

Cutting off the end of his finger was harder than Abel had expected, and he had to really bear down, grunting as the blade crunched through, just above the knuckle. He whimpered at the hot wave of agony. His head spun, and his hand throbbed. The Ravening Deep would not spare him from pain, it seemed, and he wondered at the stoicism of the priest in his vision. It hadn't been human, or not entirely so, and perhaps that accounted for the difference.

Abel picked up the severed end of his finger with his unharmed hand and looked at the bit of flesh for a moment. I have a hangnail, he thought, or I used to. Then he flung the finger into the tub. He hoped the chanting from his vision wasn't necessary. He did not know the words.

Abel bandaged his hand and stumbled to his bedroom, where he fell into a deep and dreamless sleep that lasted until the next morning.

When he woke, he went into the bathroom, and the water had changed – it was no longer clear, but opaque, the gray-green of the sea seen on a stormy day. Abel barked out a laugh, elated and astonished. He hadn't really *doubted* his visions; they were too powerful for that, but it was still amazing to see his god's promised miracle in action. He resisted the urge to reach in and feel around under the surface. Things were growing there, remarkable things, and he must give them time to develop.

Abel was hungry, and there wasn't much to eat in the house, just a tin of ancient cornmeal and another of ancient flour, abandoned when he lost the place. He considered going out for groceries. Instead, he walked outside, down to the stony shore. In this little protected curve of the coastline, the waters were calm, and the waves were not breakers but ripples. The day was cool, the air full of salt, and the cries of the gulls forlorn. Leaden clouds pressed down as far as Abel could see in every direction.

He rolled up the legs of his pants and waded into the water, then dropped to his knees, immersed to his chin. His thoughts were disjointed and feverish, a jumble of associations flooding his mind: births, baptisms, drownings.

But as he felt the steady and constant motion of the water around him, an engine that had turned without human intervention for millions of years and would continue to do so long after all the humans were gone, his thoughts settled and became more orderly themselves. Somewhere out there in the water, there was a vast emptiness where his god should be. His god was dead, its kingdom conquered, its works broken. But Abel could bring his god back to life, and in return, Abel would be rewarded. He'd *already* been rewarded. Rewarded with purpose.

After a long time in the water, Abel rose, and felt refreshed. His hunger pangs were gone, and his hand no longer throbbed at all. The pain was gone, but the bandage was tighter now, and uncomfortable. As he walked to the shore, he unwound the bandage, and was unsurprised to see his pinky finger had grown back. The digit had a new little kink in its length, though, like it had considered and abandoned the idea of growing a fourth knuckle, and the fingernail was thick and striated like the shell of a clam, but the digit curled when he tried to bend it, and it felt normal enough.

Abel turned and faced the sea. "Thank you, Asterias." But that felt wrong. His god was not in the sea. His god had been stolen away, the last fragment of its greatness hidden somewhere inland, forgotten in a crowded room.

Abel walked back up to the house, determined to find and restore the god.

When he entered the living room, he saw the wet footprints on the floor immediately. Unnerved, he picked up a poker from beside the cold fireplace, wishing he'd kept his beautiful knife closer to hand. He hadn't expected to need a weapon; the house was remote, and he hardly had enemies. The tracks came from the hallway, from the direction of the bathroom, and continued toward the kitchen. Though Abel had cut off his finger hoping for a miracle, he hadn't truly *expected* one. How much power could a dead god possess, after all, and who knew what truth could be found in visions?

When Abel went into the kitchen, fire poker held high, he found a man, naked and dripping wet, standing at the counter with his back turned.

"Who are you?" Abel demanded, hoping but not quite daring to hope.

The man turned, and Abel looked into a face he'd seen so often in the mirror. This stranger had Abel's same dark eyes, same long face, same unruly hair, same slightly crooked nose. The man had been stuffing dry handfuls of cornmeal into his mouth, and when he spoke, little yellow grains spilled down his chin. "Brother," the creature croaked. "I am your brother."

Abel lowered the poker. "You... came from me." Like Eve from Adam's rib, he thought, and then flinched at the blasphemy. No. Not blasphemy. Because *that* God was not *his* god.

The impossible creature turned and fumbled at the sink until a weak flow ran from the tap, then drank from cupped hands, washing the dry cornmeal down. It – he? – turned back to Abel and spoke again, this time in a more even voice. He didn't sound *quite* the way Abel sounded to himself, but close. "I am a comet."

Abel frowned. "A... comet?" Did he mean he came from

space? Had *Asterias* come from space, a refugee from some shattered world, sailing through the cold void until crashing untold millennia ago into the ocean, adapting to a new world, making a new kingdom on earth?

"Starfish," the creature said, and beckoned. Abel joined him, unnerved at standing beside a naked replica of himself who stank of brine. The creature drew a seven-pointed star in a spill of cornmeal on the counter, beside the overturned canister. He drew a wavy line down the center.

"Some... some starfish reproduce like this, by dividing themselves in two. Each half becomes a new creature." Then he drew a line at the base of one of the seven arms. "But there are others, in the Pacific, who shed their arms instead. The severed arm grows into a new starfish. You see? The process is called autotomy. From the Greek. It means... self-severing." The creature grinned at Abel, and its teeth were straighter and whiter than his own. "Self-amputation. Like you." He mimed a chopping motion. "That amputated arm of the starfish is called a comet." The creature thumped himself on the chest with a fist. "I am your comet."

"How do you *know* all this?" Abel said.

The comet cocked its head. "I know only what you know, brother. Uncle Jericho came back from Hawaii and told us about the starfish. Mother went to the library and found a book about it. She read to you from it on the afternoon of March 13, the year you turned nine. It was raining. Your mother was in her favorite housedress–"

"You remember all that?" Abel was agog. He'd known the ritual would create another person, to expand his congregation, but he hadn't expected *this*, a version of himself, but with an improved mind? It was eerie, it was alarming, and it was exhilarating. Together, they would restore their god to glory.

"Of course I remember," the comet said. "I am all that you were, and more." He held out a hand and clasped Abel's. "We're closer than brothers, but brothers will do for a name. You can call me... Seth."

"Seth, like Abel's brother, from the Bible?"

"One of his brothers," Abel said grimly.

"This Seth... this double... had all your memories?" Diana shuddered. Abel didn't blame her.

"More than that," Abel said. "He had all my memories, and could recall them at will. Every instant from the moment I was born. He had perfect recall for every event, every conversation, everything that happened around me, even if I wasn't even paying attention at the time. He could recount conversations held by strangers across the room when I was a child. The full potential of the human mind, unlocked by an inhuman mind."

Abel took a sip of his coffee, now gone cold. He'd never told this story to anyone before. His only close confidants in the past six months had been his own comets, and they knew everything he knew, by definition. Abel was aware how unlikely his tale sounded, and expected her to throw him out now that he'd told it. "You must think I'm a madman."

"I have never seen anything quite like... what you've described," Diana said. "But I've seen some other things that—"

She was interrupted by a shrill ringing of the telephone

from downstairs. Diana rose from her spot on the other side of the counter and frowned. "I'm sorry, I should run down and answer that. I don't usually get calls on Sundays when the shop is closed."

Abel nodded and watched her depart. He looked around her kitchen, so much cheerier and cleaner and more homey than his own. Though "his kitchen" wasn't his own anymore. It belonged to the comets, like everything else he'd once owned. Specifically, it belonged to his other "brother", the comet who came after Seth, the one who'd replaced Abel as high priest, and who'd assumed Abel's identity. That was the comet that called himself "Cain". A little joke. Adam and Eve's first son, and the biblical slayer of his brother Abel. The fact that the monster had a sense of humor, however rudimentary, just made everything more disturbing.

Even worse, Abel knew Cain was nearby, just across the river, the certainty of his presence throbbing in Abel's skull like a rotten tooth. Abel no longer had visions, not since he lost the amulet, but he still felt connected to his comets, the copies he'd spawned directly as well as the ones they had spawned in turn – his grand-comets, as it were. There were at least half a dozen duplicates of him in Arkham now, moving in inscrutable circles, going about treacherous business. Drinking made it harder for him to sense them, too, which was another reason he'd turned to the bottle.

But now that he'd met Diana, with her connection to the Lodge, and her clear suspicion of the Order… maybe he could do something besides getting drunk and waiting for Cain to kill him. Maybe he could stop his comets from fulfilling their goals. In order to restore the Ravening Deep,

Cain had to gain access to forbidden parts of the Silver Twilight Lodge, and Abel had no doubt his comet was working to solve that problem even now. If Abel could get there *first*, though…

He heard Diana's footsteps coming back up the stairs, returning to him, just as hope had.

CHAPTER FIVE
Rituals

"Shall we send a car?" said the woman on the phone.

"I can walk over later this morning, unless it's urgent." Diana didn't want to get into any car that Sanford sent. Once she was in a car, she could be taken *anywhere*. She didn't think she'd let any of her recent misgivings show, or given anyone reason to doubt her loyalty, but who knew what Carl Sanford could see? Some believed the Master of the Silver Twilight Lodge could read minds, or see into your secret heart, or catch glimpses of the future – the latter theory whispered by those who envied Sanford's luck in the financial markets.

"Oh, no hurry," the Initiate working as Sanford's assistant said breezily. Diana didn't know her name; Sanford's assistants tended to come and go, as they either excelled and were promoted or disappointed and were expelled. "He's going to be working in his office until lunchtime at least – that is, if he even remembers to eat. You know how absorbed he can get."

Such pretensions toward familiarity with Sanford were

common among the Initiates, who wanted to believe they were close to the inside of things. They should be happy they remained in the outer reaches of Sanford's orbit and beneath his notice. Diana wasn't anywhere near the true center of Sanford's world, but she was already far closer than she wanted to be.

"Let him know I'll be along as soon as I can." What could the leader of the Order want? To send her on another incomprehensible errand? To make her participate in another ritual? She wasn't sure she could do that, but pretending to go along and further gaining Sanford's trust was her best hope to someday bring him down, so she might have to grit her teeth and bear it.

Diana hung the candlestick phone on its little hook. Her phone was one of the new models, with a rotary dial on the front so you could place calls directly, without having to speak to an operator. Her customers, the wealthy women of Arkham, could be counted on to notice such details. If you wanted to move among the upper echelons, it was vital to look like you belonged there, and Diana took great pains to do so. That attention to every little detail would be beneficial if she embarked on the double life she was contemplating.

She went back upstairs, where Abel sat staring into his cold mug of coffee, absorbed in thought. He was a striking man, underneath all the grime and stubble and liquor, with dark and soulful eyes and a strong jaw, though his face was a bit long, putting her in mind of certain portraits of Puritans hanging in the town's municipal buildings. He was a true son of New England. She was inclined to believe his tale, outrageous as it was, because she knew there were strange powers abroad in the universe, and it was easy to believe the great sea contained unknown horrors. Besides, who would make up a tale so outlandish?

The problem was, she hadn't heard *enough* of his outlandish tale. She hadn't heard the part that mattered most to her.

"Is everything all right?" Abel's voice had grown more firm the longer he talked, and now there was no trace of weakness or quaver.

"I'm not sure," she said. "That was one of the Initiates at the Silver Twilight Lodge. Carl Sanford would like to see me right away."

"The magus," Abel murmured.

"I've never heard anyone call him that. Some call him the master."

"The magus is what my one of my… comets calls Sanford."

She resumed her place across the counter from him. "Why are your comets interested in the Lodge?" That was the part *she* was interested in.

"I was getting to that," Abel said. "It's a long and bloody story, but since you've been summoned, I'll skip to the end. I was ousted, and our group was taken over by another comet, a monstrous creature named Cain. He looks like me… he looks human… most of the time. But he's not. We have reason to believe the last remnant of Asterias is being held prisoner by Carl Sanford, and Cain intends to get it back."

Asterias! Abel said that so matter-of-factly, when talking about an impossible thing. Her understanding of the impossible had shifted recently, but even so… "You really think Sanford has captured a god?"

Perhaps it wasn't so unlikely. She'd seen Sanford traffic with inhuman creatures; that was the very thing that had changed her from curious Seeker to terrified apostate, after all.

The moment of her horrific awakening came during a ritual held in the subterranean depths beneath the Lodge, in a dank stone chamber lined with wrought-iron braziers that sputtered sickly flames and miasmic smoke. Her memories were hazed with that smoke, and mingled with the countless nightmares she'd had since. The nightmares sometimes happened when she was awake, superimposing themselves on the real world when she caught a whiff of burning leaves or an unidentified chemical stink. The details were slippery, but the impression was clear.

The chamber was crowded with figures veiled in robes, sumptuous black and arterial red, denoting their ranks; she was in coarse black, but with gold thread at the sleeves. She'd sipped from a cup earlier, something to "heighten her senses", but it just gave her a sense of unreality. The figures all swayed and chanted, and she spoke with them, the alien words filling her mouth, though she couldn't recall memorizing them.

When she raised her eyes to the center of the room, she saw the raised dais of black stone, with two figures upon it. Tears sprang to her eyes: one resembled a mummy, a dried-out husk of a person, her withered hand wrapped around a large silver key. The other was a young man, curled up, arms and wrists bound, face hidden under a hood. He whimpered, and shifted, and she saw his face: was that Walter Evans? He was an Initiate, wasn't he? His mother, Grace, had come to her shop once or twice…

Sanford was there, overseeing the grim business on the slab, resplendent in ornate robes. Strange glyphs cut into the stone began to glow, emitting a flat, straw-colored light. The chanting of the cultists was joined by another voice, a series of gibbering moans and clicks, teasing a meaning that she couldn't quite comprehend. Her mind struggled with the sounds, and then understanding pierced her brain like a splinter under a fingernail: the dried husk had been a young woman, and her death was an offering to open the way, mere grease for the machinery of a summoning.

The boy, Walter... he would be the first meal.

She stumbled to her knees, and she wasn't the only one, but her fall was weakness, while for the others, it was more like reverence. A wave of force broke across the dais, and the air itself seemed to split, revealing a gash in reality that spilled out darkness like ink. Things reached out of the opening, twisting writhing grasping things, and seized Walter, who screamed... but not for long. A chemical reek struck her, some malevolent intelligence groped across her mind, and then horrible slurping, crunching, moaning noises filled her ears. She wanted desperately to flee, but she couldn't. She gazed down instead, at her lap, and – there was a blade in her hand. An ornate and bloody dagger. Why? Had she... did she... why couldn't she remember? Why didn't she *want* to?

Her hand tightened on the knife. Could she charge the dais? Raise the blade? Plunge it into that monster, still crawling from the darkness, and send it back wherever it came from?

Sometimes, in her dreams, she did just that, with... mixed results. In reality, as best she could recall, she'd simply dropped the blade and stumbled to the back of the chamber, turning her face away from the horror.

Another Seeker had joined her, and spoke softly, as if to a skittish cat. "Diana, isn't it? Your first summoning? Not something that happens every day. You did well." He took her hand and led her toward the far door, chanting turning to cheers behind them. "It's hard, the first time you see something like that." He was an archivist, she thought, at the historical society, and his voice was kind. "You might have an odd dream or two later. There's a doctor in the Lodge who still prescribes laudanum, which is a great help. Let me know if you'd like some."

"He... that man... Walter..." Diana said.

"He chose to take part in the rite willingly," the archivist said, a little stiffly. "Our master guided him to his proper path."

"I... but what did they summon?" She was both bothered that she hadn't gotten a good look at the thing in the circle, and grateful she'd been spared the sight. "What did *we* summon?"

"Something our master has a use for," the archivist said, and took her back into a place of light. Except, in a sense, the darkness of that place had never left her, and she feared it never would.

There were at least two monsters in that chamber: the thing pulled from the darkness, and Carl Sanford. He'd manipulated Walter, surely. No one would offer themselves up like that unless they were deceived or deluded. What lies had Sanford told, in order to trick that poor boy and bring that monster into the world? Had the girl come willingly at all? Either way, Sanford had traded *people* for a *thing*, for some unknown but grim purpose, and the other members were celebrating! She had fallen among evil men and women, and it had happened so gradually, she hadn't even realized it.

If Sanford was willing to sacrifice innocents, and even his own people, to summon such a monster, he must be willing to do anything to further his occult goals, and someone like *that* shouldn't be allowed to wield power – not over other people, and not over the mysteries of the world. Diana could not be party to such horrible acts. Diana had to *oppose* them. At that moment, she ceased to be a faithful Seeker, and became an enemy of the Lodge, and all her thoughts turned toward stopping Sanford from ever sacrificing anyone else for dark designs again.

Abel said, "Diana?"

She blinked. "Sorry. I was just remembering… What did you say?"

"That my comets and I did a lot of research, and questioned people, and performed certain, ah, rituals, and, yes – they all point to Carl Sanford having possession of at least a piece of Asterias."

What could Sanford do with such a thing? Could he use it to make comets, like Abel did with the amulet? *Had* he? "And this Asterias could regenerate fully from such a piece?" she asked. "Like those starfish you talked about, spawning from a severed arm? The god could come back?" Would Sanford *want* to revive such an entity? It was in his nature to use any path to power available to him, and she feared what he might do.

Abel shrugged. "That's the theory. If the proper rites are performed, in the right place, in the right way, the god will return to life and power. I didn't doubt it when I was under the influence. I don't doubt it now. I only fear it."

"You'll have to tell me about your fall from grace," Diana said. "But later. I need to go to the Lodge now."

"Could you… would you… keep an eye out? If we can find that fragment before my comets do, we may be able to destroy it, and end the threat of Asterias forever."

She laughed, a little bitterly. "If I see a piece of a god sitting on a shelf, I'll be sure to tell you."

He scowled, a stubborn and mulish look. "It would look like a biological specimen, probably in a jar—"

"That's not the problem," Diana said. "Sanford doesn't leave items of power just lying about. If this god fragment is in the Lodge, it's likely locked away someplace that Seekers don't usually go. I'm sure Sanford has a vault, probably more than one, but I don't know where they're located. I've been deep into the Lodge, a few times, and there are more rooms and basements in that place than seem possible. I saw a room…" She shook her head.

"What?"

She took a breath, and let it out slow. "Once, walking down a corridor underground, led by a Brother of the Dark, I passed an open doorway, and when I glanced inside, it seemed to lead outside, to a vast gray plain… and there were stars in the sky, glowing red. I paused, trying to make sense of what I was seeing, and the Brother seized my arm and told me not to dilly-dally. My point is, the piece of your god could be anywhere, and it's not such an easy place to search."

Diana rose. "I'd better not dilly-dally now, either. You can stay here until I get back, if you like. We still have much to discuss."

"I cannot thank you enough for your kindness."

"It's only partly kindness," Diana said. "Your research might have uncovered things about the Lodge that I need to know. Things that can help me in…" She trailed off, unsure how much to say, or how to articulate it.

"In what?" Abel said. "My goal, insofar as I have one, is to stop the rise of Asterias. What's yours?"

"Carl Sanford is a master of monsters," she said. "He made me complicit in his dark work. I could not live with myself if I allowed him to continue perverting the nature of reality. I have to try to stop him. If what you say about this Asterias is true, Sanford may have plans for the dead god, and I don't want those plans to come to fruition." She considered Abel carefully. He was too wretched to lie, she thought. A broken man, but perhaps he could be mended. They had similar goals, and she needed allies. "I will do anything I can to oppose Sanford."

Abel nodded. "Then I'll stay. We're sailing in the same direction, and I'd much rather sail together."

CHAPTER SIX
The Lodge

Diana dressed in a simple but elegant two-piece cotton day dress with a low waist and a straight skirt, dark blue with a pattern of tiny white flowers, and a simple strand of pearls. She perched a straw hat with a matching dark blue ribbon on her head and slipped on a pair of Oxfords. Her strappy heels were more fashionable, and showed off her ankles to better effect, but she was walking over to French Hill, and she didn't relish the idea of catching a heel in those cobblestones. She didn't want Sanford or anyone else at the Lodge noticing her ankles anyway.

Mid-morning in early autumn was a beautiful time to be out and about in Arkham, and the Merchant District was sleepy, since it was Sunday. She turned off Main Street and headed east along Church Street, past the more established shops, and the titular old churches, though neither set of venues were bustling. She dreamed of moving her store over here – Main Street, despite its name, was a less important thoroughfare than Church, and a more fashionable address would help her business thrive even further.

She paused, slumped, then straightened her spine and adjusted her hat in the reflection of a shop window. She was still thinking about her little ambitions, her plans to find greater security and success, but she was setting herself against the Silver Twilight Lodge, and that sort of conflict wasn't likely to end well for her.

Unless... Could there be a way to stop the Lodge without losing everything she had in the process? Carl Sanford was the key – without him at the head, leading the group's incursions into occult matters, the Lodge would become as harmless as all other fraternal societies. If she could take down *Sanford*...

"Ignore the monsters and the magic," she murmured as she turned onto South French Hill Street and began to ascend toward the Lodge.

What if she could gather evidence of everyday, ordinary criminality? Incriminating information about Carl Sanford himself? He didn't hesitate to break the laws of nature and God, so she didn't think he'd pay much attention to mere human laws. If she could find proof of criminal activities, proof she could anonymously turn over to the local police – or even the state, since the Lodge probably held sway over the city and county forces – then maybe she could send Sanford away, without anyone even knowing she was involved.

It wasn't quite a plan, but it was, at the very least, an idea. She would keep her eyes and ears open for incriminating evidence.

Diana ascended French Hill, gazing up at the dark, thorny spire of Bayfriar's Church. Some of the oldest homes in the city were located in this neighborhood. Grand Georgian piles with black iron gates and ornamental shrubbery, though there were still brick row houses and smaller dwellings with Dutch roofs interspersed.

Some of those grand homes had been a lot more grand twenty or thirty years ago, too; some very old families lived here still, but many of them weren't as rich as they used to be. This street was lined with trees and well maintained, though some of the little alleys and thoroughfares that twisted up between the houses and over the top of the hill were showing their age, and in the steeper places, there weren't alleys at all, but narrow flights of stone stairs, many with crumbling risers.

The Silver Twilight Lodge was perched high on French Hill, with a view of Arkham spread out down the slopes below. Diana paused before the rust-flecked iron gate, as always troubled by the apparent decrepitude of the place.

The Lodge was an immense Victorian mansion, though it was clearly not a private residence anymore – Diana thought you could always tell when a place had been transformed into an institutional structure, somehow, like the building was missing its soul. The Lodge might have been a funeral home or the administrative offices of a failing charity organization. The lawn was untended, full of long grasses just beginning to go brown. The trees dotting the lawn were sick, trunks mottled with fungus, and if they weren't dead, they were nearly so, their spreading branches so many widowmakers in waiting.

She pushed open the gate, which didn't creak, despite its look of disrepair. The walkway, at least, was kept neat, a row of pale stones free of weeds, forming a narrow path that meandered a bit on the way to the front porch and the front doors. The first time she came here, she must have shown her surprise at the state of the place, because her guide chuckled and said, "I know, it's a bit of a mess, but we prefer to devote our resources to our charity and good works, rather than putting on a fancy façade."

When Diana approached the porch, a figure stood up from a chair placed deep in shadow: a tall woman, with red hair and green eyes, in a dress that had been nice a decade or two ago – the sort of outdated garb that would never grace a rack at Huntress Fashions.

"Hello, Sarah," Diana said. She looked around for the woman's constant companions, a pair of immense black mastiffs, but the beasts were nowhere to be seen. Maybe they were lurking in the long grasses. Or gnawing the bones of a trespasser...

Sarah Van Shaw was the warden of the Lodge. Diana still didn't know exactly what that *meant*, but she suspected anyone who tried to gain access to the house without an invitation wouldn't make it far, and might not ever make it off the property again.

"Diana," the woman said, sounding, as always, as if she were amused by a private joke – and the joke was probably on you. "You're here to see the master, I presume."

"When he calls, I answer."

"The master has his eye on you," Van Shaw said. "Some find ambition in a woman unseemly, but the Order is untroubled by such distinctions. Fortunately for both of us."

The idea of any commonality between herself and this

strange, intimidating woman struck Diana as repugnant, but she smiled affably and said, "Once they gave us the right to vote there was no stopping us, was there?"

Sarah opened the door and gestured for Diana to go inside. She stepped into the anteroom, where all pretense to disrepair vanished. There was a fire burning in the great hearth, and as always Diana's eyes scanned across the spines of the countless books on the floor-to-ceiling shelves on the opposite wall. There were valuable first editions here, though the truly precious volumes were kept elsewhere – there were rumors of some so precious and dangerous they were kept chained in a basement. Even so, this was a library to boggle the mind of the farm girl Diana had once been. She longed to sit on the Chesterfield sofa by the fire and peruse a few titles, but there was no time. When Sanford called, you came.

She proceeded past niches in the walls that held bits of statuary from the ancient world, squat and ugly things that possessed no beauty, though their antiquity demanded respect. Incense burned in one niche, thickening the air with cloying smoke. This anteroom was a disorienting space, the ordinary mingled with the strange and disturbing, and she suspected that combination was deliberate, meant to keep visitors on their back feet.

She went through the door that led deeper into the Lodge – it was often kept locked, but it opened for her now – and into a large meeting room dominated by a gilt-inlaid table, flanked by austere high-backed chairs. Sanford was seated there, talking in a low voice with the perky Initiate who'd called Diana. Sanford took note of Diana's arrival and patted his assistant on the hand. "Leave us alone for a few moments, would you?"

The Initiate, a young blonde woman wearing elbow-length white gloves, gave Diana a bright smile and then disappeared through one of the room's many doors.

"Greetings, Seeker," Sanford said. He was an older gentleman, though she had trouble guessing his precise age – the years didn't weigh on him as heavily as they seemed to do on most people. He had silver hair, though, and a neat beard to match, and wore a suit of refined cut and obvious expense – menswear was not her specialty, but she could recognize quality. The only time she'd seen Sanford wear anything other than a suit was the night of that horrible summoning ritual, when he wore robes like the others, except for fine scrollwork in golden thread around the neckline, sleeves, and hem.

Sanford's eyes moved up and down her body, though she'd never gotten a sense of lustfulness from him – it was more like he was conducting a thorough inventory to determine what use she might be. She hoped the intensity of his gaze did not extend to the inside of her head – if he could sense thoughts, *she* might never leave the property again. "Have a seat, Miss Stanley." He patted the chair the blonde had departed.

Diana sat beside him, glancing at the files on the table before her. She noted the names of some of the most prominent citizens in the city on those folders – at least a few of them were people she'd seen at Lodge meetings, and several others had passed through her store, or at least their wives had. "Thank you for inviting me," Diana said. "It's always a pleasure to serve the Lodge."

"We never talked about the ritual. The one you assisted with, some weeks ago." As if she could have forgotten. "What were your impressions?" His voice was mild, and she tried not to show her nervousness.

"It was... extraordinary, master. Though I didn't entirely understand it."

He nodded. "I wouldn't expect you to, at this stage of your development. I confess, inviting you to help with that rite was a test, of sorts. Some people... well. They don't know how to process an experience like that. Their minds are weak, and they recoil. Then we tell them the impossible things they saw were hallucinations, brought on by tainted whiskey or too much heat and incense."

They did rituals like that often enough to have such processes in place? Diana was appalled, but kept an expression of bland interest on her face. "I never doubted the evidence of my senses."

"I'm told you were troubled by the disappearance of the postulant." Sanford looked at her levelly.

She didn't dare lie, but she could shade the truth. "I was surprised."

"It's quite a surprising thing. The young man lacked direction and meaning in his life, but the Lodge provided him with a greater purpose. What he wanted most of all was to break free of the shackles of the mundane – he was oppressed by the *banality* of the world, you see. I can relate. I offered him an opportunity to explore... other realms, and he leapt at the chance. The ritual sent him on his way."

"He's alive, then?" Diana's heart thrummed with hope.

Sanford shrugged. "The place he wished to explore is not

without risk. But I prepared him as well as I could for what awaited him, and I hope he is thriving there. He may even return someday, with new wisdom. Stranger things have happened."

Diana's hope evaporated. She'd spent enough time around horse manure to recognize it when she smelled it.

Sanford clapped his hands, once, sharply. "But enough about our intrepid postulant. I am interested in you. You acquitted yourself well on the errands we sent you on after your ascension to Seeker, situations that brushed up against the uncanny, and I invited you to the summoning because I wanted to see how you reacted to a true confrontation with the underlying reality of the world. You acquitted yourself admirably – no screaming, no gibbering. Your mind, it seems, is made of stronger stuff than most."

"Thank you." This was her moment. The opportunity she'd been waiting for. If she could gain his trust, if she could gain *access*, she might find what she needed to take Sanford down. "I just want to learn, and be of service."

He chuckled. "You want to *move up*, Miss Stanley. You came to Arkham two years ago from a hardscrabble farm, the last living member of your family, and you transformed yourself into a successful businesswoman. You've made connections with some of the most powerful and prominent people in town. Arkham can be an insular place, and hard for outsiders to thrive in, but your charm and work ethic have paid off. You aren't satisfied with a comfortable little life, though. You want more. What do you want?"

"I want... what you said. To move up." In truth, she wanted security – to be free from the worries about money that had defined her father's existence on the farm. She wanted freedom from precarity. But if Sanford thought she wanted more than that – if he saw in her a kindred spirit fueled by poisonous ambition – she would exploit that misapprehension. "I always knew there was more to life than just working hard and dying alone. There *has* to be. There are secrets. You know them. I want to know them, too."

"The thing about secrets is, there are always more of them," Sanford said. "The word 'occult' means 'hidden' – and if we could uncover *all* those secrets, they wouldn't be hidden anymore, would they? But I do know a few things. You could learn them, too. And reap the benefits. You are on the cusp of ascending to the next level – to becoming a Sister of the Dark. Would you like that? To gain access to a whole new understanding of reality?"

"I would like nothing more." And access to your account books, if possible, Diana thought. There was no way Sanford's business dealings were unimpeachably honest. A man who would break natural law and summon monsters wouldn't feel beholden to follow *mortal* law, and that might be an avenue to bring him down.

"I thought so." Sanford smiled indulgently. "I just need your help. Proof of your loyalty, and usefulness." He tapped the files on the table. "These are notes regarding some of our members, plus one or two prominent individuals who are not part of our Order, but who are nevertheless worthy of attention. I have grown… troubled… by some of these people, of late."

"In what way?" Diana asked.

"They are behaving peculiarly. These two, for instance, Colonel Mott and Doctor Undercliffe, are both Initiates, and unlikely to ever rise any higher, as they lack the curiosity necessary to become Seekers. They've hated each other for decades, something about an insult delivered to one of their sisters at a cotillion when they were at university together – I can't be bothered to remember the details. They are formal with one another, if they interact at all, but last week I saw them sitting in the Initiate's lounge, heads together, talking like old friends. Neither one was drinking, either, though I sometimes think they both joined us just for access to the Lodge's liquor cabinet. When I strolled over to them, they reverted to their old ways, stiffening up and glaring daggers, but it was clearly pretense."

"Perhaps they are in the midst of a reconciliation?" Diana said.

"Perhaps," Sanford echoed. "But consider Doctor Kulten. He is an emeritus professor at Miskatonic University, once a scholar of the ancient epics, but long since in mental decline. He sometimes escapes the attentions of his nurse and wanders onto the porch here and stands, confused, on the threshold. Yet not two days ago I found him in this very room, attending one of our regular meetings, and speaking with a level of erudition and authority he hasn't possessed in ten years or more." Sanford shook his head. "Something strange is happening to our members, and I've heard whispers of curious behavior on the part of other eminent citizens. Personality changes, mainly."

Diana blinked, but schooled herself to show no other reaction. This Kulten had regained his memory? Abel's comet had demonstrated remarkable feats of memory, apparently… could there be a connection?

Sanford went on. "Most people are creatures of habit, and when there are significant deviations from those habits, it makes me curious. There are many possible causes for such changes, but I've ruled out the involvement of the Yith, and of Kamog and similar entities—"

"I'm sorry?" Diana said. She thought she'd seen mention of the Yith in one of the texts she'd read, though she couldn't recall the context, and Kamog she'd never heard of at all. Maybe these oddities weren't related to the comets. Maybe there were more strange things in the world than she could comprehend.

Sanford sighed. "Yes, of course, those are matters known only to higher ranks than you have yet attained, Seeker. Suffice to say that I have explored the most obvious explanations, and remain uncertain of the cause for these changes, if indeed these situations are related. If these changes portend a threat to the Lodge, I have to be cautious. But it occurred to me that *you* know many of the people involved, through your shop, and they are unlikely to see you as a threat, since, forgive me, you are a tradesperson. You could contrive reasons to enter their homes, delivering dresses and scarves and the like, and observe them, eavesdrop a bit, and look for clues that might offer an explanation for their recent… peculiarities."

"You wish for me to become a spy?" she blurted.

"You are a Seeker," Sanford said. "The name of your rank indicates your function: to pursue knowledge. I want you to pursue this knowledge for me."

"I... of course, master. Where should I begin?"

"I think with Mrs Cornelius Berglund."

"Cornelia?" Diana said, surprised.

"I always wondered if Cornelius married her *just* because he found the similarity in their names amusing," Sanford said. "Given his hideous propensity for puns and wordplay. It's a mercy for his students that he left the university. I can't imagine having to listen to him prattle week after week in a lecture hall..." He shook his head. "But Cornelia. Yes. She bears closer examination, and her husband does as well."

"I saw her just last week," Diana said. "She was inquiring about some French silk scarves I received. She seemed normal enough to me."

"She was seen driving a car yesterday," Sanford said. "She does not drive. Perhaps the matter of these scarves will give you a pretense to visit her home?"

"Of course. May I ask... why do you wish to begin with her?"

"Cornelius is helping me with a delicate matter." Sanford's expression clouded. "I would be vexed to discover he's been compromised, and unable to fulfill his duties. I have no reason to think anything is amiss with him... but if his wife has changed, it seems reasonable to assume that he might have, too."

"I didn't realize the Berglunds were members of the Lodge."

"They are not. Occasionally I find it necessary to seek outside help. Cornelius has connections I needed."

Diana wanted to inquire about the nature of that help, but she knew it was pointless. Sanford would never share more than he wished to. "I'll get started right away." She would investigate on her *own* behalf more than Sanford's, though. If she found something she could use against the Lodge, or something that could help Abel in his fight against the comets, she'd keep it for her own use.

"Good. And do be cautious. I've seen no sign that the... altered individuals are dangerous, but until we understand more about what's happening, it's best to assume they are." He patted her hand. "Go forth, Miss Stanley, and seek."

CHAPTER SEVEN
The Thing in the Basement

Like much of Arkham, the train station had once been a grand old thing, and looked even worse now because you could see remnants of its past glory. As Ruby disembarked, she wrinkled her nose at the sight of the main depot, like a castle gone to ruin. The tracks were flanked by huge stone towers of no obvious purpose, looming over the trains freshly arrived from Boston and about to head to Kingsport, like monuments from a fallen civilization. *Look upon my works, ye mighty*, she mused.

Ruby only had a single valise, but she caught the eye of a porter anyway, a young man with an open face. He hurried over, favoring one leg. Poor fellow had a limp, and still had to haul people's bags. At least her request wouldn't require much effort from him: "Could you call me a cab, sir?"

"There should be one waiting on the curb," he said. "Not too much demand on a Sunday afternoon." He led her through the station, cheerfully peppering her with inquiries about whether she'd been to Arkham before, and what brought her here, and how long she'd be staying: "No, this is my first time; I'm visiting a cousin; just for a few days." She had, of course, been to Arkham before, but she'd taken pains to look like an entirely different person on this trip: her hair color was different, and she was dressed like a country mouse, all drab and gray and without a whiff of discernible style. On her last visit to the city, she'd been rather more stylish, but she'd also stolen something valuable from Carl Sanford and the Silver Twilight Lodge, and she had no desire to be recognized.

The porter led her to the curb, where a couple of grimy yellow taxis idled, and introduced her to the cabbie, a sleepy-eyed Irishman with a tam-o-shanter jammed on his head. She gave the porter a coin and slipped into the back seat while the driver stowed her bag in the trunk. It was a good thing she wasn't in a hurry. She'd seen snails move faster. "Where to, ma'am?" he asked once he settled himself behind the wheel.

That "ma'am" was a good sign – she'd used makeup to alter her appearance, aging herself up just a touch, nothing dramatic, and she'd done her best to walk like someone with aching knees. "Over to French Hill," she said, and gave him an address.

He grunted and pulled away from Northside Station. Soon they were trundling down narrow streets, close enough to the Miskatonic River for Ruby to catch glimpses of the brown water through gaps between rundown old warehouses. They trundled down to the Peabody Avenue bridge, and then across the water. Ruby looked out the window, east, toward the small island in the river. She couldn't recall its name – if it even had one – but she'd heard strange rumors about it on her last visit: that in the old days, a witches' coven met there, and consorted with the devil. The island looked like nothing but a drab clutch of trees to her, with a few broken stone pillars poking out here and there, but with all the things she'd seen, and stolen, who was she to deny such possibilities?

They made it to southside, where the streets were in better shape, and there were a lot more shops than warehouses. There were nice neighborhoods on the north side of the river, too, especially around Independence Square, but French Hill had that height advantage, allowing its residents to lord it over the rest of the populace.

The cab took her up and over the hill and stopped on a steeply canted street, in front of the address she'd given. Ruby paid the man, thanked him, and pretended to search through her handbag until the taxi had driven out of sight. She hadn't given the driver the address of the house she was visiting, of course. Such caution was more than habit for her at this point – it was more like instinct.

She strolled a couple of blocks, turned down another block, took the next right, and then stopped in front of her destination. The house was by no means a mansion, but it was quite nice, two stories tall, painted white, with neat blue trim. The small front yard was crowded with statuary in brass and stone.

Her client, Cornelius Berglund, was the scion of a once-wealthy family fallen on hard times a generation or two back. In order to make a living, he'd sold off their ancestral home and most of their furniture, silver, and art. In the course of so doing, though, he became something of an expert on antiques, and had pivoted into a career as a dealer, initially in Colonial-era artifacts, but later antiquities from overseas. He wasn't scrupulous about how he acquired his wares, and Ruby had asked around about him. Through mutual friends, she met a thief who'd acquired a silver tea set made by Paul Revere for Berglund, who vouched for the man: "He paid what we agreed, and he didn't ask me any questions. I'd work for him again." That was good enough for her.

She intended to have words with Berglund, though, about his inaccurate intelligence regarding the lawyer's schedule. Ruby didn't like running for her life, and she intended to make Berglund pay her extra for the trouble. She glanced around to make sure she was unobserved – it was Sunday morning, and everyone was still asleep or at church, she suspected – and went up the steps to the front door. Before she could raise her hand to knock, the door opened, and a handsome woman of middle years greeted her with a smile – the lady of the house, presumably.

She was in a fine blue silk dress and elbow-length gloves, rather nice for just swanning about at home, and Ruby wondered if she was on her way out somewhere. When she smiled, she revealed lipstick on her teeth. "You must be the young lady Cornelius was expecting! Why, he didn't think you'd be here for another day or two at the earliest."

Berglund had told his wife about her? Well, actually, that made a certain degree of sense – trying to keep a visit from a strange young woman secret might lead to *more* trouble, if she caught wind of it. "I had an opening in my schedule," Ruby said. She also had a policy of refusing to follow any preset schedule. Never be where anyone expected you to be, when they expected you to be.

"Come in, come in! I'm Cornelia. You're in the antiques business, too? Brought some bauble for Cornelius to appraise, as I recall?"

Cornelia and Cornelius? The world had such things in it. "I dabble," Ruby said, stepping over the threshold. Ruby automatically began to inventory the house for any precious objects that might be worth coming back for later, or telling one of her acquaintances in the business about in exchange for a cut. The main room of the house didn't offer much of interest – some mediocre canvases on the walls, tending toward harbor scenes, and some ugly statuary that reminded her of similar pieces she'd passed over during her *last* visit to Arkham. Otherwise the furnishings were firmly conventional, solid wooden furniture showing off uninspired New England craftsmanship, and a scattering of colorful but unexceptional rugs to warm up the hardwood floors.

Cornelia took Ruby by the elbow, an unasked-for intimacy that Ruby decided not to shake off for the sake of the business arrangement. She led Ruby through the dining room and into the kitchen. Ruby had expected to do the exchange in some pretentious study with her employer dressed in a suit, trying to impress her, but Cornelius Berglund was sitting at a cloth-draped table in the kitchen. He was wearing shirtsleeves, with a large mug steaming before him. At a glance, the mug appeared to contain plain hot water, which was a whole new level of abstemiousness in Ruby's experience. More interestingly, there was a swollen bruise under his left eye, and a large bandage wrapped around his left hand. It was hard to imagine this stolid sixty-something man with unfortunate muttonchops getting into a fistfight, but Ruby couldn't imagine how else you'd come by a shiner like that.

"Miss Standish," he said, and that was bad, because he shouldn't know her real name; he'd met her through a mutual connection who'd obscured her identity. Coming to Arkham under her *real* name would have been a profoundly bad idea.

She'd learned to trust her instincts, and her instincts were telling her to beat feet, but when she turned, Cornelia was blocking the doorway, beaming at her affably. Ruby was calculating whether she'd be able to bull-rush her way through the woman when Berglund said, "I'm sorry. That was rude. We can use your other name if you prefer – Edna Glasby, was it?"

"How did you find out my name?" she asked levelly.

He waved that away. "I am a man of many connections and resources. I am always careful to find out who I'm really doing business with. There aren't that many young lady – cat burglars, is that the term? – who operate on this coast, and none of them are named Edna Glasby."

"Edna's a hot new prospect with a lot of potential," Ruby said. "You should have given her a chance." She sighed. "Listen, if you did your research, you know I don't love spending time in Arkham, so let's just do our business and get it done. I have your ruby, if you have the rest of my money." She opened the top of her handbag, as if to draw out the jewel, but instead put her hand on a pearl-handled derringer, a gift from an old girlfriend. If Berglund was any kind of a shrewd operator, he'd know he could just sell her to Carl Sanford, and keep the ruby for free. This had just turned into an entirely different sort of transaction, and she'd be lucky to get out without spilling blood.

"I will gladly pay you, but I will pay you even more for information." Berglund opened the lid on a wooden salt cellar and spooned a generous heap of crystals into his mug, gave it a stir, and took a sip. Who on earth drank hot salt water? Was it some kind of old home remedy?

"I'm not in the business of information, Mr Berglund. I acquire things. How about we just–"

"The Silver Twilight Lodge," Berglund said. "You've been there, in the vaults. You've stolen from Carl Sanford, and gotten away with it."

That was enough. Ruby took one step back and one to the side and drew out her pistol, pointing it at Berglund, but with Cornelia in easy range, too. "I am going to walk out of here now, and you are not going to follow me."

"We just want information," Berglund said. "We'll pay you." If he was bothered by the gun, he didn't show it.

Cornelia took a step toward her, and Ruby said, "Hold it! I'll shoot him."

Cornelia looked at Berglund, head cocked. "You'd kill my husband? That's fine. I have another one."

That threw Ruby enough to make her brow wrinkled, though not enough to make her aim waver. "What are you talking about–"

A door at the other end of the kitchen swung open, and a man who looked exactly like Cornelius Berglund stepped out. This Berglund was dressed in pajamas, and he carried a claw hammer with something dark and red on the head. As Ruby gaped, she saw a drop of blood fall from the hammer and spatter onto the tile. "You've got a twin?" Ruby swung the gun in an arc, unable to cover all three of them at once.

"A twin?" the Berglund at the table said. "Yes, I suppose so. But only recently."

Berglund's double with the hammer chuckled. Though he wasn't *quite* a double – one of his eyes was noticeably lower than the other, and his nose was crooked, not like it had been broken, but like it had grown wrong in the first place. There was also a *lot* more hair coming out of his ears, long and coarse as cat whiskers.

"Why don't you put the gun away before someone gets hurt?" the Berglund at the table said. "Just tell us everything you know about the vaults in the Lodge, and whether you saw a particular item while you were there. This doesn't have to get *messy.*"

"All right. That sounds reasonable. Let's discuss my fee." Cornelia was no longer blocking the doorway, and Ruby decided to sprint for the gap. She pivoted to run–

–and fell forward when someone grabbed her right ankle and yanked. She sprawled down face-first, pistol flying across the tile, where Cornelia picked it up, clucking her tongue.

Ruby looked back – into the face of another Cornelia, who was *under the table*, her head now poking out from beneath the tablecloth, her hands still grasping Ruby's ankle. Ruby screamed, as her mind rebelled at the improbability of *another* twin. Could that be possible, some kind of twisted dual marriage?

It didn't matter who this woman was: enough to categorize her as the enemy. Ruby kicked back with her other foot, wishing she was wearing spiked heels, but there was a satisfying crunch when her heel hit the double's face, and it's grip loosened.

Ruby scrambled upright… and then kept rising. The Berglund with the hammer had her crushed in a bear hug from behind. The first Berglund rose from the table, sighed, and reached into his pocket for a handkerchief. "This could have been so civilized," he murmured.

Ruby kicked and flailed, but it didn't make any difference. Berglund pressed the cloth, reeking of some sweet substance, against her face. Her panic rose, and then receded in the waves of chemical stink. Everything began to swim and shimmer, and then everything went away.

Ruby woke, her head aching, and shifted, only to hit some restraining force. Ropes? Was she tied to a chair?

People were talking, male and female voices, and so she kept her eyes shut and her chin on her chest, listening. It sounded like Berglund and Cornelia… though who knew which versions? They were *both* twins? And named Cornelia and Cornelius, as if *they* were the twins. What twisted family dynamic had she stumbled into?

"…need to bother Cain," a Berglund said. "I'm sure I can get her to tell us what she knows without bothering him."

"But what if she can't remember?" a Cornelia countered. She didn't sound like she was talking through a broken nose, so it was probably the one who'd met Ruby at the door. "You know how terrible these people's memories are. If

Cain brings the amulet and initiates her into the mysteries, she'll have perfect recall of every turn and passageway in the Lodge. If she saw the fragment, even from the corner of her eye without consciously noticing, she'd be able to tell us."

Ruby ground her teeth. They wanted something from the Silver Twilight Lodge, and thought she could help them get it? She wasn't going back there. She was lucky to have escaped unscathed last time she stole from Carl Sanford. She couldn't imagine what she knew that might be helpful to them, either; she'd tricked her way into the Lodge once, but the same approach wouldn't work a second time.

"Cain is busy – you know it's a delicate time," Berglund countered. "He trusted us to handle this part of the operation, and he called it a 'longshot' anyway, so think how impressed he'll be if we manage to find out–"

He was interrupted... seemingly by himself. "We should tell him the longshot paid off, shouldn't we? Look, I'll just ask Cain what he thinks. I know he's making deals right now, but this is the most important thing – this is the *mission*." This was the second Berglund, the one with the hammer; his voice was a little mushier than his twin's, as if he'd suffered a broken jaw and was still healing.

After a long moment of silence, Cornelia said, "Perhaps... I should go with you."

"You first generations think I'm not capable," the mushy one said, voice quivering with fury. "I'm not *lesser*, all right? If anything I'm closer to god than you are. Might I remind you that Cain himself is a comet made from a comet–"

"It's just better if we go together," Cornelia said in a

soothing tone. "It's not a criticism. We have total faith in you. Cain will know it's more serious if we both come, that's all."

"Fine. Do or don't. I'm leaving." Heavy boots tromped upstairs.

"I can get what we need out of her," the remaining Berglund said.

"I don't doubt you, dear. Do look in on my sister when you have time? She's upstairs in a salt bath, but that broken nose will take time to heal."

"Of course, darling. Good luck with that brute. I should have never made the beast."

"It's good you did. We needed the help. That Ruby Standish may be tiny, but she's fierce."

Ruby felt a little thrill of pride, then was annoyed at herself for caring about what Cornelia thought. She heard the tromp of more footsteps going upstairs, and then silence.

Ruby cracked an eye. She was in a basement, all stone and clutter, which she'd surmised from the musty, damp smell. The room was illuminated by a single weak, bare bulb. Berglund – the one with the shiner and the bandage – was sitting in front of her on a folding chair. "Oh good," he said. "You're awake."

Ruby lunged at him, prepared to bite his nose right off, but jerked up short. She wasn't just tied to a chair, loops of rough rope were wrapped around her body, pinning her arms to her sides. The chair was, in turn, tied to some sort of support post, stealing her leverage. She might still be able to work her way loose, but it wouldn't happen quickly, and Berglund sighed and took her derringer out of his pocket when she started wiggling.

"You know, you should be grateful."

"You should be grateful you're still breathing," Ruby retorted. "If you didn't have wives hidden under every piece of furniture in the house, I would have shot you."

"Don't be too impressed with yourself," he said. "This was all a trap, you know, even if it's not quite the same trap anymore. Carl Sanford knew I had certain connections in the illicit antiquities trade, and thought I might be able to reach you. He's still upset about your little escapade. I don't know what you took from him – I get the impression it wasn't even that important, on its own merits – but he can't bear the fact that you violated one of his inner sanctums and got away without consequences."

"You're a member of the Lodge?" Ruby said. She'd asked around, and her informants assured her he wasn't, though it wasn't as if the Order published an official membership list.

He sighed. "I was, once. Just a lowly Initiate. But I hesitated, you see, at a crucial moment during one of Sanford's little tests. The ones you don't realize are tests, until it's too late. I wasn't expelled, but it became apparent there was no chance for me to advance, and the atmosphere became so unwelcome I withdrew. It's a shame, because the members of the Order like to deal with each other. They give each other inside information, they send opportunities to one another. I missed out on a lot of opportunities. So when Sanford offered to promote me to Seeker if I'd help him catch a thief…" He shrugged. "It was a good deal."

"It's generous of him to let you lick his boots again." Ruby's bravado was always the last bit of her armor to go, but she was getting worried. She'd made it out of the Lodge once before, but if Sanford was on his way here… if he took her down to those basements, with their impossible corridors, the ones that still appeared in her dreams… she didn't rate her chances of ever seeing daylight again very highly. Last time, she'd had a special compass to show her the way. This time, she'd be on her own.

"I was supposed to call him as soon as you arrived, and keep you here until he could collect you." Berglund shrugged. "Since we made that agreement, however, my priorities have changed. As have my loyalties. If you tell me what I need to know, I won't hand you over to Sanford. How's that for a deal?"

She'd had worse offers. "What do you want to know?"

"When you were in the Lodge, did you see something that looked like a preserved anatomical specimen? A lump of pebbled flesh, no bigger than a human hand, probably in a glass jar, adrift in preserving fluid? It… there might have been eyes, on the specimen."

Ruby opened her mouth to say no, of course not, but… hadn't there been something of the sort? Not in the main vault, but in a chamber she passed along the way, a side room stuffed with dusty curiosities that made her think of a forgotten storage room in the back of a natural history museum. There were taxidermied animals that had never been recorded in any zoology textbook, and wired-together skeletons that were somehow both doglike and batlike, and, yes, there'd also been bottles and jars with specimens inside, including one that held a lump of greenish flesh dotted with half a dozen blankly staring eyes. What could they want with some creepy anatomical specimen? If it was valuable, it wasn't any sort of value her keen eye for treasure had recognized.

"Maybe," she said. "Untie me and take me upstairs and out of this house, maybe to a nice café, and I'll tell you all about it."

"I don't think you understand the situation," Berglund said. "You can tell me now, or my... associates... will do things their way instead. They can make you talk – they can make you *want* to talk. Well. Not *you*, exactly." He sighed. "I'd rather not do it that way. I think there are too many comets running around now already, and we have a history of becoming a bit fractious and having schisms – Cain had to do a *purge* – so I'd just as soon find out what I need to know from *this* version of you, and–"

A chime rang from upstairs, and Berglund frowned. It rang again. "I don't know why I let Cornelia install that doorbell," he muttered.

"Better go see who it is," Ruby said. "I'd hate for you to miss anyone important. Could be another young woman you want to betray and kidnap."

He grimaced and rose. "The things I do for a god... I'll be back shortly. Take this opportunity to think about what's best for you. If you value your life, and, if you believe in such things, your *soul*, you'll tell me what I wish to know."

Berglund went up the stairs, leaving her alone again.

Amateurs. She was bound, but they hadn't tied her wrists together, just wrapped her body in rope. There was enough slack for her to work her hand down to her thigh, where she had a slim knife in a sheath on a strap. They'd done a slapdash job tying her up and hadn't even searched her for weapons! She got the knife free and began to awkwardly saw through the bottom loop of rope, her wrist aching from the necessary angle. She worked as fast as she could – she only had until Berglund sent whoever'd come to the door packing.

After slicing through two coils, the ropes were loose enough for her to shimmy and stand up, the remainder falling down around her ankles. She looked around for windows or a cellar door leading to the outside – she would have scrambled up a coal chute at this point – but this was just a stone-lined hole in the ground. She'd have to hope the door to the kitchen wasn't locked, and if it was, she'd have to get the drop on Berglund when he came back down.

Before she went up, she caught a glimpse of something stuffed under the stairs. Knowing she shouldn't look, but unable to stop herself, she knelt and peered. It was an old tarp, stained with something wet and dark and fresh, wrapped around a form that… well, it looked like a body. Or bodies. There was no denying that. With a trembling hand, Ruby reached out, and peeled back the top of the tarp.

She looked into the ruined faces of Cornelia and Cornelius Berglund, skulls cracked from hammer blows, but still recognizable. Ruby whimpered and scrambled backward, choking back a scream and turning it into a whimper.

What was happening here? Fratricide, sororicide, triplets turning on their own? That was absurd, but what were the alternatives? She'd brushed up against the uncanny before, and now she felt *buried* by it. Were these shapeshifters?

Monsters who stole human faces? Dark creatures with a thousand masks? Who *were* these doppelgangers, and what did they want with a bit of dead meat from the Lodge? What had she gotten herself into?

Then the door at the top of the stairs creaked open.

CHAPTER EIGHT
Seth

Abel paced around in Diana's apartment, peered out her windows, and felt the psychic itch of his comets, moving around on the other side of the river. Diana wanted him to wait here until she returned, but he could bear waiting no longer. The hope newly kindled within him demanded action. He would track down Cain, spy on him, and find out what he was doing... and whether he was close to finding a way into the Lodge, and bringing Asterias back to life and glory.

He felt less awkward about bathing now that he had the apartment to himself. Abel washed off the stink of his recent derelict days, then returned to the cache of old clothes Diana had provided. Pants that fit well enough when he rolled the cuffs up, a shirt that was baggy but serviceable, and best of all, a round-brimmed fisherman's hat that would serve to obscure his features if he kept his chin down.

He considered a nip from the bottle of sherry by the armchair, but, no. He needed to feel the connection to his comets strongly so he could track them down, even if it meant they could also sense him clearly. He didn't even know for sure if alcohol made him "fuzzy" to the comets anyway – the theory was based on a single comment Seth made one night near the end, when Abel got drunk and Seth said, "I don't like how that feels – you're going all blurry on me." The comment might have been metaphorical, for all Abel knew.

Now that he was sober enough to think clearly, he wondered if being on this side of the river, all alone, made his location *more* visible to his comets. If he was on the north side, where so many of his copies and their copies were operating, his own presence might disappear into the noise of theirs, and make his position harder to pinpoint.

He wasn't sure what would happen if his comets did find him. They didn't seem to want him dead. Cain could have killed Abel during their last altercation, but instead he'd beaten him, and laughed, and told him to await the future with the rest of the humans. Cain, it seemed, had plans for him, and those plans didn't bear thinking about. Abel had been tempted to flee Arkham forever, but he'd come back, desperate to do *something* to stop the chain of events he'd set in motion. He just didn't know what. The comets probably didn't even see him as a threat.

They'd been right. He hadn't been a threat. But meeting Diana had awakened him, inspired him, and even shamed him. If she could set herself against the power of the Silver Twilight Lodge, he could be courageous, too.

Abel let himself out of the shop by the back door, making sure it locked behind him. He didn't have keys, but he'd come back later and hope Diana was home. If nothing else, her shop would be open tomorrow, and he could catch her attention then. It wouldn't be the first night he'd slept out on the street. Sleeping under a roof was the novelty these days.

The morning was crisp and clear and beautiful and quiet. The pull of his comets drew him north, but if he tried to follow that interior compass and walk straight toward them, he'd end up walking into the murky flow of the Miskatonic River. Instead he set off east down Main, heading for the nearest bridge. He had a long walk ahead of him, which meant a lot of time with his thoughts. The alcohol had been helpful for avoiding those, too.

Abel had initially come to Arkham in the company of his first comet, Seth. "I'm hardly going to name myself after Abel's *other* brother," Seth said over their first meal together, and that little biblical joke had jolted Abel. He'd been thinking of Seth as a sort of homunculus, or witch's familiar, something created to do his bidding and help him restore the glory of Asterias... but Seth was a *person*, with his own thoughts and wishes and urges. He may have started out as a copy of Abel with perfect recall of all his memories, but he would soon develop in his own way, the two of them diverging like separate branches from a tree.

"Do you feel like me, inside?" Abel asked, sharing bread and butter and salt (Seth went heavy on the salt) and tinned anchovies thick with grease. "In your head? I mean..."

"I understand what you mean." The comet considered the question. "It's more that you... provide the shape for me. You're a vessel that I'm poured into. I have your memories, of course, but also your habits of mind, and your ways of thinking about problems, and your basic personality. But there's something of Asterias in me, too. You are animated by your soul, but the source of my life is a gift from our god."

"I must seem like a lesser being to you," Abel said.

Seth shook his head. "You have the amulet, blessed by Asterias. I am close to our god by nature, but the amulet makes you even closer, and stronger than me, too. I have visions that show me the will of our god, but the visions you experience with the amulet are so much more intense. When you wear the amulet, if you immerse yourself in sea water, you heal, and while I heal faster than a human does, I don't heal anywhere near as quick as that. If I were to cut off a finger and cast it into the sea, it would grow into a copy of me, too, eventually… but it would take years for my comet to mature, while I was fully grown from your finger within a day. The amulet is concentrated power, blessed by Asterias, mixed with the god's essence or blood when it was forged in the fires of a volcanic vent beneath the sea. You bear the sigil of the Ravening Deep. You are the one chosen to lead us, and restore our god."

"I just got lucky," Abel said. "Anyone could have found that island. Or no one."

"Just because Asterias is dead does not mean he is powerless," Seth said. "That temple is holy, and I believe the Ravening Deep guided the waves that brought you to the temple. Asterias sensed greatness in you. An opening in your soul that only our god could fill."

Did he guide the storm, too, then? Abel wondered, but didn't say, because questioning his god must be blasphemy, and he didn't think Seth would take kindly to that, even from the chosen one.

"We must begin the great work now," Seth said.

Abel nodded. "I know. I made you to help me, and we can make more brothers, too, if need be. But I'll be honest. I don't know where to start. Some piece of Asterias survives, I saw it, but I can't see *where* – I get glimpses of a room, but there is no detail, and no context."

"I have examined those visions from every angle, in their every detail," Seth said. "I can look at our memories as easily as you could study a photograph or a map. And I have to agree. Our god is on a shelf in a room, and I cannot ascertain anything more specific. Our god doesn't even know its location – the Ravening Deep was dormant during its travels from the sea to the shelf, I think. Our god was truly dead until you found the amulet, and formed a connection that quickened what little life remained. But… you do know where to begin, Abel, because *I* know where to begin. What did Mother always tell us, when we were young?"

"A lot of things," Abel said. She'd been a fount of maxims and little wisdoms and tidbits of trivia.

"'If you want to know something, go to the library,'" Seth quoted. "'If anyone ever knew it, it's written down in a book.'"

Abel snorted. He did remember his mother saying that. The little library in their town, run out of a dusty old one-room schoolhouse, mostly held yellowing magazines and well-worn copies of the classics, not the secrets of the universe, but his mother's faith in the power of the written word was unwavering. "You think we're going to find information about Asterias in a book?"

"I do," Seth said. "Our god wasn't killed millennia ago,

like some I could name. Don't you sense that Asterias was alive and well more recently? The war that killed our god happened decades ago, maybe a century at most, and people, or things like people, worshipped Asterias. A power like that, located not so far off the coast of New England… There *must* have been stories, rumors, folk tales, legends, whispers. If we can track down those whispers, maybe we can find out how our god died. And what became of its immortal remains."

"I don't think the library here in town is going to be much help," Abel said.

"We should go to Miskatonic University."

"In Arkham?" Abel's family had taken day trips to Arkham several times. "Mother took me to a museum there, once. I remember there were these carved masks I found terrifying."

Seth nodded. "I remember." Of course he did. He could probably look at the memory and read the little identifying labels stuck on the wall beside the masks. "The museum is associated with the university. Miskatonic is famed for its anthropology department, and their library is supposed to be one of the finest on the East Coast. If there's information about our god anywhere, it will be there."

There were trains to Arkham, but the nearest train station was so far away a car would be just as quick. "We'll need a vehicle," Abel said. "I still have some money, but buying a car would wipe us out."

"Don't worry about that," Seth said. "I have an idea."

Abel wasn't comfortable with committing crimes, but he *was* on a divine mission, so he sat in the diner and drank coffee and ate steak and eggs and said hello to everyone he knew while Seth took their father's old revolver from its hiding place under the floorboards and robbed the pawn shop with a bandana over his face.

Shouldn't have bargained with me so hard over the necklace, Abel thought. Even if the owner recognized him under the bandana, Abel's presence in the diner was a perfect alibi.

He got back to the house, and Seth was there, upending a pillowcase full of loot onto the table. "I got all the cash, of course, but also all these rings and watches – we can pawn a few when we get to Arkham."

"You didn't run into any problems, then?" Abel asked.

"Nothing I couldn't handle," Seth said. "I got us this, too." He reached down under the table and drew out a shotgun. "The owner pulled this on me, so I took it away from him."

Abel swallowed. "Did you… did you hurt him?"

Seth shrugged. "Shot him in the shoulder. There was no reason to kill him, with you out in public like you were." Seth was nonchalant about committing such an act of violence. Abel had been in his share of fights over the years – growing up by the docks was rough-and-tumble, and he'd thrown a few punches as an adult, too, usually when somebody (including him) had too much to drink. But he'd never fired a gun at anything but bottles and tin cans.

"I ran out the back and was well on my way before I even heard sirens," Seth continued. "I got away clean, don't worry. I called our friend at the bank and asked if he knew anyone with a car to sell, too."

We're doing this for god, Abel told himself, and pushed

his misgivings away. No one had died, after all, and now they could fund their mission.

Seth took care of picking up the car – it was a 1922 Dagmar, a six-cylinder, with a dent over one fender, but otherwise a beaut. Abel whistled when he saw it come purring into the driveway. "I was expecting a beat-up old jalopy."

"We found a motivated seller, trying to catch up on mortgage payments before his house gets seized. Our pet banker put us in touch. He was a good investment."

Seth had gotten a close shave while he was in town, while Abel had the makings of a full beard. "You can always shave if we need to alibi each other again." Seth wore a wide-brimmed hat jammed low on his head while Abel sported a newsboy cap. They still looked like brothers, but were less obviously identical now. They didn't want to draw too much attention.

They spent another night in the house, discussing strategy, then set out for Arkham, first on side roads, then joining up with a highway, and they made good time. Abel hadn't done much driving in his life – he'd spent a lot more time on boats than in cars – but Seth had a real knack for it. Abel commented on the disparity.

Seth shrugged. "Oh, I just remember every time I've ever been in a car, every situation, and that helps. I've got good reflexes, too, better than human – so do you, with that amulet on."

"You don't think of yourself as human, then?" Seth had made such comments before.

"I guess I think I'm something new. Or… something old, and long forgotten, that's come back again."

Most of their conversation was more fun than that, as Abel took advantage of Seth's perfect recall of their shared experiences to clarify his own foggy memories. "Now, was that the Christmas Father tried to teach me to ride a bike?"

"No, no, you got the bike a year after, that was the Christmas you got that old sled..."

They hardly talked about Asterias at all. They didn't need to. They both knew their purpose.

When they arrived in Arkham, it was nearly dark. They motored on through its narrow streets. "When I was in town I called and got us a room at the Independence Hotel, by the square," Seth said. "Mother said she always wanted to spend a night there, and we can afford it now."

"You think of everything," Abel said.

"It's why you made me." Seth grinned. "So you don't have to."

The hotel towered over the buildings in its vicinity, eight stories of red brick standing tall among shops and offices. They let a valet take the car – their guns were stowed in their bags – and strode into the lobby side-by-side, Abel's hat tilted back, Seth's pulled low. Abel had never stayed in a place so fancy; he'd barely ever walked *past* a place so fancy.

The lobby was floored in gleaming black-and-white tiles, the walls were black marble shot through with streaks of gold, and that great dome of a ceiling sported a mural of important-looking figures doing important-looking things. Abel imagined the mural transformed, the center of the cupola painted with the seven-pointed star of Asterias, with devoted followers arrayed around the sides, offering up sacrifices and worship. Purpose thrummed through him.

They were going to change the world. Their god was coming back, and this time, it would come back stronger. So strong it could never die again.

"I reserved a room for my brother and myself," Seth said to the fussy-looking man at the counter, who brightened when he flipped through the ledger.

"One of our finest suites," he said. "And you'll be with us for, let's see, two nights?"

"At least," Seth said. "We've got a little business in town, and we'll see how soon we can wrap it up. Could be you'll have to put up with us a little longer."

The man chuckled the way those who were paid well to chuckle at the jokes of customers usually did. "I'll just get your keys, Mr Chesterfield."

"Chesterfield?" Abel whispered to Seth as the bellboy pushed a luggage rack along after them toward the elevators.

"Well, I didn't want to say Davenport, and 'Chesterfield' was just the first thing that came to mind. Would you have preferred us to be the Sofa Brothers? Mr Chaise Longue?"

Abel tried to hold back laughter but couldn't stop himself from letting out a snort.

The next day, after a luxurious evening spent in feather beds, they went to the university. They parked on the edge of campus and made their way further in on foot. Class was in session, and serious-looking young people bustled to and fro. They asked directions once, but it wasn't hard to spot the library once they got close – three stories high, dominating its section of campus, an imposing structure in a neo-classical mode.

"Orne Library," Seth read. "I wonder who Orne was?"

"That little detail isn't tucked away in your memory vaults?"

"Ha, no. I don't know everything. I just know everything I know." He grinned. "This is exciting." They went together into the library, glancing around at the polished desk staffed by three librarians, the rows of open stacks, and the bright chandeliers hanging overhead, casting a warm and even light. The two of them made straight for the imposing card catalogue, rank upon rank of wooden cabinets full of small drawers – the full catalogue took up an entire wall. "If there's anything written about Asterias, it'll be in here," Seth said.

Abel made for the subject headings first, looking up "Asterias", and was thrilled to see card after card… until it became apparent they were all references to books about marine life, "asterias" being part of the scientific name of the common starfish. That wasn't the god's *true* name, Abel knew that, just one of its many titles, but still, he'd hoped.

He moved on, looking up "gods" and "gods, sea and ocean" and everything related he could think of. There were references to legends about something called Dagon, and Mother Hydra, and Y'ha-nthlei, but none of it seemed to have anything to do with Asterias. The world was full of mysteries and terrors, it seemed, but none of them were any use to *him*. He slammed one of the card catalog doors shut in frustration, earning him a sharp look from one of the women behind the desk. He gave her a sheepish grimace and mouthed "I'm sorry."

"I've got something," Seth said. "I just started looking up variations on everything related to Asterias I could think of, and I found this."

Abel hurried over and looked at his card. It wasn't a subject entry, but a title card: *The Ravening Deep; and Other Curiosities of Coastal Lore,* by someone called Willum Stillwater, PhD, published 1905: "A compendium of lesser-known legends from the coastal communities of Massachusetts, New Hampshire, and Maine." They noted the call numbers and went to the stacks, scanning the numbers until they found 398, then checking the spines on the shelves. "It's not here," Abel said.

"Librarian." Seth said and marched to the desk, Abel trailing after. "Pardon me, miss," Seth said to the youngest and most approachable-looking of the three women behind the desk, as she stood sorting through checkout cards.

She glanced up, dark eyes curious, and looked from one to the other. "Oh, my, are you twins?"

"Just brothers," Seth said. "I'm the younger one." He winked.

She smiled. "How can I help you?"

"We're looking for a book – we found the title in the card catalogue, but it's not on the shelf."

"Let me see what I can track down," she said, and took the title and call number. After perusing her records she sighed. "We had one copy, but it was checked out years ago and returned with severe water damage and pulled from circulation. Doesn't look like we ever replaced it. Let me see… it looks like we have the manuscript in special collections. The author was a professor in our anthropology department. Are you students here?" Abel and Seth exchanged a look and shook their heads. "Accredited researchers?"

"Not technically," Seth said.

She shook her head. "Then I can't help much, I'm afraid. Access to the special collections is restricted."

Frustration welled up in him again. You'd think things would go more smoothly when you were on a mission from a god! Were they going to have to break into the library after hours? Did this place ever even close? Maybe there was a better way... "He's a professor here, you said?" Abel asked. "Perhaps we could go by his office–"

"He's retired, I'm afraid," she said. "I wish I could do more."

"The thing is, well, miss, our mother recently passed." Seth looked at her with soulful, pleading eyes. Abel wondered if *he* could manage a look like that. "She grew up on the coast, and she used to tell us stories she'd heard as a girl, but my brother and me, we can't agree on some of the details, and it's all just... slipping away. It's like we're losing her a second time. This book would be a great help to us, if there's any way to find a copy."

She leaned forward, but shook her head again. "If it were up to me, I would, but I'm just a graduate student here, and my boss would have my head." She cocked her head. "But come to think of it, he *was* a professor here, so maybe you should try Keene Books, downtown. They have an extensive section devoted to local history and local authors."

"You're a lifesaver," Seth said, and turned to leave, Abel following. His heart was thumping with anticipation. They had a thread, and they were going to follow that thread wherever it led.

•••

Abel snapped out of his reverie – he'd somehow made it almost all the way across the bridge, lost in memories. Those first days with Seth had been so pleasant, so, well, *fun*. He'd reveled in the sense of purpose, and the belief that he was chosen, working with his brother to do great things. That was before they met the professor. Before Seth made Cain. Before all the blood.

And before Abel realized the cost of bringing his god back to life.

Someone leaning on the railing ahead of him stepped into his path, and Abel mumbled an apology and tried to go around, keeping his eyes on the pavement. Someone else stepped into his way, deliberately, and Abel looked up. Three people arrayed themselves before him, all strangers, one rough-clad like a dockworker, another in a suit with a vest, the third a woman with a pinched expression that didn't match her girlish flowered day dress.

"Do I know you?" Abel asked.

"Cain told us he could feel you coming," the woman said. "He says you need to stay on the other side of the river, out of the way, for now. He doesn't need you yet."

These people must be comets, but Abel couldn't sense them. Did that mean he could only sense comets made from *himself*, or from his own twisted progeny? There were enough of those in the city, half a dozen at least nagging at the back of his mind, but if there were more, unknown to him... Arkham could be infested. Arkham could be *overrun. Anyone* could be a double, in Cain's thrall. His skin crawled and his heart thundered. Danger everywhere! How could he function in a world like that? *Knowing* the world was like that?

Abel backed away, holding up his hands. There was no other foot traffic on the bridge, and precious little in the way of passing cars, and those that went by paid him no mind. People in Arkham kept their eyes on their own business. "I was just out for a walk. I'll, I'll go back–"

"We can't kill you," the man in the vest said, drawing a blackjack out of his pocket. "Cain has plans for you. Heretics don't get to die easy in the street. But he did say we should give you a little reminder of your place."

The comets closed in, and Abel turned to run, but something struck the back of his head, and his vision exploded with stars of darkness.

CHAPTER NINE
Unlikely Allies

Diana had expected Cornelia to open the door – that was what happened last time she'd dropped by the Berglund house to make a delivery. She had a satchel with several fine silk scarves inside, and a whole line of patter to talk herself in, but that dried up when the door opened to reveal the scowling face of Mr Berglund instead. He didn't look good – there was a bruise growing under his eye, and one of his hands was bandaged. Maybe Sanford was right, and there *was* something strange going on. Had the Berglunds gotten involved in some sort of unsavory business with rough people?

Wait. The bandaged hand. Abel's tale of growing comets from his own severed fingers returned to her. People were *changing*, Sanford said. Could those changes be related to the cult of Asterias? Was their new leader infiltrating Arkham society, making copies of people? But why duplicate Cornelius Berglund? He wasn't even a member of the Lodge. How could he help them get the fragment of Asterias?

She had to maintain appearances, and not let her suspicions show. "Oh, hello," she said. "I'm not sure if you remember me–"

"Diana Stanley," he said. "Huntress Fashions. What do you – how can I help you?" He smiled at her, trying to look friendly and failing.

"I was hoping to speak to Mrs Berglund? She wanted me to bring her some–"

"Silk scarves, yes, I remember."

Diana was surprised. In her experience, the older husbands of Arkham took little interest in the sartorial choices of their wives.

"I'm afraid Mrs Berglund is out running an errand."

"Oh?" Diana glanced around, and didn't see their shiny black Packard. "I didn't realize she drove. You always bring her to the shop–"

"She learned," he said. "She wanted more independence. You're an independent woman yourself, so I'm sure you understand the appeal. Driving isn't so difficult. She's watched people do it for years, after all. You just have to pay the least little bit of attention. I'll let her know you stopped by."

This was no good at all. "I'm sorry, Mr Berglund, but could I come inside, just for a moment, to… freshen up? It was a long walk, and…"

He clearly wanted to say no, but he was ostensibly a gentleman, and bound by certain courtesies. "Wish you'd called first," he grumbled. "I could have spared you the walk. Come in, come in, you know where the downstairs bath is. You used it last time you were here."

How had he recalled *that*? He'd barely grunted a greeting at her when she passed him on that visit, and he'd been reading a newspaper in the living room at the time. Unless… oh, no. Abel said the comets had extraordinary powers of memory. Berglund's comment was hardly proof he was a comet, but it was troubling.

"I'm ever so grateful," Diana said. She wouldn't have an opportunity to snoop much, but at least she could tell Sanford she'd tried, and that his suspicions were correct. Something was odd here. People as settled as the Berglunds didn't change their habits, not at their age. She stepped inside and went toward the hallway, Berglund following rather too close behind her.

Something thumped above them, and a groan drifted down the stairway. Diana frowned. "Is that – oh, but you said Mrs Berglund was out."

He scowled again. "Her sister is visiting. She's not well. I'd better go up and check on her. I'll be right back."

As soon as he vanished up the stairs, Diana hurried to the living room, glanced around, saw nothing, and went to the kitchen. There was salt spilled on the dining room table and a handbag hanging on the back of a chair. The bag didn't look like something Cornelia would carry; she was partial to immense purses, and this was smaller and more modern than her taste. Maybe it had been a gift from her husband. He hardly struck Diana as the attentive type. There was nothing else of interest–

Except… were those drops of blood on the tile, by the door to the basement? Diana walked over, feeling half entranced. The door was secured by a sliding lock, and she eased it open, then put her hand on the knob. If Berglund caught her here… well, she could always claim she'd heard a noise. Even the finest houses on French Hill weren't immune to rats in the walls, so it was plausible. She turned the knob and took a tentative step onto the wooden stairs. A bare bulb illuminated the cluttered space below, casting deep shadows.

"Hello?"

A wild-eyed woman in a frumpy dress appeared at the bottom of the stairs and rushed toward her. "Go, go," she hissed. "We have to get out of here, they're murderers, they took me prisoner, let's *go!*"

Diana could hardly do anything but comply, so she about-faced back into the kitchen as the woman barged by her. The stranger skirted around the draped table for some reason and snatched up the handbag from the back of the chair. "Come on, you're in danger too, if you aren't one of *them*." She opened the back door and slipped out, and Diana followed, a little dazed by the suddenness of everything. The stranger – who was younger than she looked at first glance, judging by how nimbly she moved – flew across the backyard and scrambled over the board fence.

Diana glanced back at the house, shook her head, and then hurried to the fence herself, getting a running start before leaping, her bag banging against her side. She hauled herself over the fence, not as smoothly as the stranger had, but creditably enough. She'd grown up on a farm, and though working at the shop was hardly physically strenuous, she was still in fine condition, a regular walker up and down the city's hills, and a frequent swimmer at the Arkham Natatorium.

The two of them were now in the backyard of a house facing a different street, and the woman – had she really been kidnapped? – was hurrying toward the side gate. Diana caught up with her. "Who are you?" she said.

"Edna Glasby. Who are *you*? What were you doing in that house of horrors?" She opened the gate and walked out as if she had every right in the world to be there, glancing up and down the empty sidewalk, and then setting off toward the north.

"I'm Diana, Diana Stanley, I run a shop. I was just making a delivery–"

"Do you have a car nearby, shopkeeper? I need to get to the train station. Hmm, no, they might look for me there. It's better if I drive out of town."

"No, I walked over. I don't own a car."

The woman huffed. "I need to get off the street at least, lie low for a bit–"

"You can come to my shop," Diana said. The offer was instinctive – the urge to help out a fellow woman in need. But it was also a smart move. This woman was yet more evidence in support of Sanford's theory that something strange was happening, and she might have information about what that something strange *was*. Though Diana had a sinking feeling it had something to do with Abel and his comets. "It's closed on Sunday, and no one would look for anyone there."

The woman glanced at her. She really was quite young, maybe even younger than Diana herself. Why had she made herself up to look so frumpy? "I... that's kind of you. You don't even know me."

"Someone recently told me I'm an independent woman. If I don't use that independence to help other women, what good is it?"

The woman nodded, but didn't smile. "Is your shop nearby?"

"Just in the Merchants District."

"Then let's go. But stick to the side streets, if you would?"

They made it to the shop without incident. As they walked, Edna laughed and told frivolous stories and gave every impression of being out for a lighthearted stroll with a friend. When Diana remarked on this, Edna said, "If you're on the run, you never want to look like you're on the run."

"Are you an actress?" Diana asked.

"My line of work often requires a certain amount of acting ability, yes," Edna said. At Diana's shocked look, she burst out laughing, and the genuine sound was much more pleasant. "Oh, no, I don't mean – I'm not a lady of the *evening*. Though I do work a lot at night. I'm sorry, I'm just – I think I'm a little giddy. I didn't think I'd make it out of that basement."

They approached the back door of the shop. "We should call the police," Diana said, unlocking the door and letting them in. She'd considered making an anonymous call to the authorities to report Walter, the boy from the ritual, missing, but had decided they'd be unlikely to believe her outrageous story without proof. Surely the testimony of a kidnapping victim would spur them to action, though!

"No police," Edna said.

"But–"

"No police," Edna said. "If you don't agree to that, I can't come in with you. I'll just have to take my chances on my own."

"I will agree… if you explain," Diana said. "If you tell me the truth."

Edna grunted. "Yes. All right. Fair. But I don't think you'll like the explanation. You seem like a fine upstanding citizen. Someone who doesn't get down in the dirt too much."

"I may be more acquainted with the dirt than you imagine," Diana said.

They went into the shop, and Diana sat Edna down in the back room. "Let me just run upstairs for a moment to check on something," she said. Before Edna could ask any questions, Diana hurried up and checked the bedroom and bathroom. Abel was gone, but he'd left a scrawled note on the countertop.

Gone to check on some things. Back later. Thank you again.

Well, at least she wouldn't have to explain Edna to him, or him to Edna, right away. Explaining *everything* required a level of understanding she lacked anyway. "Come on up!" she called from the top of the stairs.

Edna stepped into the apartment, looking around. "Nice place. All yours?"

"My castle keep. Well, I don't own it, but I got favorable terms from the landlord." A fellow member of the Lodge, of course, who'd slashed her rent in half once she became a Seeker, because membership has its benefits. "Can I get you anything? Water, tea, coffee?"

"Coffee. I need fuel if I'm going to explain things like you asked."

Diana filled the pot and lit the stove. "Can you start with... what did you mean when you called it a house of horrors?"

Edna settled down on the stool Abel had used that morning and put her head in her hands. "I don't even understand what I saw, Diana. Do you know them well, the Berglunds?"

"Cornelia is a good customer."

"Not anymore. She's dead. I saw her body in the basement, wrapped in a tarp, and it wasn't natural causes."

Diana stared. "You don't... do you mean to say Cornelius killed her?" He'd barely even paid attention to his wife, and it was hard to imagine him killing anyone.

Edna sighed. "This is the part you won't believe. Cornelius is dead *too*. I saw his body, right next to his wife's. I don't know who let you in, who trapped me in the basement, but it's not Cornelius. The thing is, I saw *two* of him, and two of her, too, I thought they were twins, but... maybe triplets? Can they *both* be triplets?"

"I think I would have heard. That's the sort of thing people comment on." Diana's mind whirled. She'd seen Berglund, too, and had no doubt it was him, or someone who looked just like him. The conclusion was inescapable: Berglund *was* a comet. Cornelia too. It was the only thing that made sense, if you could call *that* "making sense". "Edna... do you believe in magic?"

"I used to say I just believed in people who *believed* in magic," she said. "I thought they were deluded or gullible. But I've seen some things. I saw something impossible just today. If it's a choice between believing in magic or disbelieving my own eyes, then I guess... sure. Magic. Do you? Believe, I mean?"

"I don't just believe. I know." She poured a cup of coffee. "Do you take it black?"

"As the woods at night," Edna said. "You *know*, huh? You're going to have to explain that."

"I will. But you said you'd tell me the truth, and I want to hear the rest. What were you doing in that house?"

"I'm in the antiquities business," she said. "Just like Berglund. He was supposed to buy something from me." She opened up her purse and removed a red gem set in a dark metal setting, and placed it on the counter. "This. But when I got there, he locked me up."

"Why?"

"I don't know."

Diana looked at her closely. "I don't believe you. People are dead, and you aren't being honest with me. I'm going to call the police–" It was a shot in the dark, and mostly a bluff, but it worked.

Edna took her hand. "Wait. Stop. All right. Honesty is not... it's not exactly a virtue in my line of work. I'm a thief, Diana. Berglund hired me to steal that ruby. That's why I don't want to get the law involved. There are too many scenarios where I end up behind bars. Anyway, the whole job, the ruby heist, it was all a setup. A trap. Berglund, the job, it was all just bait to lure me back to Arkham. Have you heard of the Silver Twilight Lodge?"

Everything was coming back to the Order. Sanford's tendrils were everywhere. How could she stop him, when she could barely comprehend the scope of his machinations?

It was like trying to tear down a mountain with her bare hands. But she had to try. If she could stop Sanford, maybe it would finally banish the nightmares… "It's hard to live in Arkham without knowing about them." Now *she* was being dishonest. Diana would come clean later – she didn't want to distract Edna by explaining her own complicated relationship with the Lodge yet.

"Yeah, well, you probably think it's a social club. It's not. The Silver Twilight Lodge is neck-deep in the occult. And I… I stole something from them, a while back. The guy who runs the place, Carl Sanford, he wasn't too happy about that, and he's been after me ever since. Turns out he hired Cornelius to track me down and hire me, all so he could trap me."

"Your name isn't Edna Glasby," Diana said. She knew who this woman was. Sanford had talked about her. It was one of the only times she'd ever seen him lose a fraction of his cool. Diana wasn't high enough in the Lodge to know what Ruby had stolen, but she knew Sanford wanted her punished even more than he wanted his property back.

The woman sighed. "I was getting to that, yeah. You saved my life, so you deserve to know my name, anyway. I'm Ruby. Ruby Standish." She smirked. "Stanley and Standish. We oughta start a law firm."

"Ruby…" She let out a slow breath. "I'm surprised you trust me enough to tell me all this."

"Like I said, you saved my life, and that earns you some consideration. Besides, I'm about to skip town, and once I do that, I'm *never* coming back here. I might even leave New England entirely."

Diana didn't want her to leave. Ruby knew things. She'd gotten one over on Sanford once. She could be a resource… perhaps, even, an ally. "Ruby, I'm about to tell you something that will make you want to run away. But please don't. I'm on your side. It will just take me a moment to explain how and why."

Ruby stiffened. "I can't say I like those terms, but I'll try to abide by them."

"I am a member of the Silver Twilight Lodge – no, please, wait!"

Ruby had leapt up from the stool the moment the words were out of Diana's mouth, but she hesitated. "Hand me a big knife, and I'll listen for another minute."

Diana nodded, drew her butcher knife from the block by the stove, and slid it across the counter, hilt first. Ruby snatched it up and backed away toward the stairs. "OK. Talk."

"I *did* think it was a community organization." Diana backed up too, leaning against the sink, to give Ruby space. She hoped the woman wouldn't flee. "That's why I joined – to make connections in the business community, and among the city's elite. My membership was just about building my business and putting down roots in Arkham. I've only been here two years, and it can be hard for outsiders to gain a foothold. But then I started getting invited to help with certain rites and rituals, and recently I saw Sanford… *summon* something, a shapeless monstrosity covered in mouths, and he killed people to get it. I realized the Lodge is monstrous. *Sanford* is monstrous. I am trying to gather evidence to get him locked up, to stop the Lodge from doing such horrible things."

"A redeemed cultist, huh?" Ruby considered. "You're a member of the Lodge… but you didn't lock me up in a basement and threaten me with my own gun. I guess I've jumped from the fire back into the frying pan. It's not good, but it's an improvement. So. That's all our cards out. Where do we go from here?"

"I have a few more cards," Diana said. She was pleased that Ruby hadn't fled. For all her professed desire to flee, surely she'd want to understand what was happening here? Ruby was a curious and quick-witted person, and if Diana could pique her interest… "I think I understand what happened with the Berglunds. I met a man last night…"

She told Ruby about Abel Davenport and Asterias and the cult, which seemed a lot more believable now that they'd both encountered unnatural doubles with strangely perfect memories.

Ruby sat back down, and put the knife down, too. "That's… Diana. They were going to do that to *me*. Cut off my finger and throw it in a tub full of salt water and make a copy of me, so they could interrogate me – her, it – and find out where their little piece of a dead god is. I thought I was in bad trouble. I thought I might die. I didn't realize there was a *worse* option than dying."

"Do you know where the fragment of their god is?" Diana asked.

Ruby shrugged. "I mean… I might. I guess. I think so. I saw something, anyway, in a jar, with little eyes all over it. It sure didn't seem godlike, and I don't think Carl Sanford knows what it is, because it wasn't even locked up tight. He just kept it on a shelf with a bunch of other junk. I get the sense he sweeps up whatever occult items he can find, whenever he can find them, you know? He probably has people scoping out estate sales and combing through antique shops all the time."

"How did *you* reach the vault?" Diana asked. "The Lodge is hard to navigate on the lower levels. Did someone give you a map?" They could certainly use a map.

Ruby shook her head. "The lady who hired me had this doodad that was 'attuned' to the relic she wanted me to steal. I guess they were connected, once upon a time, part of a whole. She rigged up a sort of compass, and that led me to my target. I don't have the compass anymore, she took it back, but..." Ruby sighed. "I could still find my way down there again. I have a good memory for stuff like that."

So. Ruby *was* the map. Maybe Diana could actually do this; help Abel, stymie Sanford, and strike a blow against the Lodge all at once. She said, "Ruby, will you stay and talk to Abel?"

"I need to get out of town. Even if Berglund isn't reporting to Sanford anymore, these – what did you call them, comets? They'll be looking for me. They think I can help them bring their god back to life."

"I don't think leaving town will help," Diana said. "From what Abel told me, these comets are zealots, and... well. There are probably a lot of them. If Sanford is right, the comets are replacing all sorts of prominent people in Arkham, and they even make copies of their copies. Their supply of manpower is basically infinite, as long as they can find a body part and some brine to grow more soldiers. Do you want to look over your shoulder for the rest of your life?

Wondering if even your closest friends and confidants are *really* who you think they are?"

"That doesn't sound like much fun," Ruby said. "But if this cult is infiltrating the Lodge, maybe they'll find someone else who knows where the little bit of broken god is, and then they won't need me anymore."

"I don't think there are many people who've been to the vault you broke into," Diana said. "Only the highest-ranking members of the Order, and those people would be hard to compromise. They're paranoid, and they have defenses. But even if you're right, and the cult does succeed without you…" She trailed off.

Ruby stared at her for a long moment. "Then they'll resurrect a monstrous sea god. Which will do who knows what kind of damage. Right." She groaned and put her face in her hands. "You're trying to appeal to my better nature, Diana. That's usually like trying to get blood from a stone. But in this case… They kidnapped me. I'd like to give them a black eye for that."

"The best way to stop them from hurting you is to stop them entirely," Diana said. "If we can get our hands on that piece of Asterias, and destroy it, the cult will have no purpose, and with luck they'll just fall apart."

"After we murder their god? You think they'll leave us alone then? Just say, 'oh well, you beat us fair and square, have a nice life?'"

"It's… well. It's not a *complete* plan," Diana admitted. "But we can talk to Abel. He might have ideas about how to stop the comets, too. I still haven't heard the whole story of how he went from being their high priest to being…"

"A drunken heretic? Yeah. I'd like to hear that one myself." Ruby tapped the side of her mug. "I can't believe I'm saying this, but… give me a refill."

Diana poured, and then her phone rang downstairs. "Oh, I hope that's not Berglund," she said. "I'll be right back." She hurried down and took the call.

"Miss Stanley?" a brusque voice said. "I'm calling from St. Mary's Hospital. We have a patient here who asked us to call you, says his name is Davenport?"

CHAPTER TEN
New Friends and Old Books

"I'm fine," the man coming up the stairs grumbled. "They just roughed me up a little."

Ruby put down the book she'd been reading and rose, nodding to Diana when she entered, a pale man with shadowed eyes leaning on her. Diana helped him to the armchair, and he dropped into it. Diana said, "I'll get a glass of water," and left Abel and Ruby looking at each other.

"You must be Ruby," he said at last. "Diana told me you might be able to help us."

"Helping myself might end up helping you, is more like it." She folded herself onto one side of Diana's small sofa. "I guess you aren't the muscle of this operation, huh?"

"It was three against one, and they had a sap," Abel said. "But… no. Probably not. What I have is information, mainly, and the ability to sense when these people – some of them, anyway – are close by."

"I can see how that would be handy," Ruby said. "How's your head?"

"Aching. Makes me wish…"

"What?"

He sighed. "My old patron gave certain gifts. Healing. Freedom from pain." He shook his head. "Price was too high, though."

"I hate all this spooky stuff," Ruby complained. "I've heard stories, and seen some things, and I stole a statue once that I was sure was looking *back* at me, but I always wanted to believe it was delusion, or the opposite of wishful thinking. There's no denying what I saw in the Berglunds' basement, though." She sighed. "No use pretending the world isn't what it is."

Diana returned with a glass of water for Abel and a bottle of something dark brown. "Drink?" she said to Ruby.

"Always," Ruby said, and accepted a glass. She sniffed and then sipped. Whiskey, and not the fake stuff colored with caramel. "Canadian?" she asked.

"Lodge membership has its benefits." Diana joined her on the couch.

"I could use one of those," Abel said.

"Doctor said no," Diana replied. "Stick to water."

This was a lot to process, but Ruby had always been good at rolling with the punches. Life had thrown enough of them at her, after all, and it was better to get on with difficult things than to sit around and lament the necessity. That didn't mean she couldn't complain a *little* bit, though. She said, "Here I am, sitting with a pair of reformed cultists. Bravo. I'm glad the two of you rehabilitated yourselves." Ruby looked from Abel to Diana, took a sip of her drink, and then said, "But I'm just wondering. Did it ever occur to either of you not to join a cult in the first place?"

Diana winced, but Abel chuckled. "In my defense, I started the cult. Or... restarted it. I just didn't realize right away that I was riding a tiger. Asterias saved my life, and I thought that meant I *owed* it my life. But not at the cost of other lives. Then I realized people would have to die to bring my god back, and that a lot more people would die *after* we brought him back. Asterias isn't going to be in a forgiving mood if it returns. The Ravening Deep will do whatever it takes to make sure it never dies again."

"Tell us what we're up against here," Ruby said. "Diana filled me in on some of your story, the part she knew, but I gather there's a lot more. I haven't decided if I'm on board with helping you two or not. I always do my research before a job." She also wanted to make sure that Abel was truly opposed to bringing this dead god back to life – that he was actually an apostate, and not just another cultist who'd lost his position and wanted to win it back. That moment before, when he said he missed the gifts of his horrible god, made her wary.

"I'm a little groggy still," Abel said. "I got a good knock on the head."

"The doctors said we shouldn't let you fall asleep yet anyway," Diana said. "Talking will be a good way to keep you awake."

"If you drift too far off, we'll shove you back on course," Ruby said.

"All right, then." He held up his water glass to the lamp and looked at the light shining through. "I should start by telling you about Seth, and how we first came to Arkham..."

●●●

The bookshop was a few blocks off the heart of downtown, tucked away on a side street, with a hand-painted sign above the door: KEENE BOOKS * RARE AND ANTIQUE VOLUMES * LOCAL HISTORY. They went inside, a bell above the door ringing to herald their arrival, and Abel immediately sneezed from all the dust.

Keene Books was one of those cramped shops with just as many tomes stacked on the floor as there were on the shelves, head-high towers of crumbling paper and boards that created their own corridors and islands, defining the shop's interior geography. Abel just glimpsed a counter, with a sleepy-looking man perusing a volume with an unlit pipe in his mouth.

"Afternoon, gents," he said, not closing the book before him. "Here for a browse, or do you come with intent?"

Seth got straight to it. "We're looking for a book called *The Ravening Deep* by Willum Stillwater."

"Old Professor Stillwater." The bookseller shook his head. "Shame about him. He was bright as a torch in his day. Didn't used to have that book in stock – they didn't print too many. But you're in luck. His daughter is trying to make some room in his apartment since she's living there full-time now, and she brought in a bunch of things to sell. All the *good* volumes got snapped up by the university, those vultures, but she did have a few of the contributor copies his publisher sent him, so..." He stood up as he talked and began to make his way through the rows of books, toward the back, Abel and Seth following. "I'm Keene, by the way. My people opened this shop pretty much when the university started up. We still make most of our money buying and selling textbooks and the required reading every year…"

Seth made interested noises as the bookseller rambled, until they reached a back room with a LOCAL HISTORY sign over the door.

"Now this particular book isn't really local, but this is also where I keep the local authors." Keene plucked a slim volume from the shelf – there was a bad drawing of a lighthouse on the cover – looked at the flyleaf, and told them the price. Seth reached into his pocket and handed over the funds right there, then plucked the book from Keene's hands. The shopkeeper's bushy eyebrows went up. "I've never seen anyone so excited about *this* book before. It's a bit dry, you know, for all that the subject matter gets bloody."

"It has sentimental value," Seth said, already headed for the door. "Thank you!"

They didn't return to the hotel; they didn't even return to the car. Seth found a bench by a fountain square a couple of blocks away from the shop and sat down, Abel joining him. He opened the book, scanned the table of contents, and flipped to the page headed "The Ravening Deep". The two of them leaned their heads in and read together.

Abel sighed and looked apologetically at Ruby and Diana. "If Seth were here, he'd be able to recite the whole article, word-for-word, like the page was open right in front of him. But since all we've got is me, you'll have to settle for an overview.

"Basically, Professor Stillwater was an anthropologist, collecting the folklore of the coast, gathering the stories fishermen and sailors told. As a fisherman myself, I can assure you we have a lot of stories, and most of them are nonsense. Stillwater tracked down one particular old-timer with an outlandish tale and went to his house. The old fellow, who wasn't named in the article, was quite a character. He had a sort of bulgy-eyed, toadlike look about him, common to certain communities on the coast, likely due to generations of inbreeding. He'd moved inland to avoid some sort of trouble, but he liked talking about the old days.

"He told the professor a story he'd heard from his mother, about a giant undersea monster who lived at the bottom of a castle of coral and stone, and was tended by seafaring worshippers who brought the monster things – maybe even people – to eat, in exchange for blessings. I remember one line: 'These weren't blessings like you're used to hearing about in church, promises of future bliss – these were blessings you could make use of right in the here and now.'

"The old man said the creature had a lot of names, including 'The Ravening Deep' and 'The Great Divider' and 'The Seven-Pointed-Star'. It was a thing of terrible appetites and equally terrible power. But the part that had Stillwater the most interested was, the Ravening Deep was supposedly *dead*, which was unusual in tales like that. Legendary sea monsters make better stories if they're still out there, alive and lurking, after all."

Abel closed his eyes, and Ruby thought he was trying to summon up a memory. The perfect recall of the comets would be a nice thing to have, in some respects… but there were plenty of things in her life she was happy to forget about forever, so, on balance, she preferred being human.

When Abel spoke again, his tone was closer to a recitation. "For you see there was a great war, between the dwellers in the deep and the worshippers of the Star. The dwellers feared that the Star would grow and spread and overtake the whole of the sea, and swamp their secret city Y'ha-nthlei in its own revolting flesh. The war was long and costly, and much blood mingled with the waters, for the followers of the Star were a multitude that constantly grew. But the dwellers lived long, some say forever, and they were hard to kill, while the thralls of the Star were weak in comparison, and in time the dwellers breached the temple, and set upon the Star with their spears and hooks and claws. They rent the Star to pieces and burned its flesh in secret volcanoes beneath the sea, not even daring to feed the Star to the sharks, lest the monster poison them."

Ruby tried not to shiver, but she couldn't help it.

Abel opened his eyes. "That's not word-for-word, but pretty close. Then Stillwater wrote up some bits of speculation, about how the story might be related to tales of the fall of Atlantis and mer-people and such. The important part came at the end. The old man could tell that Stillwater didn't believe it was a *true* story, of course. So he said, 'I have proof. A piece of that dead god washed up on the shore, and my own mother picked it up, and saved it, all those years ago, and I inherited it when she underwent her great change'. The old man heaved himself up from his chair and went into another room and returned holding a gallon jar full of murky fluid. There was what Stillwater called 'a good-sized hunk of some poor dead sea beast, all pebbled flesh, perhaps a bit of whale skin or a segment of an unusually large starfish'. The old man said, 'It mayn't even be all the way dead, for sometimes, when you thump the glass, it opens its eyes, and it has oh so many eyes'. But though the old man banged his knuckles against the jar several times, the bit of dead flesh didn't stir, and the old man gave up. I do remember the last words he spoke, or at least, the last ones that Stillwater recorded: 'Mayhap it sleeps. Mayhap it will wake again, in time.'"

"That lump of flesh sounds like what I saw in the vault," Ruby said. That fact made his whole outlandish story sound plausible. There really *was* a jar, and now she knew what was inside it. "Except it *did* have open eyes. I'm not saying the thing was alive, they looked like dead eyes to me, but it sounds like the same specimen. How did it end up in the Silver Twilight Lodge? How did you find *out* it was there?"

"I didn't, not exactly," Abel said. "Cain did. And you should know about Cain, because if he realizes we're trying to interfere with him, he is going to kill us all." Abel paused. "Or kill you, at least. I fear he has plans worse than death for me, since he's kept me alive this long."

"Keep talking, then," Diana said.

CHAPTER ELEVEN
Stillwater

Abel continued his story. "We went back to our room, and argued about what to do next…"

Seth paced around the hotel room, annoyed and excited all at once. "We have to find that professor and make him tell us where this old man lived. Our god could still be there, right in his house!"

"The book came out twenty years ago, and the account is doubtless from even earlier," Abel said, trying to temper his comet's expectations. "If the man was already old, he's probably dead by now."

Seth waved that objection away. "Maybe so, but it's a place to start. This is an actual lead, Abel, can't you feel it? Asterias is shifting the current in our favor."

It was the only clue they had, and in the end, it wasn't hard to track down the professor. Seth called the anthropology department, claiming to be a former student who wanted to write a letter to his favorite professor, and the secretary obliged without hesitation. The address was in the tangle of residential streets around the university, and they set out the next morning – a compromise, since Seth was in favor of charging over that night.

Abel wasn't expecting much. He'd noticed the bookseller's comments about Professor Stillwater's mental decline, and wondered how Seth had missed it. But then, Seth was probably just choosing to ignore it, and hoping for the best. Abel believed in the power of Asterias – the god had saved his life, after all – but Seth seemed to believe the dead god would make fortune fall in their favor, and Abel had his doubts. It was called The Ravening Deep, not The Solver of Problems. Abel's initial wonder at his new powers had ebbed, and he was beginning to wonder what *sort* of god he'd pledged himself to.

After a breakfast in the hotel's opulent dining room, where Seth drank too much coffee, they set out in the car. They parked on a steep hill, and Seth leaped from the car and hurried up the cracked sidewalk, Abel at his heels. The professor's house was narrow, dark, and tall, with an unkempt front lawn, but overall the structure was not in visible disrepair. Seth was already hammering away at the brass door knocker by the time Abel stepped up beside him.

The door opened a crack, pulling the knocker out of Seth's hand in the process. A woman with dark hair and shadowed eyes peered out at them. "Yes? How can I help you?"

"We're old students of Professor Stillwater's, in from the coast," Seth said. "We've been following up on some of the research he did, and we have some fascinating information to share with him."

The woman looked at them for a long moment, then sighed. "My father is… retired. He doesn't do that kind of work anymore. He doesn't do much of anything anymore. I'm sorry." She started to shut the door, and Seth stuck his foot in to stop her, like an overzealous salesman.

"Please, miss, we'd really love to see him. It's been years, and he was such a profound influence on us. He set us on our whole *path*." Seth had begging-puppy-dog eyes and such an earnest tone even Abel found it plausible.

She cocked her head, looking from one to the other. "Are you brothers? Brother... folklorists?" She almost smiled. "Like the Grimms?"

"Seth and Abel Davenport," Abel said, putting a little gravel in his voice, so its uncanny resemblance to Seth's would be less noticeable. "And sure, just like Jacob and Wilhelm Grimm, only a lot less famous, and instead of the Black Forest, we gather stories along the New England coast."

She snorted, then eased the door open. "Sounds like my father did influence you. I'm Ellen Stillwater. You can come in and say hello, but I warn you my father is no longer the man you knew. He has good days and bad days, and it's too early to tell which one today will be, but even on his best days..." She shook her head. "He doesn't recognize me most of the time. Don't expect him to recognize you."

Miss Stillwater led them into the foyer, past tall bookshelves with just a few leaning volumes gathering dust among candle-ends and forgotten coins. She took them into a small room off the hall, where a man with patchy white hair sat hunched in a chair with a blanket over his knees, facing an immense landscape painting that depicted crumbling rock formations arcing out of the ocean. Or... *were* they formations? The structures looked more like fortifications, with the suggestion of arrow-slit windows, and were those tiny figures climbing up the sides, or just darker sections of the paint? They didn't look human, though Abel couldn't have said how the artist conveyed that in just a few brushstrokes. The piece unsettled him.

The old man didn't respond to the three of them entering the room. Miss Stillwater said, "I used to put him by a window, but he seems to like looking at that painting more. He bought it in Boston from a painter named Pickwick or something. Said the painting showed the reality beneath the reality." She shook her head. "He was getting a little fuzzy even back then. Papa?" She stepped forward and touched the old man's shoulder. "Papa, some old students are here to see you."

No reaction. She dropped her hand, looked at them, and shrugged. "I'll make some tea. You can talk to him. He might hear you." Miss Stillwater left the room, plodding like there were weights hanging around her neck.

"Poor woman," Abel murmured when she departed, but Seth was already kneeling in front of the professor, looking into his face. Abel joined him. Stillwater had been shaved, and his hair was combed, but his eyes were like empty windows.

Seth snapped his fingers in front of the man's face. "Stillwater? We need to talk to you. If you're still in there..." He stood up, fists clenched at his sides, shaking his head from side to side. "This is no good. This violates the will of Asterias."

"We should leave," Abel said. "We'll find another way.

Miss?" He called down the hall. "We won't trouble you any further. Thank you for letting us stop by." He grabbed Seth's hand and dragged him out of the house. "We'll ask around," Abel said as they returned to the car. "Maybe Stillwater had an assistant, or–"

Seth stopped. "We'll just take his finger."

Abel looked at him, frowning. "What?"

Seth gestured at Abel's chest. "We'll put the amulet around the old man, chop off his finger, and grow a comet. The comet will have perfect recall, with all the professor's memories, so he'll be able to tell us–"

Abel recoiled from his twin. "Don't be ridiculous. You can't cut off a sick old man's finger, that's – it's a crime. It's monstrous."

"He won't even notice, he's so far gone, and even if he did suffer, what does it matter? This is the will of Asterias!" Seth's eyes shone.

"And do you think *Miss* Stillwater would sit patiently while we fill her bathtub with brine and chop off bits of her father? The ritual requires fresh blood to work, so we can't wrap up his body parts to go."

"We could… sneak back in, grab the old man, bring him home to the farmhouse, do it there…" Seth trailed off, but the wheels were clearly turning in his mind.

"*No*," Abel said firmly. "I forbid it. Do you hear me, Seth? I am the chosen one, the prophet of Asterias, I bear the amulet, and I *forbid* this. We will find another way."

Seth wrinkled his brow, looked like he was about to argue, and then slumped. "I… yes, brother. Of course. You guide us. I'm sorry. We're just… we're so close."

"Let's go home," Abel said. "We've found all we can in Arkham."

So they did.

"That's when things turned, that moment outside Stillwater's house," Abel said. "I just didn't realize it right away."

"What do you mean?" Diana asked.

Ruby had a pretty good idea. "Seth went through with his plan anyway, didn't he?"

Abel nodded. "I woke up at home the next morning tied to the bed. There's a lot of rope in a fisherman's house, and Seth was better at knots than me, since he remembered every one he'd ever seen tied. He was standing over me, holding the amulet, the string looped around his fingers. He didn't want to wear it – I think he was afraid to. But he said, 'I'm going to need help,' and put the string over his neck. The amulet touched his chest, and he sort of shivered, all over, and his eyes closed. I was yelling this whole time, telling him to let me go, but he ignored me. He got my knife and cut off his pinky finger right there, using the top of the dresser for a chopping block. Then he went away, and came back with his finger bandaged up, the amulet in his other hand, and sat by the bed. 'This is how it has to be, Abel,' he said. 'Nothing matters but the resurrection of our god. I know this part is too hard for you – you're too human to do what's necessary. I will take this burden from you, because I love you.'"

"If that's love, you're lucky he didn't hate you," Ruby said.

"He did love me, though." Abel sounded sorrowful. "He just loved Asterias more." Abel told them how Seth fed him soup and responded calmly whenever Abel raged and made demands. How Abel fell into a fitful sleep. How when he woke up the next morning, there were *two* comets standing over him, both wearing his clothes.

"I could recognize the new one immediately, and not just because he had all his fingers. He was just... wrong, in ways I couldn't quite put my finger on. The way his eyes lined up, or didn't, quite. How sharp his teeth looked. These deep lines on his face that didn't match mine and Seth's. His fingers looked too long, and he moved in a sort of eely way, like he was slithering through the water even when he was walking around on dry land."

"I think when you make a copy of a copy, things start to go wrong," Ruby said. "I saw that with the Berglunds. Some of the doubles were a little... off."

Abel nodded. "Seth said, 'I think we'll name our new brother Enos', after the son of Seth in the Bible, you know, but the new comet said, 'I will choose my own name when the time comes. May I wear the amulet, brother?' Seth tightened his grip on the amulet and said, 'I think I'll hold onto it'. Then he leaned over and patted me on the cheek and said, 'We'll be back with the professor, don't you worry'. I shouted at them, told them not to do it, that they'd better not hurt that old man or his daughter..." He shook his head. "They just left. But the new comet, he looked at me before he left, a long look, and then he licked his lips, and I swear, his tongue was black."

"Did they get the professor?" Ruby said.

"I remember this," Diana broke in. "I didn't remember the name, Stillwater, but I heard about this a while back. There was a break-in, a murder, and a man disappeared. That was your comets?"

Abel nodded. "I don't know exactly what happened. They never gave me details. But Miss Stillwater must have gotten in their way, and they killed her. Seth was upset about that, at least. I think the other one, the new comet, did the actual killing. He doesn't mind killing much. People don't matter to him at all. Only Asterias does. But after Miss Stillwater was dead, they bundled the old man away and brought him to the house and put him in the bed – they moved me to a chair, tied me there sitting up, which was a change, at least. They put the amulet on the professor, and chopped off his finger." Abel put his head in his hands, and his shoulders shook. His voice came out muffled and weak.

"He screamed when they did it. He wasn't so far gone that he couldn't feel pain. He didn't live long, after that. You have to be alive, I think, for your comet to grow, and he lasted that long, but then his heart gave out, or something. "

"But you got a comet of Professor Stillwater out of it?" Ruby said. "One with his mind intact?"

"We did," Abel said. "And, heavens help me, once the whole mess was done, and the old man buried in the basement… I told Seth and the new comet that I didn't approve of their methods, but I still believed in the mission, and since they'd already done what they'd done I wanted to be part of things again. They believed me." He looked up, and his eyes were haunted. "I wasn't even lying. I did want to see things through. Seth untied me, and gave me the amulet back, but the new comet, he was watching me. He didn't trust me."

"The old man," Ruby said. "Professor Double. What did he have to say?"

"He sobbed, mostly, so it was hard to get anything useful out of him at first. He was bereft, you see, because he was now devoted to Asterias, and he'd actually *seen* a piece of our dead god. He'd held the jar in his hands. If he'd known what it was, he could have achieved the resurrection all those years ago. The knowledge that he'd failed to save his new god... it almost broke him. But he did finally tell us where we could find the man from Innsmouth. His house was just a few hours' drive away. So the next day we set out, and took our new Stillwater with us, even though he was practically hysterical, because the man we were looking for – his name was Lambton – knew the professor already. We thought seeing a familiar face would help us get in the door easier."

"Did it?" Diana asked.

"There was no door. It was torn off the hinges. The windows were broken, and the whole house was empty, except for dust. After we had a good long look, Seth drove into what passed for town and asked around – he made like he was interested in buying the property. Seth was always so good at that sort of thing, talking to people. A gift from our god, I guess."

Ruby noted the past tense but said nothing. Abel would get to that in time, she supposed, but it seemed like a safe bet that Seth was gone, and probably not from natural causes.

Abel went on. "We found a local busybody sitting on the porch at the general store who was happy to gossip. It turned out Lambton had died years before – killed, actually, a grisly unsolved murder. Seth blew right past that and asked what happened to all Lambton's furniture and things – said he was interested in antiques, that kind of nonsense. The busybody told him, quote, 'a fella came up from the city and bought all his books and things at the estate auction, and took it all away in a truck'. A little more questioning, and it turned out the city in question wasn't Boston, but Arkham, and we got a description of the buyer–"

"A small man," Diana said. "Older gentleman, but still hale. Silver hair. Neat beard. Dapper dresser."

"Carl Sanford," Ruby said.

"That's how it turned out," Abel said. "Though getting the name wasn't that quick for us – we spent two days in that county, with Seth sweet-talking himself into a records office and finding a receipt from the estate sale. It didn't say 'Carl Sanford' on it, either, it was something like 'Silver Imports Ltd', I forget the exact name, and then we had to do *more* research. But, yes, eventually, we figured out Carl Sanford bought up everything. Including, we assumed, the jar holding the piece of Asterias. We didn't know who Carl Sanford was at the time, apart from a prominent citizen of Arkham. So we decided to return here, and do more research, and find a way to take back our god." He sighed. "That was two months ago."

"How did you end up on the outs with your brothers?" Ruby wanted to know what had converted Abel from reluctant cult leader to out-and-out adversary, but before he could answer, there was a pounding at the door downstairs.

Diana startled, then rose and looked out the window,

down into the alley. When she turned back to them, her eyes were wide, and her face was pale. "It's *Carl Sanford.*"

"This is what you need to tell him," Ruby said instantly.

BOOK TWO

THE MAGUS

CHAPTER TWELVE
The Magus

After rather longer than should have been necessary, Diana opened the door to the back of her shop. She looked a little flustered, which was appropriate. When the head of your order showed up with a pair of large men – Brothers of the Night both – flanking him, it *should* make you flustered. Perhaps she'd needed extra time to get dressed for visitors. That could explain the delay. But so could other things.

"Hello, Diana," Sanford said. "I had my assistant call you, but there was no answer. I was hoping you'd get in touch after visiting the Berglunds. I was worried something might have happened to you." That wasn't precisely true. Sanford didn't worry about many things. But he was curious. "I am glad to see you appear unharmed. Perhaps you have a few moments to talk to me now?"

"I... yes, of course." She straightened, putting the steel back in her spine, and that pleased him. Diana had the potential to be a useful tool.

Sanford looked left, and then right. Sunday night in the

Merchants was quiet indeed, and a cool fog was creeping in from the river, muffling the world further. "Did you want us to talk here in the street?"

She blinked, then laughed. "Of course not. I'm sorry. We can talk in my office."

"My associates will wait here." Sanford trusted the two of them as much as he trusted anyone... but that didn't mean much, especially lately. Diana was an exception. He did trust her – or at least, her self-interest, her ambition, and her desire to rise in the Arkham social scene. She also wasn't important enough to the Lodge to be worth coopting, if, indeed, people *were* being coopted.

Sanford didn't have time for this sort of distraction. He had a meeting tomorrow at the Independence Hotel with an out-of-towner, pursuing a deal he'd been working on for months, and this was a terrible time for a disruption. But the world never much cared for anyone's convenience, did it? If strange things were afoot in his city, he needed to know.

He followed Diana into the back room of her shop, which he inventoried with a glance – fine fabrics and the various tools required for alterations, nothing of interest to him – and then into the small office at the back. She sat behind a desk, and gestured to a chair on the other side. Sanford sat down in it, amused. Usually he was the one sitting behind the desk, and a rather more impressive desk at that, but she was clearly striving for a sense of control. She hadn't invited him up to her apartment. That was not surprising. She was not comfortable around him – that showed intelligence – and allowing him into the place where she ate and slept would feel too intimate. He could have suggested they move upstairs, to assert his own power, but that would be petty. He *had* real power, and thus, there was no need to make a great show of it.

"May I offer you anything to drink?" Diana said. "Water, tea, or I keep champagne on hand for my customers."

He shook his head, once, a simple negation. "I just want to know what happened when you visited the Berglunds."

Diana closed her eyes, clearly preparing herself. "I am… still trying to figure out what happened."

"Simply tell me your experiences. I will assist with any necessary interpretation."

She wrung her hands, then stilled herself. She looked directly into Sanford's eyes when she spoke. Interesting. That was something liars did, because they thought it made them seem honest and forthright. It was also something nervous people did to hide their nerves, though.

Many people believed that Sanford had the ability to see into their minds, to tell truth from lies and divine hidden motives. In fact, he was simply a sharp observer and an astute listener, and hardly needed recourse to the supernatural to figure out whether people were lying or scheming. For one thing, almost *everyone* was lying and scheming. He listened to Diana with interest and growing alarm.

"I went to see the Berglunds, and something was clearly wrong. Cornelia was upstairs, moaning, in some kind of distress, and wouldn't come down. Cornelius said it was just a migraine, but…" Diana shook her head. "There were drops of blood on the floor in the kitchen. Cornelius had a bandaged hand from some kind of wound. I got the sense there were other people in the house, too – I could hear thumping, and people moving around. Something strange was going on."

"Do you have any idea *what*?" he asked.

She hugged herself, shivering a little. "Cornelia called down from upstairs, and Cornelius went up to check on her, so I took the opportunity to look around a little. There was blood by the basement door, so I went down, and… and… Master, it doesn't make any *sense*."

This was interesting. He leaned forward. "Tell me what you saw."

"I saw… it's not possible, but under the stairs, wrapped in a tarp, I saw… Cornelia and Cornelius. They were *dead*. But they couldn't be, because I just saw him upstairs, and I *heard* her, I know her voice." She hunched further into herself, and when she went on, her voice was small. "That's why I didn't come to you. I fled the house. I came back here. I've been going over and over it in my mind, trying to understand, debating whether to call the sheriff. I've seen… things… helping out with your projects at the Lodge, so I know there is more to the world than I was taught, but something like *this*? Master, what's going on?"

"I truly don't know." Sanford was so troubled by the presence of unknown supernatural entities here, in *his* city, that the truth slipped out. "I've never heard of anything quite like this before. There are illusions, used to hide your identity, but who is doing the hiding? Or perhaps they're shapeshifters of some kind, pretending to be other people – there are stories about those. But such creatures are usually solitary, and it sounds as if Cornelia and Cornelius were *both* replaced, and I have reason to believe others have been, too... and why target the Berglunds anyway? I thought there might be a conspiracy to infiltrate the Lodge, but they aren't even members. One hates to speak ill of the dead, but Cornelius was a blowhard and Cornelia was a fool, and they don't offer anything of particular value to the sort of people or creatures who could manage such a convincing imposture." Sanford leaned back, steepling his fingers under his nose. "This is very curious, Diana. Did you see anything else at their house? Strange books? Unusual objects?"

She shook her head.

"Did this ersatz Cornelius say *anything* that might shed light on their motives or their nature?"

"No, I... wait." She tapped her forefinger against her pursed lips. "I... they were upstairs, talking, so I couldn't hear well, but they said something about a person named... Cain? 'Tell Cain he has to help us', something like that?" Diana shrugged. "I'm sorry. That's all I can recall."

Cain. The name meant nothing to Sanford, but it was a place to start. He rose. "Diana, I wish you'd come to see me immediately, but I understand you were distressed, so I will not hold it against you. In the future, however, do not hesitate to report to me directly. You are a member of my Lodge, and as such, you are under my care, and I will protect you." As long as doing so protected him too.

"What should I do now, master?" she asked, rising.

"Nothing for the moment. I may call upon you later with another task, once I gather further information. In the meantime, you should remain attentive, and report any strange behavior by Lodge members and other citizens to me immediately."

Diana nodded, and led him to the door, where his Brothers of the Night were waiting, watching the foggy night. "Have a pleasant evening, Miss Stanfield," Sanford said. She wished him the same – little chance of that, sadly – and shut the door.

Sanford glanced at the upstairs window above, where her apartments were, and thought he saw a flash of motion at the glass. Well, well. Perhaps his Diana had a gentlemen caller, and that's why she hadn't invited him upstairs. It could explain her nervousness, too. He dismissed the issue. He was hardly in a position to quibble about morals. Morals, in fact, were the invisible fetters that so often held one back from greatness.

"Gentlemen," he said. "We're going to call on the Berglunds."

One of his associates stayed in the car, to watch the street, and the other accompanied Sanford to the steps of the Berglund house. It was dark, well after the dinner hour. The moon was a sliver of polished bone overhead, and the air cool, though not as misty up here on the hill.

They were close to the Lodge. Too close, if what Diana said was true. Sanford didn't like the idea of some supernatural infestation on French Hill – at least, not one he didn't control himself.

Carl Sanford was not an evil man. He knew this, and further knew it wasn't the deluded self-justification of a villain who claims a righteous cause to soften his atrocities. He has *done* evil things, at times, but always with a greater purpose in mind. There were forces that wanted to destroy the world – or worse, *unmake* the world – or still worse, negate the existence of the world entirely, and retroactively. Sanford considered himself a bulwark against those corrosive forces. He had no interest in seeing the world and its people eliminated or undone, and indeed, he had often intervened to help ensure the continued survival of humankind when it was threatened by hostile or (and in some ways these were more disturbing) indifferent forces.

The world, to put it crudely, was where Carl Sanford kept all his *things*, and the people in the world were the things that most amused him. Thus, he was a champion of humanity, standing for them against the forces arrayed in the deep caverns, and beyond the stars, and behind the sharpened curves of conventional geometry.

To stand against such forces often required mastering them, and taking their powers for his own, but what better hands *were* there for such powers?

He rapped on the Berglunds' door with the head of his cane. A few moments later it opened, and Cornelius – or an undetectable copy – blinked at him in alarm, dressed in a flannel robe. One of his hands was clumsily bandaged. "Ah, Sanford, what – what are you doing here?"

"You were meant to call me, Cornelius," Sanford said. "About our little thief. Do let me in. I don't do business on *stoops*."

"It's getting late, and Cornelia isn't feeling well–"

"Let me in, or Brother Cluny will." Sanford did not bother to gesture at the hulking Brother of Night beside him, but the Brother cracked his knuckles. Cluny was not a professional leg-breaker – he'd inherited a block of office buildings and spent most of his time playing golf – but he was large and had a mean scowl. For people like Berglund, a show of overt force was all you needed. The truly dangerous people in Sanford's circle were far less obvious. Sarah Van Shaw, for instance, wasn't physically intimidating, but between her and her vicious "dogs", she was by far the more dangerous.

"Yes, please, of course, come in." Cornelius moved back, and Sanford moved in.

"You don't mind if Brother Cluny takes a look around the house?" Sanford said.

"What?" Cornelius goggled, tightening the belt on his robe. "Why would you want to–" He moved to block Cluny from charging up the stairs. Cluny looked at Sanford, who shook his head, and the beefy landlord stood back and crossed his arms.

"To make sure you aren't hiding the thief here, of course," Sanford said. "You made a side bargain, didn't you?" Sanford clucked his tongue. "Tut-tut. I was going to let you keep the jewel, but you wanted more, I suppose. What did the thief offer you?"

Berglund stiffened. "She offered me nothing. I haven't even met with her yet. I expect she'll come in tomorrow."

"I have it on good authority that she passed through the train station *today*." This was a bluff – he had people watching the station, of course, but Ruby Standish was adept at blending in, or standing out, whichever better suited her needs.

Cornelius was not rattled. He scowled. "Then perhaps she's enjoying an evening on the town and intends to come here in the morning. I *will* call you, Sanford, once I have her, you may be assured of that."

Sanford turned to peruse some unlovely statuary on a nearby shelf. They were copies, anyway. "What happened to your hand?"

Cornelius looked at the bandage wound around his fingers. "I picked up a piece of broken glass and cut myself. Nothing serious."

"I've seen more than a few maimed limbs in my time, Cornelius. It looks to me like your smallest finger is missing."

He put his hand in his robe. "Nothing so dire as all that, I assure you."

"Mmm. Who's Cain?"

Cornelius stiffened, then looked panicked, eyes cutting up toward the stairs and back to Sanford. "I don't know anyone named Cain. I think you should leave. I'll call you when Ruby, when the thief, when I find her–"

"I heard Cornelia is unwell. I should check on her." Sanford headed for the stairs, and when Berglund tried to block him, he gave the man a chilling stare. Cornelius had all the backbone of a limpet, and he should have slunk out of the way... but he just returned the stare. He definitely wasn't himself... so, then, who was he? Sanford intended to find out.

"Let's just *take him*," a voice from the direction of the kitchen said. "Wrap him up and give him to Cain. We'll never have a better chance!"

"What in the hell?" Brother Cluny said, and Sanford looked toward the new voice. There was a man standing in the kitchen doorway, holding a claw hammer in one hand.

He looked like Cornelius's dissolute twin, his unshaven face snarling, his left eye drooping, his hair unkempt.

"Interesting," Sanford said. "Cluny, kill that man." He pointed toward the double while returning his gaze to the other Cornelius, who looked terrified.

You didn't become a Brother of Night without proving – under difficult conditions – that you would follow the orders of the master without question, and Brother Cluny reached into his suit coat and brought out a straight razor, flipping it open.

That blade had belonged to certain British murderer, one who'd dabbled in forbidden arts and used the corpses of his victims to fuel his research, and it had unusual properties. The other Berglund lunged forward with his claw hammer, bringing it down in a vicious overhand swing, intending to break Cluny's wrist.

Instead, the hammer struck the blade of the razor when Cluny moved it to block. The hammer rebounded as if it had struck an iron bar. The other Berglund howled at the pain doubtless vibrating through his hand and up his arm. Cluny swung his razor in a smooth, flat arc and turned his face away from the blood that burst from the double's throat.

"Cornelius?" a querulous voice called from upstairs. "What's happening?"

The surviving Cornelius spun and started up the stairs, but Sanford reached out and grabbed his ankle as he began to climb, making him fall and bang his face against the wooden risers. "Don't be tiresome," Sanford said, stepping forward and planting the base of his cane between the man's shoulder blades. He pressed down. "Tell me what you are.

Tell me what you're doing in Arkham. Tell me who this Cain is."

"You can never kill us all," Cornelius said. "We serve that which when divided multiplies." He rolled over and, with more strength than Sanford would have imagined he possessed, wrenched the stick out of Sanford's hands. He rose, brandishing the weapon – and then came the *pop* of Brother Cluny's small revolver. A hole appeared in the false Cornelius's throat, and he gurgled, and fell. People imagined gunshots were loud, and they could be, but the sound of a .22 could be dismissed as a backfiring car or the crack of a tree limb if it was noticed at all.

"They die like people, anyway," Cluny said. "They don't bleed ichor, like that thing in–"

"Shh," Sanford said. "There is still someone upstairs. At least *one* someone."

Sanford retrieved his stick and mounted the steps, Brother Cluny moving along behind him. After a moment, Sanford paused, and unsheathed the sword hidden in his cane. They resumed their climb as Cornelia – or something that sounded like her – shouted: "What was that noise? Who's there? What's happening?"

Sanford stepped into the bathroom, where Cornelia rested in a bathtub full of murky water. She had a bandage across her nose and two black eyes. Someone had struck her hard in the face. "You look terrible, my dear," Sanford said. "I was just wondering. When did you get *two* husbands? Surely a single Cornelius Berglund is already more than the world requires."

She started to lever herself out of the tub. Why on earth

was she wearing a nightgown in the bath? Well, it was hardly the oddest thing he'd seen in this house. "What have you done to them?" she demanded.

"Killed them for refusing to answer my questions," Sanford said. "Tell me: who is Cain?"

She stood, dripping, and, to Sanford's horror, she giggled. "He is our prince, our priest, and our prophet."

"I see. And where might I find him?"

"He is everywhere, because he is our creator, and *we* are everywhere, because we serve that–"

"Which when divided multiplies, yes, I heard. Could you be more specific? That title, or is it a description, does little to enlighten me." Sanford's knowledge of esoterica was broad, and those phrases had a faint ring of the familiar, but he was annoyed at being in the dark. He was a keeper of secrets, not the victim of them.

"You don't get to know. Not yet. But once Cain takes you, and you undergo the sacrament, you won't *need* to be told. You will simply know, as all of us know."

"Is that really how it works?" Sanford leaned against the pedestal sink, giving Brother Cluny a clear shot through the doorway, should he need it. "You'll do some ritual, and then I'll see the light and be inspired to join your cause? Because I understand the real Berglunds are both dead in your basement. You are cheap counterfeits." But *good* counterfeits, and that worried him. Sanford wasn't in the habit of trusting many people anyway, but he could generally at least trust that people he dealt with were *human*.

"Oh, well." She waved a hand. "*You* won't join us, not the you that stands before me. We'll have to discard this version.

But the new you will be better, because you will serve our god, and be blessed and joyful in service."

"Let's go back to the Silver Twilight Lodge, my counterfeit Cornelia. You've been eager to see the innermost secrets of that place for a long time. Now you'll have your chance." He had researchers on his staff who could discern what manner of creature this false Cornelia was, and interrogators who could pull more useful and concrete answers out of her–

"Die!" someone shouted from the hallway, and Brother Cluny grunted and fell, tackled by another figure. Sanford had the impression of a woman furiously slashing at the man, but he kept his focus on the Cornelia in the bathtub, and it was good he did, because she launched herself at him.

Fortunately, she slipped on the wet tile, and lost control of her charge, and he was able to adjust his stance and allow her to impale herself on his sword. She reached out to him as she slid forward, the sword moving through her abdomen and out her back, and he expected her to grasp him by the throat. Instead, she caressed his cheek. "Cain is coming for you," she murmured. "You will join our fellowship, and be glad."

Sanford stepped to one side, pointed the sword at the floor, and watched her body slide off. When she hit the floor, he delivered a short, decisive thrust to her heart. Sanford then stepped into the hallway, where the other Cornelia was sobbing and slashing at the throat of an already very dead Brother Cluny with a pair of nail scissors.

Sanford stabbed her through the heart, too, this time from the back, then stepped over the mess in the hall and went down the stairs. He hadn't gotten much blood on him, at least, but he still blotted at his face with a handkerchief. Killing worked up a sweat. He hadn't personally taken a life in some time, and seldom needed to sully his hands with murder at all. But he didn't think this was homicide, precisely. More like *homunculi*-cide, perhaps.

The Berglunds had a phone, and he placed a call to the Lodge. "I require the warden," he said to the Initiate who answered. A few moments later, Sarah Van Shaw's crowlike voice said, "Master?"

"We have a bit of a mess to clean up, Sarah dear." Clearing the dead bodies out of the house and covering up the crime scene was just the start. There was a much bigger mess in Arkham, and he'd need to sort that out, too. Curse it all, he had other business to attend to, meetings and deals and machinations. The last thing he needed was some upstart cult running rampant in Arkham. But dealing with them would fall to him, as such things always did. Heavy lies the head that wears the crown, he thought.

Sanford went down to the basement to confirm that the bodies of the Berglunds were there – he might as well verify as much of Diana's story as possible. They were indeed wrapped in a tarp under the stairs. There were things Diana hadn't mentioned, though, notably several loops of rope around a pillar, partially cut through. Perhaps the rope only appeared after Diana departed, or perhaps she was simply distracted by the more disturbing presence of two corpses… but perhaps something else. Maybe Diana had withheld the detail for her own reasons. Sanford was not one to leap to conclusions, but he believed in leaving himself open to the consideration of possibilities, especially the unpleasant ones.

He went back upstairs to meet his people, who would take care of cleaning up the scene. They'd take the bodies of the doppelgangers back to the Lodge for study, and the original Berglunds would be found elsewhere, the victims of a vicious and senseless attack on the street.

Sanford would return to the Lodge, and begin the process of eradicating this new rot from Arkham before it could further threaten his enterprises. They'd already spoiled his trap for the thief Ruby Standish, and it irked him that she might slip his grasp again. Someone would answer for that, and Sanford knew that someone's name, even if he didn't know anything else about him.

"Cain, Cain, Cain," he murmured. "I simply cannot wait to meet you."

CHAPTER THIRTEEN
The Rise of Cain

"Yes, I *do* think it was a good idea to tell Sanford about Cain."
Diana did her best to strike a soothing tone. Ruby could be
forthright, and Abel had a stubborn streak, and she didn't
want to see those qualities come into conflict; the stakes
were too high for infighting. "That's why I went along with
it."

Ruby nodded. "Of course it's a good idea. It's mine. The
comets put you in the hospital, Abel. Now, after what Diana
told him, Sanford will be out there hunting these monsters,
using all his considerable resources against *them*. He'll stop
looking for me, or at least make me a lower priority, which
only helps us. And he'll be distracted by rooting out this
conspiracy, and *that* will make it easier for us to get into the
Lodge vaults and lay our hands on your god in a jar. When
you have the chance to pit two enemies against one another,
you should always take it."

"It's just risky, is all." Abel paced back and forth, fretting.
"What if Sanford realizes what Cain is looking for? The
treasure he's had in the Lodge all this time? You say all

Sanford cares about is power, Diana, so what if they form an alliance to resurrect Asterias together?"

"Is Cain the allying type?" Diana asked.

Abel snorted. "All right. That's fair. Probably not. But if they meet, Cain will at least try to chop Sanford up and make a double out of him, and that double could lead Cain straight to the jar. That's his whole mission here in Arkham, infiltrating the Lodge, and if he can get his hands on Sanford, he'll be done. Nothing will stop him after that."

"Carl Sanford is hard to catch, and harder to keep," Ruby said. "There's a reason the comets haven't snatched him up yet. He's got as many protections as those vaults of his. Maybe more, since he considers himself more precious than any object, no matter how powerful."

"There's no use talking about it anymore," Diana said. "The die is cast. Sanford *is* distracted, now. I bet he went straight to the Berglunds'. That means Cain and his people – or whatever they are – will probably be distracted soon, too. The question is, how do we take advantage of the chaos we've just created?"

"We're all too tired to do anything tonight anyway," Ruby said. "I say we give these fresh tensions a day to simmer and start boiling, and tomorrow night, we see about breaking into the Lodge."

"So soon?" Diana blinked. She'd known that was coming, that such a step would be necessary, but everything was happening so fast. Were they being decisive and swift, or acting in haste?

"The sooner the better," Ruby said. "I'll admit it: Abel has a point. Sanford is powerful. He might get answers out of the comets. Zealots can be chatty. We don't want to give Sanford time to realize what he's got floating in that jar downstairs. Right now, that piece of Asterias is pretty easy to reach – it's not locked away behind barriers of magic and steel, like some of Sanford's other, prettier treasures. Getting our hands on it should be an easier heist than my last adventure at the Lodge. Even if they've improved security since then, they probably did so for the vaults, not a storage room off to the side. So, yes. Tomorrow night."

"Tomorrow *afternoon*," Diana countered. "The Lodge is busiest at night. During the day, often there's no one present but the warden and an Initiate or two working inside. On the upper levels, at least. I don't know what all goes on down below. We just have to make sure Sanford isn't on the premises himself. I can call his assistant, and see if he's available to talk, and if he's not, we can go in. If he is there, we can give him a fake lead on Cain, and send him on a wild goose chase to get him out of the way."

"I prefer operating under the cover of night, but OK," Ruby said. "We'll just have to figure out how to get past that warden."

"How did you avoid her last time?" Diana had never gotten details about that.

"I messed with her dogs," Ruby said. "Set snares, nothing that hurt them, but they were tangled up and yelping, and when she came running to check on them, I just circled around. That trick won't work again, though. She'll know to be suspicious."

"I can distract her," Diana said. "She knows me, and she knows I'm working with Sanford on something. She won't suspect me of anything."

"That doesn't help with the dogs, though," Ruby said. "We need to distract *them*, too, in a way that won't make the warden suspicious."

Diana slumped. There were rumors about how viciously the dogs treated interlopers; the nastiest rumors said some of those trespassers were buried in the back lawn. "Hmm. Maybe if we got some sleeping pills, put them in some meat…"

"Why don't you just walk in?" Abel said. "Diana is a member of the Lodge in good standing, and we *know* Sanford wants to capture Ruby. So, Diana, you pretend you captured her, and just walk her in. Say you're supposed to put her in a holding room downstairs, and offer to stand guard over her." He shrugged.

"The old fake prisoner trick?" Ruby tapped her fingertip against her lips. "I guess it's a classic for a reason. It could work, if Van Shaw doesn't decide to cut me into little pieces first."

Diana nodded. That could work. "Sanford would want to deal with you directly," she said. "He's only mentioned you once or twice in my presence, but the fact that he mentioned you at all means you got under his skin. He doesn't like it when people take things that belong to him. If we work fast, and get you out of the Lodge before Sanford can return, we can just say you escaped again. I might even keep my cover as a loyal Seeker intact."

Ruby yawned. "Good enough. We'll work out the details later. But first, I need some sleep. I'll take the sofa."

Abel insisted that Diana take her own bed again, and went

downstairs. There was a divan there, for the spouses or friends of her clients to rest on while measurements were taken and samples cooed over, and that was a softer place to sleep than most he'd endured lately. He lay on his back, his feet dangling off the end of the divan, and looked at a triangle of light on the ceiling, shining in through the front windows from the streetlights.

Something was nagging at him. Why had Cain's thugs prevented him from making his way across the river? Cain was up to something over there, but Abel couldn't imagine what. The Silver Twilight Lodge was over here, just a long walk to the southeast, on French Hill. There must be something integral to Cain's plan on the north side of the city. What could it be? There were the tall buildings downtown, the train station, the newspaper offices, Independence Square, and a lot of docks and industrial buildings. Certainly nothing that would obviously help Cain get his hands on the fragment of their god.

Abel tried to think the way Cain would think, but he'd never had the knack for that, despite the fact that, in theory, Cain was just a copy of him – or, rather, a copy of a copy. Cain had always been *off*, ever since Seth first made him, but it had taken a little time before Abel realized *how* strange the new comet was.

"How did you end up on the outs with your brothers?" Ruby had asked. How indeed. He'd have to tell them about it, in the morning, before they made their infiltration of the Lodge.

Abel turned over on the divan, away from the shape of light, staring instead into the darkened recesses of the shop.

His mind painted the shadows with figures from memory.

This time, Abel and the comets didn't stay in the hotel – they still had decent funds, but they thought a set of triplets traipsing through the grand lobby might draw attention, so they rented a shack in Rivertown instead. Abel hated how much at home he felt there, with the wind blowing through the cracks in the walls and the tattered nets hung from the ceiling and the stink of old fish everywhere. They weren't far from their target, at least: the Silver Twilight Lodge, a rambling old pile up on French Hill. The question was, how to get inside.

"A machine gun would do the job," the new comet said. His voice always had a peculiar rasp, like he'd been shouting himself hoarse the night before. "Three machine guns, even better. We kick in the door, kill anyone we see, and tear the place apart until we find our god."

"Going in hard won't work, Enos," Seth said. The new comet hadn't acknowledged that name, but they had to call him *something*. They were all sitting around the scarred wooden table in the shack's front room. "Someone will hear the gunfire and call the police. And anyway, we don't know what it's like inside there. The place is huge, and our god could be anywhere. It would take us hours to search. We'll have to sneak in, but it won't be easy."

"Perhaps we will be able to sense the Ravening Deep's location when we draw near, as we sense one another. Perhaps the amulet will even strengthen the effect," Enos said as he stared at Abel. He didn't blink anywhere near enough. "That would make the search faster."

Abel shrugged. "Maybe. I didn't feel anything when we walked by the Lodge. But we don't even know if that piece of our god is still there. This Carl Sanford bought the jar, probably, but maybe he sold it to someone else, or he keeps it someplace else, or hell, maybe he didn't know what it was, and he threw it in the trash–"

Suddenly Enos had Abel's shirt front bunched up in both fists. The new comet snarled, face inches from Abel's. "Do not blaspheme. We have been *led* here, carried on the tides of fate by the will of Asterias. Do you not believe? How can you, our *priest*, lack faith?"

Seth stood up, patting Enos on the shoulder, drawing him back, soothing him. "Take it easy, Abel is just working out the angles and the possibilities, it's OK–"

"You are not worthy to wear that amulet." Enos trembled. "You are only *human*."

Abel stood up. The power of Asterias coursed through him, the amulet burning cold against his chest. Sleeping and eating were largely optional now, his strength was greater than an ordinary man's, and his endurance was far greater than even an extraordinary one. He was *chosen*, and he would not be disrespected again. He'd let his grip slip once, and this snarling zealot was the result.

"And you're a fingernail clipping off a fingernail clipping, *Enos*. You're lucky I didn't tear your head off and throw you back into the sea for the cousins of our god to eat. I forgave Seth for making you. I understood his desperation, and he is my brother, the first of my congregation. But *you*." Abel spat on the wooden floor. "If you aren't useful to me, then you're a problem, and problems are chum for the water."

Enos stormed out of the shack, and Seth sighed, slumping down in the chair. "I'm sorry, Abel. I should have talked to you more before I made him. Tried to convince you, instead of tying you down and taking the amulet."

Abel shrugged. They'd been over all this before. "You did what you felt Asterias called you to do. I disagree with your methods, but our goals are still the same."

"And we're close to achieving them. Surely you see that?"

"I guess. I don't know how, though. Maybe I should try to join the Lodge, so I can at least get a look at the inside."

"We could just find someone who's already a member," Seth said. "Do what we did with the professor, make a copy."

Abel shuddered. "Because that worked out so well?" The professor's comet had wept and screamed and wailed, unable to forgive himself for failing to restore Asterias when he had the chance, and the night before they came to Arkham, he'd walked into the sea, disappearing beneath the moonlit waves, and never returned. "If we go down that path again, more people will die."

"We're talking about the restoration of the divine," Seth said. "What cost could stand up against that?"

"There's another way," Abel said. "People don't have to die. One murder was too many, and I won't preside over more. I'm going for a walk."

He went outside and walked toward the misty waters of the Miskatonic. He looked left, toward the Black Cave, a local landmark that swirled with dark stories. He'd like to leave Enos in that cave. He looked right, toward French Hill, toward the Lodge, toward–

He heard the scuffle of a footstep behind him, and then

something struck the back of his head, and an explosion of stars filled his vision. He shook his head a moment later, woozy and disoriented. *Why am I on my knees?* Then he gagged, because someone was pulling the amulet from behind, choking him on its string. He scrabbled at his throat, and then a knee pressed into his back, pushing him forward against the cutting pain of the necklace. This couldn't be happening. He was the chosen one! He couldn't die here, with his work unfinished, murdered by some mugger–

"You are not worthy," a familiar voice hissed in his ear.

His terror turned into a colder variety of fear. Then the string snapped, and Abel fell forward into the mud. He rolled over, and looked up at Enos, who stood over him, the amulet clutched in his fist. As Abel watched, the new comet tied a knot in the string.

"Making comets from the Lodge members was *my* idea," Enos said. Abel started to rise, but the comet put a boot on his chest and pushed him back down. Then he kicked him in the ribs, once, twice, three times, until Abel curled up on himself. Enos spat into the mud beside him. "Seth said he'd talk things over, convince you to follow the right path, but I listened at the window, and you're still so *stubborn*." He held out the necklace, the amulet swaying. "You are just a human. You wear this amulet, and you take on the semblance of us, the true servants of Asterias. But you aren't one of us."

"I *made* you," Abel said. He tried to sit up, ribs aching, but Enos put the boot on his shoulder and shoved him back down.

"You are the soil, but we are the trees. Seth was afraid

to wear the amulet at first, did you know that? Afraid that doing so was blasphemy. He used this relic to make me, but he took it off again right away. He said it made him feel like there were oceans inside his mind. He was frightened of the vastness the amulet revealed. But I am even closer to Asterias than Seth was, more pure, and I wonder. If the amulet gave you, a pitiful human, such powers, what might it do for someone like me, a true son of the Ravening Deep?" The comet dropped the necklace over his head and put the amulet against his chest. He shivered. "I am now the head of our religion. You may call me… Cain."

Then the comet leaned over, and looked down at Abel. The weathered lines on his face were darker than before, and as Abel watched, they became darker still, and then – Cain's face *unfolded*. The flesh peeled back, unfurling from the center point of his nose in all directions, until it formed a seven-pointed star of flesh. Cain's head now resembled a flower, with petals made of triangular flaps of skin.

No. Not a flower. A starfish.

That peeling-back of the skin should have revealed muscle and blood underneath, and the shape of the skull under that, but Cain had been transformed by the amulet, and in a far more extreme way than Abel had been.

The unfolded flesh revealed the mouth of a starfish, a ragged circle surrounded by spines, big enough for Abel to shove his fist inside, though he thought if he did so, he'd draw back the spurting stump of his wrist.

"*I am chosen now*," that rasping voice said. Cain leaned forward, and Abel stared, transfixed with horror, as tendrils wriggled inside that mouth.

"No!" Seth shouted from behind Cain. "No, don't kill him, please, he *made* us, brother."

Cain paused, then turned. "Kill him? No. He must see the world that is to come. He must see me succeed where he never could. But you… you are weak, too, it is harder to forgive you, since you are closer to the divine." Cain bent and picked up an oar – probably what he'd hit Abel with – and struck Seth across the face. The other comet fell like a piece of timber. "I will make *new* brothers," Cain said. "Better ones."

Abel scrambled to his feet and rushed away, terrified that Cain would change his mind about sparing him. He felt an aching absence within his mind where he'd been able to sense Seth before, like a tooth had been ripped from his head.

Cain shouted after him. "Run, worm, and await the coming of Asterias with the other human meat! You have given up your place and your name! Cower in the shadows and await the rise of my god! When the Ravening Deep is reborn, we will meet again!"

Abel fled Arkham, and over the course of the next day, hitchhiked home. He went to the bank, planning to cut off Cain's resources, only to find that his accounts had been closed and his assets transferred away. Cain, or Seth, or both, must have planned this, to cut him out.

His flight clarified his mind, though. He couldn't just run away. There was a monster out there, wearing his face, and using his name. Abel wasn't a killer, and Seth a somewhat reluctant one, but Cain would drown the world in blood to see his god resurrected. Abel had to do something.

He sold a few things from the house and made his way back to Arkham, determined to stop Cain. He even got his hands on a pistol. But when he tried to get close, he could feel a dozen new comets, all over the city. Cain must have cut off his fingers, grown them back, cut them off, and grown them back again, or else made doubles of his own doubles – how strange and inhuman would *those* creatures be? Abel's reverence and gratitude toward Asterias were gone, replaced by horror. Cain and his progeny were the true children of the Ravening Deep. Abel had only ever been a tool for the monstrous entity to use for its own ends.

Abel watched from the shadows as Cain swanned around town, wearing new suits and smoking cigars, buddying up to the local businessmen. Abel didn't understand how he'd attained his newfound wealth until one night when a pair of Cain's comets appeared and grabbed Abel under the armpits, dragging him down an alley and stuffing him into the trunk of a car. He didn't even have his pistol with him – it was stashed under the floorboards of the shack where he was staying. Abel thought he was going to die, but instead, they drove him to a house on the north side and took him into the living room, dropping him on a beautiful oriental rug.

Cain was there, in a suit that would have done a bootlegging gangster proud, all pinstripes and diamond stickpin and mirror-shined black shoes. Cain had a sharp haircut and rings on his fingers. "Did you think we wouldn't notice you? We can sense you, fool."

Abel blinked at him. "With so many of you around, I thought I'd just sort of blend in with the crowd."

"You have a special stink about you, being fully human. We've been watching you, watching us. It's amusing. You're so desperate, scurrying around, trying to figure out what we're doing. I took pity on you. I decided to show you." Cain gestured with hands clad in black gloves, probably to hide the horror-show of his fingers grown back wrong. "This is my house. Or one of them. I bought it with cash, thanks to a generous donation from a new member of the brotherhood. It's easy to make money, for me. I just have to break into the house of a wealthy man, put the amulet on him, and cut off some fingers and toes. Dispose of the original, and the copies are happy to contribute to the cause. I have half a dozen of the most prominent people in Arkham dancing to my tune–"

"Then why don't you have Asterias yet?" Abel cut in. He couldn't stand the smug arrogance of this beast. He might die here, but he would die spitting his contempt.

Cain sat back. "Well. At first, I was just going to grab Carl Sanford, and bring *him* into the fold, but… he's slippery. Seldom alone. Always watchful. Spends most of his time in the Lodge, which, it turns out, is something of a fortress, though you wouldn't know it to look at the place from the outside. I've turned some of his Initiates, and they've given me floor plans and layouts, but they only see the surface. There's a lot more happening underneath. Getting my hands on members of the Lodge with greater access… that's a bit of a project. But I'm working my way up. The more access I get, the more access I *can* get. Eventually the Order of the Silver Twilight will have more comets than humans in its ranks. Cuckoos in the nest. Wasps in the beehive. Pick your metaphor."

"Why not just join up yourself, if you're such a pillar of the community already?"

Cain sneered, and the lines on his face darkened. For a moment, Abel was afraid he'd see that terrible face under his face again. "I could join, but it takes years to work your way up the ranks, so why bother, when I can take someone who's already done the work for me?"

"How many people have you killed so far?" Abel said.

"I don't keep track. Why would I? They're just *people*. They're nothing but food for the Ravening Deep. You stupid insect. What did you think would happen when you brought our god back to life? Didn't you realize he would want to *feed*?"

Abel had never thought that far ahead. "I didn't care. Asterias saved me. I owed it my life. I pledged myself in service. That's all."

"The Ravening Deep would have devoured you first," Cain said. "That's why I'm keeping you alive. Because it still *can*. When my god wakes, it will wake *hungry*, and I want you to provide the first mouthful." Cain flicked his fingers. "Get out of my sight. We'll find you when the time comes. We always know where you are. But stop skulking around watching us. I hate the sight of you."

"Because you hate being reminded of what you come from," Abel said. "That you're nothing but a copy of a copy."

"I came from you," Cain said. "I have never denied it. But I am you with the repulsive human parts cut out. Brothers, go dump this human in an alleyway somewhere. Give him a bottle from the crate by the back door. You might as well start drinking, Abel. It will help you pass the time until the dinner bell rings." Cain smiled, his teeth too many and too sharp. "It tolls for thee."

They did dump him in an alley with a bottle, but Abel didn't drink it. He went to the train station instead, intending to buy himself a ticket as far as he could afford to go – Chicago, maybe. He was resigned. He couldn't defeat Cain, but he could avoid becoming a meal.

Except a couple of comets came at him from both ends of an alley, offering no escape even though he could sense their approach, and grabbed him a block from the depot.

"Cain doesn't want you leaving town," one of them said. "It's too much trouble to fetch you when we wake up our god." They roughed him up a little, and then dumped him back in the alley where he'd started.

This time, he did pick up the bottle, and he kept picking up bottles until Diana found him and showed him a glimmer of light.

CHAPTER FOURTEEN
The Prisoner

To her surprise, Diana discovered she liked having people in her home. She'd been alone since her father died, and having Ruby and Abel in her kitchen, drinking coffee and eating eggs and toast with her, awakened some forgotten sociable part of her personality. The best part was, Diana could truly be herself with them. She'd become so accustomed to wearing masks – as a loyal Lodge member, of course, but also just as a businesswoman, a fashion expert, an entrepreneur – that being fully herself was like putting down a heavy load.

The mood *should* have been heavy, but Ruby was impish and irrepressible, one of those people who thrived on danger and found it exciting. Abel, too, wasn't the dour figure she'd first met, but a man energized and excited at the prospect of *doing something*. He sat at the counter beside Ruby, sipping coffee, and said, "I suppose, one way or another, all this business will soon be done."

"One way or another?" Ruby said. "You mean, we either get your bit of god-flesh, or we get murdered by Lodge members?"

"I guess there might be other outcomes," Abel said, "but those do seem like the main ones."

"What do we do with the jar after we get our hands on it, anyway?" Diana asked. "Just… burn it in a trash barrel?"

"I think fire is worth a try, yes," Abel said. "It worked for Hercules and the hydra – when he burned the stump after cutting off one of the monster's heads, it stopped growing new ones."

"A fisherman with a classical education?" Ruby said.

Abel chuckled. "My mother liked to read. She left me with a head full of stories about gods and monsters." He sighed. "I just wish I'd realized sooner that Asterias was the latter instead of the former."

"Yes, your poor judgment is unforgiveable," Diana said. "Unlike my unimpeachable sense of who to trust."

"We all make mistakes." Ruby gestured with a piece of toast smeared with sunny yellow egg yolk. "The point is not to make the same ones twice."

They finished their coffee, and Diana checked the clock over the stove. "I'm going to give the Lodge a call and see what I can find out about Sanford's plans for the day." She went down, leaving Abel and Ruby to tease each other – she treated him like an older brother, and he treated her like a bratty younger sister.

The other end of the line rang and rang, and Diana almost gave up when the perky intern from the day before answered. "Silver Twilight Lodge."

"Oh, hello. This is Diana Stanley. I was hoping to meet with Mr Sanford."

"Oh, hi Diana. Let me take a look at his schedule…

hmm." Diana heard the faint sound of pages turning. "Today isn't good."

"Oh?" she said. "Does he have meetings at the Lodge?"

"No, he had me postpone today's committee meeting. He said he had an errand that was likely to keep him occupied all afternoon, and not to expect him back after lunch. I can try to get you an appointment later this week, but I'll have to check with him." She chuckled, like Sanford was her eccentric grandfather instead of one of the most powerful men in the state, and maybe the entire Eastern Seaboard. "You know he isn't the best at keeping his staff up to date on his comings and goings in advance."

"Oh, that's fine," Diana said. "I'll see him at the next regular meeting anyway. It's nothing that can't wait." If she'd really wanted to talk to Sanford, she could have pushed – he *had* told her to call if she saw anything strange, after all – but she was happy to get the brush-off from a clueless Initiate.

Diana hung up, then let out a slow breath. Sanford was going to be out all afternoon. They were actually going to do this. Infiltrate the Lodge. Claim Asterias. Save the world. And ideally leave Diana in a position to continue working against the Lodge afterward. Her head spun with dizzy elation. After these past months of gnawing indecision, it felt so good to have a plan. She went back upstairs to share the news.

Abel said he had to run an errand, and Ruby and Diana talked out details while he was gone. One difficulty was making it look plausible that Diana *had* taken Ruby prisoner. Diana could hardly carry her bound and gagged up the walk. "I

Arkham Horror

suppose you could walk me in at knifepoint," Ruby said. "Though us shuffling along with a knife to my throat might draw attention on French Hill."

"I have my father's shotgun, but *that's* not subtle, either," Diana said. "Realistically, if I actually caught you, I'd call the Lodge for help taking you in, but that would be counterproductive."

"That's one word for it," Ruby said. "I–"

Abel came clomping back up the stairs, and dropped the key Diana had loaned him on the counter. He held something bundled up in sailcloth. "Here," he said. "This should help make for a more convincing ruse." He unwound the cloth and revealed a strange-looking pistol with a long barrel, a metal box attached in front of the trigger, and a rounded hilt.

"Some kind of German gun?" Ruby said.

"Mauser C96," Abel said. "The pawnbroker called it a 'broomhandle', I guess because of the grip. This model holds six rounds, in this magazine." He tapped the metal box. "It's loaded."

"Where did you get that?" Diana asked. She wasn't unfamiliar with firearms, since they'd had some on the farm, but it was still disturbing to have one in her house.

"I've had it for a while," Abel said. "After Cain chased me off, I took the last cash in my pockets and picked up a gun. I planned to kill him, to end all this, but I couldn't get close. He had too many comets looking out for him. I stashed the gun in an old shack by the river, and fortunately it was still there. It couldn't kill Cain, but it can help you play the part of Ruby's captor, if you like."

"May I?" Diana held out her hand, and Abel gave her the pistol. After looking it overt, Diana grunted. "The ammunition loads in from the top, I see, and the safety is here… it's a semi-automatic?"

Abel grinned. "It is. Just pull the trigger as many times as you need. You know your way around guns?"

"My father had a shotgun and hunting rifles, but he showed me how to use pistols, too – just revolvers, though. This is something else. I think I get the idea. How much ammunition do you have?"

"Just what's in the magazine now, six shots. I figured if I didn't get Cain in six tries I wasn't going to get him at all."

"Just as well. I don't intend to fire it." Diana looked up. "Ruby, would it be all right if I stuck this between your shoulder blades and walked you into the Lodge?"

"Just keep the safety on," Ruby said.

"We could unload it, to be safe," she began, but Ruby shook her head.

"We don't know what's going to happen in the Lodge," she said. "We might as well take every edge we can get."

Early afternoon arrived, and they commenced their plan. Ruby and Diana walked the first few blocks side-by-side, but when they got closer to French Hill, Diana held up the pistol, pointed at Ruby's back, with a scarf draped over the weapon and her wrist to hide it from casual glances. "This is awkward," Diana said as they walked up the hill.

"Try being me. I've got an itch right between my shoulder blades. If we had a car, you could have put me in the trunk and driven right up the Lodge's front door. Or maybe a back entrance. They have to take deliveries, right?" Ruby was babbling. Diana realized that, despite all the young woman's bravado and general air of nonchalant confidence, she was nervous, too.

"This will work," Diana said, as much to reassure herself as Ruby.

"Of course it will. I haven't blown a job yet."

They reached the Lodge, and Diana pressed the gun into Ruby's back, because this needed to look right. "Are you ready?" she murmured.

"I am. I just hope Abel is." Ruby straightened her shoulders. "Okay. I'm putting on my most annoyed and put-upon face. Let's go."

"Open the gate," Diana said loudly. "Come on, in you go."

Ruby pushed the gate open, and Diana nudged her with the pistol, urging her to take a step onto the path. A pair of black dogs, almost the size of small ponies, stepped out of the long grass on either side of the walkway. They bared their long yellow teeth, but they didn't growl or bark or make any sound at all – that was more unnerving than snarls would have been.

"Going to feed me to the dogs, then?" Ruby said, a tremble in her voice that Diana took to be genuine.

"You know me," Diana said to the dogs. "I have Lodge business."

The front door opened, and Sarah Van Shaw emerged, chewing on a chicken leg. She sauntered down the steps and along the path, stopping between the dogs. "Diana." She dropped the chicken bone and the dog on her left snapped it out of the air and made it disappear.

You aren't supposed to feed chicken bones to dogs, they could choke, Diana thought inanely. "Sarah," she said instead.

"Who's your friend?" the warden asked.

"No friend of mine, or of yours," Diana said. "This is Ruby Standish."

Van Shaw raised an eyebrow, then peered at the younger woman. She grunted. "So it is. Didn't recognize her with the hair and all. Not quite as much the fancy girl as she looks in the photos the master found."

"I didn't think this was a formal occasion," Ruby said, then winced as Diana jabbed her in the back.

"Now how did *you* come to keep company with Ruby Standish?" Van Shaw asked.

"Is this really the time and place to discuss this, warden? I've got a gun on her, but she's not the most well-behaved prisoner. Can we continue our discussion inside? We should tell the master–"

"He's across town, dealing with some damn fool nonsense," Van Shaw said. "But I take your point. We'd better get her inside, find a nice cozy room where she can wait. A room without any valuables in it."

"I thought, perhaps… downstairs?" Diana said. "No one will hear her there, and it's tricky to get out again."

Van Shaw grunted again. "That's right, you're a Seeker now, so you've been past the first threshold. Aye, that's a good enough idea. Don't want any of the Initiates stumbling on her in the main house." She stepped aside, and the dogs vanished back into the grass. "Step lively, young miss." She grinned nastily. "I'll take that pistol and escort her the rest of the way."

Diana scowled. "I'm the one who caught her, and I want to be the one to hand her over to the master."

"Fair enough. I'm not sending you home. But I'm the warden here, and I'll be the one–"

"Dump the bosses off your backs!" a man bellowed from the front gate, followed by a cataclysmic rattle. Van Shaw's head snapped around, and Diana and Ruby looked, too.

A man in shabby clothes, with a hat jammed down on his head, was banging a metal pole against the fence by the gate. "You're a bunch of rich scum, stealing bread from the mouth of the working man!"

"You've got some kind of Wobbly at the gates," Ruby said, and then shouted, "Up with the working man! No gods, no masters!"

Van Shaw slapped Ruby sharply across the face, then hissed. "Shut up, thief."

"Thass right!" the man bellowed. The dogs appeared on the other side of the fence from him, and now they were snarling, but couldn't get at him through the bars. "We're coming for you! We'll tear it all down!" He kept banging the fence and jeered and taunted the dogs.

"I think your dogs are about to get their heads caved in with a pipe," Ruby said. "It seems a shame. They're such lovable pups."

Van Shaw cursed, then jabbed a finger at Ruby and spoke to Diana. "Get her inside, take her downstairs, put her in the storage room on the left, right past the first threshold. Lock the door and wait for me outside." She hurried off across the lawn, shouting, "Get out of here, you Wobbly scum, or I'll open the gate and set the dogs on you!"

"You treat us all like dogs!" he bellowed back. "Sitting in your fancy house lording it over us! I oughta burn the place down, starting with you!"

Diana and Ruby hurried up the walk. "He's convincing, isn't he?" Ruby asked, voice sparkling with mirth. "It's almost as if he's speaking from the heart, and not just playing a role. Maybe if he survives all this he can become a labor organizer."

"As long as he keeps Van Shaw distracted, we might all live to change our careers," Diana said. There was more shouting, and more banging, and then an almost musical tinkle as Abel ran along the fence, dragging his metal pole along the bars, shouting profanities. "I don't *think* the warden will hurt him, as long as he doesn't step onto Lodge property. Not every policeman in Arkham is beholden to the Order, and attacking him in broad daylight on the street would lead to trouble and fuss."

The front door was open, and Ruby stepped inside. "I never saw this part of the house before. I came in through the back."

"We'll do a sightseeing tour later. Or not." Diana propelled her through the anteroom, into the Lodge proper.

The blonde Initiate at the long table looked at them in alarm. "What's all that noise out there?"

"Trouble with some vagrant," Diana said. "You should see if the warden needs any help."

"Oh dear, oh dear." She wrung her hands together. "Who's this?"

"Lodge business," Diana said.

"I have an appointment with the *master* later," Ruby said airily.

"I don't remember making any appointment," she said. "Maybe you should wait–"

Diana said, "I am a *Seeker*, Initiate," her voice sharp as a cleaver's edge. "My business is not yours, and you will speak of this woman's presence to *no one*, inside the Order or out."

The blonde's eyes flared with anger, but then she bowed her head. "Of course, Seeker. I hear and obey."

Diana and Ruby continued deeper into the house, down a corridor lined with portraits of stern-faced men with elaborate facial hair, then through a hidden door disguised as a wall panel into a rather less glamorous portion of the residence, where the servants once lived. The walls here were bare plaster, and the boards bare wood, though strange sigils were daubed here and there in paint, mostly red, but occasionally bright yellow. The yellow ones were hard to look at, seeming to squirm at the edges of perception.

Diana lowered the pistol, and watched Ruby's shoulders relax. It must be unnerving to have a gun pressed against you, even if you knew the wielder had no intention of firing. "Are you all right?" Diana said. "It looked like she hit you hard."

"It felt like she loosened my teeth at first, but I'm all right. Let's go. I know the way from here." Ruby moved ahead, turning down narrow corridors until she reached a door that seemed to lead into a dusty linen closet lined with empty shelves. Ruby lifted one of the shelves in the middle, activating a hidden mechanism with a click. The wall on the left side of the pantry opened on silent hinges. Ruby pushed that panel open, revealing a short flight of stone steps.

They hurried down into the dimness, the secret panel

closing up behind them. The only light was a line of brightness below the door at the bottom of the steps. Ruby opened it, revealing a stone hallway lit by a single bare electric bulb. That corridor extended for only a few feet before the passage turned left.

Diana remembered the first time she'd been shown the hidden places below the Lodge. She'd been so *excited*. What a fool she'd been. "The first threshold," Diana murmured, looking down at the dark line on the floor revealed by the opening of the door.

"Why do they call it that?" Ruby asked.

"There are many levels below the house. Past the first threshold there are rooms that Seekers like myself are permitted to visit. There are other thresholds that only more advanced members of the order can pass, and there are... rumors about them. That if you pass over some of them, you leave this world and enter another. The first threshold is also called the Threshold of Salt."

She pointed. "You can see, there are salt crystals, among other things, mixed with the stone. Supposedly it's a magical barrier. The master – Sanford, I mean, being here in the Lodge makes it seem natural to call him that – says it keeps certain 'experiments' from escaping. There's also the Threshold of Silver, and the Yellow Threshold, and others I'm not even advanced enough to know about yet, though I've heard rumors."

"You tempt me to go exploring," Ruby said. "I didn't know about all those levels. What kind of treasures do you think the old man keeps locked up even deeper? But we should focus. We won't have long before the warden comes looking for us." She set off down the corridor like she'd been here a thousand times, and Diana followed after, trying to shake off her own sense of reverence. They'd promoted her to Seeker down here. This was the sanctum, or rather, a series of sanctums, and there were floors and rooms she'd never been permitted to see, that she'd once dreamed of entering. Now she knew those tantalizing closed doors likely hid rooms full of horrors.

They moved past the storage room where Ruby was supposed to be locked up, and took a few moments to stage a scene – knocked over a wooden chair, dropped Diana's scarf in the middle of the floor, and scuffed up the dust on the floor so it looked like there'd been a struggle. Then they proceeded past a series of locked doors, encountering no cultists along the way.

They stopped before an unassuming door tucked away down a dead-end corridor beneath a burned-out lightbulb. The shadows seemed thicker there. "I've never been through here," Diana said. "I never even noticed this door before."

"I think there's something about the door that makes it hard to notice. I walked past it twice the first time I came down here before I realized it was the one I wanted." Ruby's lockpicks were in Diana's purse, and she took them out and got to work. After a few moments, the door clicked open, and they slipped inside. The hall on the other side was dark, but Ruby was prepared for that, too: there was a small flashlight tucked away in Diana's purse as well. She clicked it on, then said, "Lock that door behind us. I'm sure the warden has keys, but slowing her down can't hurt."

That done, they moved along the hallway, which had

a pronounced downward slant. "Sanford's vault is here?" Diana whispered. She wasn't sure why she whispered, but this didn't seem like a place for raised voices.

"There are some storage rooms, including the one we *want*, and then, yes, there's basically a bank vault."

"What did you steal last time you were here?"

"I wish I could tell you," Ruby said. "But my client… he paid me, fair and square, but he said it was crucial that Sanford never find out who he was, and he beckoned me over and told me to look at this page in a book, and there was this… sort of drawing, or writing, or maybe both… and the next thing I knew, it was two hours later, I was sitting in my apartment with a half-empty glass of whiskey in front of me, and there were pieces of my memory just *cut away*."

The flashlight beam played across the floor. "I couldn't tell you what my client looked like or where we met, and I don't remember what I was sent to steal, either. I can remember everything else, sneaking in, cracking the vault, but there's just this blur when I try to focus on my target." She sighed. "That's when I started to believe that all this nonsense about magic might be true."

"I wish I could cut out a few of my memories," Diana murmured. The dreams were bad. The occasional flashes of that horrible night of sacrifice that seemed to superimpose themselves on the world in her waking hours were even worse.

"You say that, but you're wrong." Ruby's voice was flat. "It's not a pleasant sensation. Come on. Not much farther now." She opened a wooden door, and groped around on the wall past it. "There's a light switch somewhere… here."

There was a click, and then a bulb on the ceiling flickered a few times before settling down to emit a weak, yellowish light. It revealed a long hallway, with open doors on either side, and a huge, closed metal door at the end, complete with a large round handle in the center, just like a bank vault.

"Not today, old friend," Ruby said, apparently to the vault. "Maybe another time. Here, we want the second door on the left, assuming Sanford hasn't done any rearranging."

Ruby took a step forward, but Diana said, "Wait. Do you smell something?"

The thief sniffed. "Yeah, it's a bit like… rotten fish? But also kind of *burned*, and there's something chemical there, too." She looked down at the floor, and whistled. Diana looked down, and for the first time noticed the bare boards smeared with a shimmering grayish substance, like snail trails. Ruby wrinkled her nose. "Looks like you have a slug problem. Big slugs."

Diana breathed in, and the scent filled her nostrils, and a whirl of memories spun in her head: a black stone, robed figures, a terrified man bound in ropes, chanting – she groaned. "Ruby. We have to leave."

"What? We're almost done."

Panic rose up in Diana like an animal trying to crawl out of her stomach through her throat. She seized the younger woman's arm. "We have to go *now*." Ruby turned to face her, frowning.

And then the horrible thing Sanford had summoned in the circle came oozing out of a doorway on the right.

CHAPTER FIFTEEN
The Guardian and the Scholar

Diana was losing her nerve, which Ruby hadn't expected – she'd been quite impressed with the woman's performance so far. The reformed cultist had played her role beautifully, brazened right past the warden and Sanford's assistant, and kept her nerve all the way down to the hidden parts of the Lodge. Why was she panicking *now*, when they were moments away from finishing their task? God, the expression on her face, Diana was *terrified–*

"Look," Diana whimpered, pointing down the hall. Ruby turned, and looked, and then flattened herself against the wall and started whimpering herself.

There was a *thing* in the hallway, filling the corridor from side to side: a greenish-black, amorphous, oozing creature. Ruby's first thought was that it resembled a tumor, but tumors didn't have waving tendrils, gaping mouths, and eyes that bubbled up to the surface and then submerged again, like bits of meat in a boiling stew. The stench was stronger now as the thing squelched toward them, and a high-pitched, horrible sound emerged from its many mouths, sounding almost like words – "teck-ah-lee-lee, teck-ah-lee-lee!"

Ruby's mind froze. She'd known there were horrors in the world, but she'd never imagined anything like *this*, a fetid mass of malleable flesh full of grasping whiplike appendages and horrible wet mouths that *spoke*. "That – there was nothing like *this* here last time," she managed to choke out.

"Sanford brought it here. Summoned it. To be a guardian. To make sure no one could break into the vault again. I… I was…" To Ruby's surprise, Diana stepped past her, holding up the gun, and advanced on the thing. Shooting it would be pointless, like shooting into a bubbling pit of tar, but maybe the noise would scare the monster away? As if anything could scare *that*, a nightmare brought to life!

"Diana, we have to run, if it's a guardian maybe it won't chase us, maybe we can get away–"

Diana took another step forward. "This foul thing… I helped bring it to life, or set it free, I don't *know*, but… I have to destroy it. I have to try."

Ruby grabbed Diana's shoulder. "Look. It's moving away from you." It was true – as Diana stepped forward, the leading edge of the thing receded, like lapping waves on the shore. Ruby had a flash of inspiration and backed away. "Diana, I think it recognizes you, or knows you're part of the Order – look! When you approach it withdraws!"

Diana cast a doubtful glance at Ruby, then took another step forward, and the monster pulled back further, piling up on either side of the hall, parting before her like a fetid sea. "It only wants *me*," Ruby said. "You can go past and reach the storage room. It's the second door on the right, the jar is on a shelf about halfway up the wall, you can't miss it. I'll… I'll find my own way outside and meet you on the street."

"Ruby!" Diana said, but she was already on her way, darting for the door. Diana shouted in alarm, and Ruby risked a look back. Diana was blocking the hall, but the guardian didn't give up its pursuit of Ruby: the oozing monster was going *around* her, crawling up the wall and onto the ceiling, clinging to the surfaces as it slid and lurched after the interloper.

This was no good. Ruby wished she'd taken the gun – maybe it wouldn't have hurt the monster, but it would have improved her morale, at least. "Teck-ah-lee-lee, teck-ah-lee-lee!" the thing squeaked behind her. Ruby made it to the door and unbolted it. Maybe the monster wouldn't follow her far – if it was guardian of the vault, perhaps chasing her away was enough?

She flung open the door and pelted out into the corridor… and the thing kept coming, making its horrible, keening chatter. How far would the creature go? Would it chase her through the house, into the street, out of Arkham, into Boston? How could she *stop* it?

Then Ruby remembered: The Threshold of Salt. Diana said that glittering strip across the floor was a magical barrier, made to stop "experiments" from escaping. If Ruby could make it to that door, it might stop the guardian, and then she could get out of the Lodge, make her way to freedom–

Ruby rounded a corner and slammed straight into Sarah Van Shaw, sending the warden sprawling. Ruby lost her footing but didn't slow down, just scrambled ahead, climbing over the warden, driving her knees into Van Shaw's abdomen as she went.

The warden snarled at her and seized her ankle before Ruby could get away, her encircling fingers as hard as ancient tree roots. Ruby looked back and kicked, driving the heel of her shoe into the top of Van Shaw's head, wishing she was wearing stiletto heels.

The warden just grabbed tighter, and then the guardian came around the corridor and flowed up the wall and onto the ceiling. It hung suspended above them both, eyes and mouths drifting across its gelatinous form, and then it reached down with a dozen thickening tendrils.

Ruby knew, she *knew*, that if that thing touched her, she would go mad – her mind would break like a cracked dam, and gibbering darkness would come rushing through. She'd been afraid before – of being caught in an act of burglary, of violent men, of being betrayed and turned into the police – but this was a whole different order of fear. This was the fear early humans had felt when a ravenous bear came shambling from the depths of a cave where they'd sought shelter. This was a fear of being *consumed*.

"The shoggoth," Van Shaw said, something like awe in her voice, and Ruby took advantage of her distraction to kick again, as hard as she could, and this time the warden's grip loosened, and Ruby got free.

She wasn't fast enough, though. The creature – the shoggoth? – flowed across the ceiling and then oozed down to the ground, blocking the hallway ahead of her. The Threshold of Salt was in view, past the guardian, but Ruby couldn't reach it – she didn't dare try to *jump* over the thing. If she missed, it would be like landing in a carnivorous bog.

Van Shaw groaned behind her, and Ruby swore and turned. She ran back the way she'd come, vaulting over the warden's supine form.

Where to go now? There was no point retracing her steps – that would just dead-end her at the vault. Ruby turned right where she'd only turned left before, and faced an unknown set of passageways, more bare plaster and wooden boards. She'd gotten directions to the vault when she first invaded the Lodge, but the rest of this place was mysterious to her. That could even work in her favor – if she didn't know where she was going, no one could predict her destination, and maybe she could throw off the pursuit by taking random turns. This was the secret basement of a secret society, after all – surely there were more hidden passages, and more importantly, hidden *exits*?

Whenever she reached an intersecting hallway, she chose a direction at random, winding her way ever deeper into the warren of the Lodge basement, racing past numerous closed doors. How could this space be so vast? The basement must honeycomb the entirety of French Hill! Or maybe space didn't work down here the way it did in other places. She'd heard a story from another thief about breaking into an occultist's mansion and finding a ballroom on the ground floor that didn't have a ceiling – instead it had an open sky full of stars he described as "festering". She'd assumed it was exaggeration, or hallucination, or both, but now… she wasn't so sure.

Ruby needed an exit, or at least a solid door she could

put between herself and the shoggoth. She focused on the necessity of escape, using her fear as fuel to make her run faster.

She pelted around another corner, then stopped short and turned back. Something had snagged her attention back there – something that seemed *wrong*...

Ruby stepped toward an alcove shrouded in thick shadows. Having seen through a similar illusion twice before, it seemed her senses were growing more adept at noticing such trickery. There was a door there, hidden in the dark, once she stopped to look for it. The door was marked with a peculiar sigil, seemingly daubed on in charcoal: a triangle or cone shape with sprouting tendrils arcing off from the top. Maybe there was another mystic threshold here that would keep the shoggoth at bay.

The door was locked, of course, but the locks down here were old – most of the security in this place was based on obscurity and the overall defenses of the Lodge above, not physical barriers. Ruby made short work of the lock with her picks, then eased open the door. There was nothing special about the floor beneath it, no sparkle of crystals in a strip on the floor, which was disappointing. The door only opened on another corridor that right-angle turned out of sight. Oh well. Putting a locked door between her and the vault guardian was a good thing, anyway.

Her mind supplied an image of the protoplasmic monster simply *oozing* beneath the crack under the door, and she shoved the idea aside.

Ruby re-locked the door and walked down the hallway, paneled in dark wood and floored with tile, an upgrade from the utilitarian passageways she'd seen so far. There were no doors lining this corridor, but there were symbols painted on the walls in black and silver and yellow paint, and the dark brownish-red of blood. The designs were doubtless mystical in nature, but they didn't make her brains boil or her legs weak or her vision go blurry – whatever they were supposed to do, they weren't supposed to do it to *her*, apparently.

Ruby turned another corner and came upon a peculiar sight in the middle of the passageway: a straight-backed wooden chair. The chair sat facing a heavy wooden door festooned with chains, with an iron grille set about head high. The passage continued beyond the chair, the walls similarly etched with symbols.

Ruby was about to go around the chair and continue on her way, wanting nothing to do with anything Sanford felt compelled to lock up so thoroughly. Then a woman's mild voice emerged from the cell: "Have you come to pry further secrets from me, Sanford?"

"Hello?" Ruby paused behind the chair, ready to take flight in an instant.

A face swam into view beyond the grille. The cell was so dim Ruby could only make out a pale face framed by locks of gray hair. There was something around the woman's neck, a heavy chain necklace, or… was it just a heavy chain?

"Interesting," the woman said. "Only Sanford comes here. He trusts no one else to speak to me. You are an intruder."

Ruby didn't run. The warden had talked about locking Ruby up in a room – would she have ended up in a cell like this, eventually? "Are you a prisoner here?" she asked.

"I am," the woman replied.

"I can try to let you out." Ruby looked over the chains, but they weren't held in place by padlocks or anything of the sort – they were welded into the iron doorframe, as if they were never meant to be loosened at all. She tugged at them, and the woman chuckled.

"Even if you could remove the chains out there, and the chains in here, there is still the matter of the sigils on the walls, which bind me as well. Carl Sanford is a very *thorough* person."

Ruby tugged on a chain one last time, then let it fall with a rattle. "How long have you been here?"

"For over a year now. Ever since Sanford discovered my… true nature and had me abducted from my office at the university." She sounded amused.

Ruby wasn't shocked that Sanford had abducted someone and locked them away under here – nothing would shock her, coming from him, except maybe a selfless act of pure generosity – but she was curious about why. "Your true nature?"

The woman cocked her head. "I assumed you came because you, too, wished to question me, and gain my knowledge. But if you are ignorant of my true nature… I was being self-centered. Solipsism is a danger when one spends so much time alone. You have come upon my cell by accident, then. I am curious – why are you down here, in this secret place, all alone?"

Ruby found something about the woman's manner oddly calming, and there seemed no harm in telling a prisoner the truth. "I broke into the Lodge to steal something from Sanford's vault. I ran into some kind of… monstrous guardian, a thing like a bubbling blob of tar, but full of mouths."

"Sanford has acquired a shoggoth?" The woman went *hmm*. "The only ones extant on this plane are in Antarctica. Sanford would have questioned me first if he'd planned an expedition to that lost city, so I know he didn't go in person. He must have used a ritual of transposition, and swapped some unlucky follower of his with the shoggoth you met. I'm sure it's quite a young specimen, if it fell prey to such a stratagem and allowed itself to be bound. I wasn't aware the creatures were still reproducing, though there's no reason they shouldn't bud occasionally, even with the cold temperatures slowing them down. How interesting. I have learned something new. Thank you. Lately it seems I only *dispense* knowledge."

"Who are you?" Ruby said. "How do you know about shoggoths and things?"

The woman clucked her tongue. "What did I say about my boredom with dispensing knowledge? But, since you were kind enough to wish to rescue me, I will return the kindness. I don't mind sharing what I know, when I am not compelled to do so under threat of torture."

The woman straightened, taking on a dignity at odds with her situation. "I am a scholar of the Yith. I came to this place, to this body, to look up certain volumes in the university library, in order to fill in a few small gaps in the understanding of my people – just minor details. I found enough of interest to occupy me for some months, however, and apparently my behavior differed sufficiently from that of my host... I see your confusion. By 'host' I mean the owner of this body I have borrowed. Carl Sanford heard rumors of my odd behavior, and suspected I might be a member of the Great Race. Most humans don't know about us, but Sanford has wide-ranging interests. He took advantage of this frail body and abducted me, which any brute can do, but he also found mystical means to trap my mind, so I cannot return home to the library. Since I cannot return, the owner of this body is trapped too – she is in a borrowed body in *my* home, and is just as trapped as I am. I pointed this out to Sanford, but he has little fellow feeling for other humans, it seems."

"You're... not human? You're from another planet? An alien?" She thought of the Martians from the *War of the Worlds*, with their tentacles and beaklike mouths, and felt her gorge rise. What was worse, aliens that looked like aliens, or ones that could pass for human? She decided they were equally horrible in different ways.

"Mmm, yes, but no. I am from... another time and another place. My people are capable of transposing our minds with those of others, across the depths of time. It is a talent we use to increase our storehouse of wisdom. We are scholars, you see."

Ruby didn't want to believe. It was easier to think Sanford just had a madwoman locked up in this basement. But after the things she'd seen today, how could she rule anything out, even something this outlandish? "I'm sorry. I wish I could let you go."

"That is apparent. You cannot help me. I could help you, perhaps, and I am inclined to do so, if only because you are in opposition to Carl Sanford, and I support anything that undermines him. Is there anything you'd like to know, my failed rescuer, to assist you in your endeavors, whatever those might be?"

"I wouldn't mind directions to a back door. I need to get out of here, and I can't go out the way I came in," Ruby responded, not expecting much.

The scholar surprised her. "If you proceed down this corridor in the direction you were going already, and take each left-hand turn as they arrive, you will eventually reach the ruins of an old kitchen. There is little left there now but rust, mice, and broken crockery, but unlike most of this basement, *that* room is part of the structure of the original Lodge. There is an old dumbwaiter there, and if you ascend the shaft, you will reach a room on the ground floor of the house. The upper dumbwaiter panel is sealed, but a human of your ingenuity can doubtless circumvent such an obstacle. From there, you need only reach the nearest exterior door or window. I can provide a list of the best candidates—"

"No, thank you! I think I can figure it out from there. If... if there's a way I can come back, and help you..."

The scholar shrugged. "While this captivity is tedious, it will not be infinite. All barriers fail eventually. My relationship with time is not the same as yours. An eternity for you is but a moment for me, and I am good at patience. But, again, I appreciate your kindness."

Ruby turned to go, then paused. "Could I ask one other thing?"

"Only one? Proceed."

"Have you ever heard of something called Asterias?"

"Asteria means 'starry' in Greek, and Asterias is a genus of sea stars – ah, but for a woman who runs afoul of shoggoths in the course of committing thefts in the headquarters of a secret society dedicated to the occult, such prosaic definitions are of minimal interest." She hooked her fingertips through the grille in the door. Her fingernails were broken and her hands were grimy. "I take it you refer to the entity known as the Ravening Deep, The Hungry Star, That Which When Divided Multiplies, The Wrong Star, and The Infinite Maw, among other appellations, yes?"

Ruby swallowed. Some of those names were new to her, and none of them were comforting. "Yes. That's it. Someone recently found the temple of Asterias, and there was an amulet there, with unusual properties, and… things have gone very strange."

"An artifact created by the worshippers of the Ravening Deep retained its magical potency, even after the demise of their so-called god? How fascinating! Hmm, what can I tell you? The origins of Asterias are unknown. Some believe it is a terrestrial aberration of nature, while others think it infiltrated this world from some other plane – my guess is the latter, though in that case, it has altered itself over the centuries to better fit into the local ecology of this planet and its oceans. The Ravening Deep is a *changeable* entity, you see. Its physical form eventually settled into a shape reminiscent of an enormous starfish, although one equipped with numerous hidden pseudopods, and with a mouth that is vast and ever-hungering. Asterias devoured everything alive in its local area, summoning sea creatures to its maw with a psychic lure, and then reached out farther with its strange mind, catching the attention of intelligent beings.

The Ravening Deep realized those were worth more as servants than food: its cultists could bring sacrifices, and so instead of consuming them, Asterias granted them visions and offered them power, giving them some small measure of its own abilities–"

"Regeneration," Ruby said. "Strength, and durability, and the power to create copies."

"Indeed." The scholar beamed like Ruby was her favorite student, and she felt a flash of pride, like the first time she'd successfully picked a lock while blindfolded, by feel alone.

"The cult grew, multiplying itself, and its members fed the Deep. The Deep grew, as well, expanding to ever greater size, spreading across hundreds of meters of the sea floor. The matter of duplication following amputation is especially interesting. The Deep bestowed that gift upon its followers, but Asterias *itself* never duplicated in the same way. The cult spoke of 'The Great Division', however, a prophesied day when Asterias would grow large enough to spawn its own sibling, which the cult would then transport to a fresh territory. From there, the two Ravening Deeps would grow, and in time, each would split again, and *those* four would grow, and then split, and on, and on… A colleague of mine with a special interest in your planet once calculated that, if left unchecked, the spawn of Asterias would fill the oceans in under three centuries. Once they consumed all the life in the sea, their mutable nature would allow them to make the necessary adaptations to spread onto land, and after that… Well."

Ruby stared at her. But that meant… "The Ravening Deep would have covered the entire planet?"

A nod. "Given time. And not much time, once a sufficient threshold of copies was reached – that is the nature of exponential growth. My colleague theorized that Asterias is the last survivor of its kind, a refugee from one other world – a world that was completely consumed by the Ravening Deep's kin." The scholar shrugged. "Of course, the Ravening Deep never got that far. There are far older denizens of the oceans, among them Mother Hydra, Dagon, and the Deep Ones. Those entities are used to thinking on *much* longer timescales than humans do, and they recognized the threat posed by Asterias and its cult. They waged a brutal war on the Ravening Deep, with many losses on both sides, but in time they breached the temple, tore the great star to pieces, and incinerated its fragments in undersea volcanic vents."

Would that it were so! It was a strange thrill, to know something this knower-of-all-things did not. "They didn't incinerate *all* of it."

The scholar widened her eyes. "Explain."

"A piece of the Ravening Deep's body washed up on the shore. That fragment ended up in a jar, in a storage room, here in the Lodge. That's what the restored cult is looking for – what I was trying to steal before they could get it. They want to use the fragment to–"

"To bring Asterias back to life – or, rather, back to strength, since so long as even a fragment of its body lives, the entity itself still clings to life. Yes. I see." The prisoner pressed her face close to the grille. "Listen to me, human – you *must* destroy the piece that remains. The Ravening Deep must not be revived. It has doubtless learned from its mistakes – if allowed to return to the temple, it will grow in hiding this time, protected by its cultists, until it is ready to divide, and then this world's doom will be assured. You must stop that from coming to pass."

"I know." Ruby wished she didn't. Things had seemed dire enough before! Maybe she should have fled Arkham when she had the chance… though then she wouldn't be here to help avert the end of the world, would she? "I understand now. The fate of the entire human race is at stake–"

"I don't care about *humans*," the scholar said. "My people have plans for this world, plans that have nothing to *do* with humans, and if the Ravening Deep is allowed to spread, *my* people will suffer too."

"I… forgot you weren't human," Ruby said. "Briefly. Thank you for reminding me."

The scholar closed her eyes for a moment, then opened them again. "Sometimes I forget I'm not human myself." She sounded sad. "Go, thief. Fight for the survival of *your* people, then. Destroy the Ravening Deep before it can consume your world."

Ruby usually liked to get in the last word, to end any interaction with a pithy remark or witty bon mot, but in this case, all she could do was nod, and rush off down the hallway.

She followed the scholar's directions and found herself in a dusty mess of a kitchen, home only to mouse droppings and a dead iron stove and broken crockery – but the dumbwaiter shaft was there, even if no dumbwaiter was in evidence. Ruby had escaped from houses by working her way up chimneys before, and this was no more difficult than that, though she crushed several fat spiders with her knees and back as she made her ascent through the dark, shuddering with revulsion along the way.

She finally spied a square outline of shining light and knew she'd reached the ground floor. Working herself around she got one heel pressed against the panel, and pushed, her calf muscles straining and her spine screaming. She thought she was going to push herself backward through the dumbwaiter shaft before the panel gave way, but then one corner tore loose, and a few short stomps popped the panel the rest of the way out.

Ruby worked her way out of the small opening, tearing her dress on a sharp corner in the process. She looked around the unadorned room, probably a place for servants to prep dishes for dinner, back when this was a grand house, and not a vile pit of secrets. There were no windows in the room, so she went through the nearest door, into a dining room, and then she knew where she was from her long-ago memorization of the Lodge's main layout.

Ruby sprinted through several rooms, and didn't slow down, even when she raced past the astonished blonde assistant, and through the anteroom, to the front door–

Which was locked, from the inside, with a key, which was not in evidence. She cursed, fumbled for her lockpicks, and made short work of the lock. She wrenched open the front door… and looked down into the snarling faces of two waiting dogs. She looked past them, and there was Abel, still in his rags, shaking the bars of the gate and shouting, but the dogs were not about to be distracted this time.

Ruby took a step backward. If she could get upstairs and climb out a window, make her way onto the roof and into one of the ancient trees, she might be able to find a branch that got close to the fence and–

A rough hand grabbed her by the back of the neck in an iron grip and jerked her backward, shaking her like a terrier would a rat.

"Ruby Standish," the warden hissed in her ear, wrenching one of Ruby's arms up behind her back. "The master will be *so* glad he didn't miss you."

CHAPTER SIXTEEN
The Hospitality of Cain

Carl Sanford's driver, Brother Altman, pulled up in front of the Independence Hotel. Altman was just as reliable as the late Brother Cluny, and while he appeared less physically intimidating, he could be lethally quick. His preferred weapon was the kukri, a large, curved knife he'd become fond of during certain excursions in South Asia, and there was doubtless at least one such blade tucked away in his well-cut suit jacket even now.

Sanford didn't expect any bladework to be necessary today – this was a business meeting, one that had been scheduled for weeks – but after his experience with the Berglunds, he was inclined to be cautious. Strange things were afoot, and there might be connections hidden from his sight.

Altman opened the door for Sanford, who sprang out, ready for anything. He didn't like supernatural disruptions in his city, especially when he didn't know the cause, but he had to admit, the presence of hidden adversaries did get the blood pumping. He'd been the master of so many things for so long that a hint of real danger was invigorating. The tussle at the Berglund house had reminded Sanford of his youthful forays into the occult, before he'd had quite so many devotees, proxies, and employees to take the bulk of his risks for him. He felt combative and energized. He would take that energy into today's negotiation, and drive a nice, hard bargain.

"Your hair is getting a bit long, Altman." Sanford had his hair cut weekly, by a barber who came to the Lodge.

"If I cut it short, you can see where my ear's missing on that side, and people stare at that more than the long hair," Altman replied.

"Fair enough," Sanford said. "Though the missing ear would make you look more dangerous, which is all to the good."

"If I looked as dangerous as I actually am, people would run screaming." Altman grinned, and Sanford favored him with a small smile in return. He usually discouraged such informality with his underlings, but Altman had been with Sanford in some dark places – a certain cave in Kashmir came to mind – and had earned the right.

"This should be fairly straightforward." Sanford strolled into the overly ornate lobby of the hotel. All that marble and gilt was so ostentatious, but it couldn't distract from the small cracks in the walls and the faint whiff of mold. It couldn't distract Sanford, anyway; maybe the dazzle worked on others, but he was not easily swayed by surface elements. "I'm meeting a gentleman who goes by the unlikely name of Mr Marius, though my sources tell me he's actually a former fisherman named Abel Davenport."

"A fisherman? Trying to pass himself off as an adept of the occult?" Altman said.

"I assumed so, at first, but in his letters and the one phone call we shared, this Marius demonstrated a *deep* knowledge of esoterica related to the sea – if you'll forgive my wordplay. He claims to possess an amulet sacred to the cult of a certain marine deity."

"Is this Esoteric Order of Dagon business, then?" Altman said.

Sanford made a sour face. He'd tussled with the Dagonites before. Those people had pledged themselves to foul things beneath the waves, for no reason other than *tradition*, as far as he could tell. Sanford couldn't understand that sort of sentimentality. If you were going to work with dangerous inhuman forces, you should at least win some material gain out of it. "I don't think so, but our Marius has been a bit vague on the specifics. He says the amulet has miraculous properties, including the ability to heal almost any injury – 'any wound short of the mortal', he said. I've been promised a demonstration, which should be interesting. That's why I agreed to meet at the hotel. If someone is getting a leg chopped off to prove the power of this bauble, I'd rather it not happen in *my* office."

"Marius wants to sell this amulet to you?" Altman said.

"Not exactly." They boarded the elevator, and Sanford told the operator which floor they wanted. They rode up in silence – Lodge business was not spoken of in front of outsiders – and stepped off at their destination. Sanford checked his pocket watch and saw they were a few minutes early. He gestured toward a pair of chairs tucked into an alcove near the elevators, and sat down beside Altman. "Marius proposes what he calls a 'joint expedition' to the site where he discovered this amulet. What that means, I think, is that I should provide the money, and he will provide the coordinates, and we will share whatever we find."

"It seems an optimistic scenario on his part," Altman observed.

"Indeed. Apparently he found some sort of temple in the Atlantic, which is plausible enough – we know there are whole prehuman *cities* in that ocean, but they are all far too deep to be reached. Marius's temple is supposedly accessible from the surface, and though it extends below the waves, there are areas of the structure that hold breathable air, and others that could theoretically be reached by diving suit."

"Might be worth a look," Altman allowed.

"If this amulet of Marius's does everything he claims, then, yes, it just might. Of course, once I know the location of this temple…" Sanford shrugged, and Altman chuckled.

After checking his watch again, Sanford rose, and they walked down the hallway. Davenport was in the "Imperial Suite", one of the large corner accommodations the hotel kept for its most well-heeled guests.

"He must have caught some valuable fish to afford rooms like this," Altman observed, and Sanford smiled.

"I gather he found some other baubles in his temple, gold chains and the like, and sold them to improve his lifestyle. He *should* have sold them to fund his own expedition, but it may be to our benefit that he did not." Sanford knocked.

The door opened, and a man smiled out at them. He wore

a white linen shirt, open at the throat, a silver chain around his neck. More oddly, he wore black leather gloves. His black trousers were pressed, but his feet were bare. There was something strange about his feet, and after a moment Sanford realized what it was – there was a membrane of webbing between his first and second toes. *Was* he a Dagonite, then? The only unusual features on his long face were deep age lines – he didn't have the bulging eyes associated with the Dagonites, but perhaps he was from a cadet branch of their twisted family tree.

"Carl Sanford and... associate, I presume?" The man's voice was rough. He sounded every inch the fisherman.

"This is Mr Altman, my personal secretary," Sanford said. "You are Mr Marius?"

The man gave an odd little bow. "I am. Do come in."

Sanford stepped inside, Altman at his back, and inventoried the room with a glance. A man in a bowler hat sat on a sofa, a wood axe laid across his knees, and through the open door to the bathroom, Sanford glimpsed a woman kneeling beside a row of salt boxes, dumping one of them into the bathtub. "What interesting company you keep," Sanford said.

"Care to hand me that axe, my friend?" Altman said. "Shaft first, if you would."

The man in the bowler looked at Marius, who laughed, and said, "Of course – that's just for the demonstration, but if you'd be more comfortable holding onto the axe until then, I have no objection."

The man reversed the axe, held it a trifle awkwardly by the head, and offered the handle to Altman, who plucked it away and then leaned the axe against the wall behind him, beside the door.

Marius gestured to the fellow in the bowler. "This is Monty, a fellow enthusiast of the esoteric." Monty nodded. Marius turned and pointed. "There in the bathroom, preparing for the demonstration, we have the lovely Glenda, who has forgotten more about sailing than I ever learned, and I've spent most of my life on boats."

"A pleasure to meet your... associates," Sanford said. "May I examine the amulet you told me about?"

Marius touched his chest, massaging something beneath his shirt. "It's an astonishing item. This amulet changed my life, and it will change yours, too, Mr Sanford."

"My life is pleasant just the way it is." Sanford tapped his sword cane on the carpet. "Let me see it now, please."

Marius reached into his shirt and drew out the amulet, but made no move to remove the chain from around his neck. He held the medallion up, tilting it to catch the light, and Sanford leaned forward to examine it. The amulet was round and silver, decorated with the raised shape of a seven-pointed star, with a round circle in the center full of inward-pointing triangles – a toothy maw?

"I don't recognize this iconography," Sanford said. "But the starfish is a symbol of regeneration..." He thought of the way some starfish reproduced by dividing themselves, creating doubles of the original, and developed a terrible suspicion. Could these people be involved with what happened to the Berglunds? Best for now to pretend he suspected nothing, and see what developed. He straightened. "What do you propose in the way of a demonstration?"

Marius spread his hands and smiled like a salesman. "The simplest thing would be to chop off someone's finger, put the amulet on them, and immerse them in that tub of salt water Glenda has prepared. Soaking in brine isn't strictly necessary, but it accelerates the process – if you're submerged, a new finger will grow back within minutes, instead of hours or days. Perhaps we might use Mr Altman as a test subject?"

Altman snorted.

Sanford shook his head. "Mr Altman has given up enough pieces of himself to the cause over the years. I believe one of your own compatriots, or you yourself, would be a more suitable choice."

"Ah, but I've done this so many times already. You see?" Marius tugged off one of his gloves, and held up a hand to Sanford's face with a flourish. He frowned when Sanford leaned in for a closer look.

"You expected me to recoil?" Sanford said. "I've seen worse than this and then eaten a hearty breakfast." The hand *was* grotesque, though. Marius had six fingers, or perhaps five and a half – his index finger had another half-length digit emerging from the second knuckle, sticking off at an angle. His other fingers appeared functional enough, but no longer resembled those of a human, or any primate: the middle finger had tiny suckers, like an octopus tentacle, while the ring finger was green and pebbled like starfish flesh, and the pinky resembled the pincer of a crab. "I must say, the healing properties of your amulet were oversold in your letter. You have not been healed – you've been transformed into the appetizer platter at a seafood restaurant."

Marius scowled, the lines on his face deepening. "The first time, the fingers grew back normally enough, but after subsequent severances, they started to go strange. I like them, though. They make me feel closer to my god – marked, you see."

Closer to *which* god? Sanford abhorred zealots. They could be useful idiots at best, and deadly ones at worst.

Marius turned toward Altman and wiggled his fingers. "Even if you lack my particular perspective, you must admit, these are better than no fingers at all, aren't they?"

"I would have to think about that for a while, to be honest," Altman said.

"You two *are* hard to impress," Marius said. "But the amulet possesses other powers. It bestows visions upon its wearer, for one thing."

"So do mushrooms that grow from cow patties." Sanford was, of course, interested in acquiring the amulet despite the undisclosed quirks of its operation, but part of negotiating was hiding any unseemly eagerness.

"You're such a jaded old sorcerer! I haven't told you the *most* remarkable power of the amulet yet, though." Marius cocked his head for a moment, fixing Sanford's gaze with his own.

Then he lunged past Sanford, toward Altman. Something was happening to Marius's *head*. Sanford couldn't quite make out what, since the man was turned away from him, but fleshy protuberances appeared to unfurl from the sides of his face.

Marius seized Altman by the shoulders and leaned forward, pressing his altered face close to Altman's own.

Altman screamed – a sound that seemed to come from the bottom of a well – and a horrible, wet crunching followed. Blood poured down Altman's shoulders and chest. He fumbled for his kukri, drawing it from its hidden sheath at the small of his back, but then he dropped the blade on the floor and went limp. Marius lifted Altman's body off the floor as the horrible sounds of mastication continued.

All this happened in an instant, and in that same instant, Sanford took a step back and tried to draw his sword from the cane. He had seen many dreadful things over the course of his long life, but it had been ages since he'd watched someone *eaten* right in front of him! There would be time to feel horror later. The most pressing matter was to stab and slash his way free of this place before he got eaten himself.

Monty was ready for him, though, and kicked the stick out of Sanford's hand before he could draw it. Sanford reached into his jacket, where he'd secreted a derringer revolver, but the woman from the bathroom – Glenda – wrapped her arms around him from behind in a bear hug, pinning his arms against his sides. She was *inhumanly* strong… which made sense. Whatever this Marius or Davenport was, he was not human, and there was no reason to think his associates would be either.

Marius let Altman's body drop to the floor. Altman's nose was gone, and his eyes, and most of his cheeks, with his teeth visible through the remaining flesh.

Marius then turned toward Sanford. The open petals of meat around his head folded inward as he moved, so Sanford caught only a glimpse of his horrible secret face: a red and green ruin of raw flesh, with a round maw at the center, lined with sharp and tiny teeth, just like the depiction on the amulet. The folds of skin flattened out, restoring the creature's human face, though not seamlessly – those deep wrinkles on Marius's face *were* the seams.

"I fear you've brought me here under false pretenses," Sanford said. There was no point in showing fear, or letting them believe they had the upper hand. The loss of Altman stung deeply, though. Sanford didn't have friends in the conventional sense, but Altman had been something close.

Monty picked up the axe by the door and gave it a twirl. "I suppose I should begin screaming and alert the other hotel guests to the presence of deranged murderers," Sanford said, in the tone of one musing aloud.

"This floor and the ones below and above are occupied by my people." Marius dabbed at the corner of his mouth with a handkerchief, though *that* mouth had eaten nothing.

Such a fool, giving away information when there was no advantage in doing so. Sanford was troubled to hear the cult was so numerous, however. "I don't think they're really *people*, though, are they? What is the point of all this, Marius? I don't understand what you think you have to gain by seizing me this way."

Marius dropped into a chair and crossed one leg over the other. He caressed the amulet as he spoke. "Have you ever heard of Asterias?"

Sanford examined the vast storehouse of knowledge in his mind, and could only come up with a footnote from a history of the Esoteric Order of Dagon. "Some sort of dead sea monster, wasn't it? A minor adversary of the Deep Ones?"

Marius leaned forward, clenching his misshapen hands into fists. "Not *minor*."

"I see," Sanford said. "I was misinformed. Please don't allow the gap in my education to delay you from getting to the *point*."

"The *point* is, you are holding the body of our god hostage in your Silver Twilight Lodge!"

Sanford frowned. "Am I?"

Marius stood and paced back and forth in front of Sanford. "The *ignorance*, the *insult*, the *degradation*! The last surviving fragment of the Lord of the Depths is rotting away in one of your storerooms, and you don't even *know*!"

"We're talking about some sort of… specimen, then? A holy relic, like the fingerbone of a saint? Something sacred to your order?" Sanford rolled his eyes. "All of *this* was hardly necessary. You could have simply offered to buy the specimen from me, or worked out a trade. You zealots always make things so *complicated*." Not that Sanford would have consented to give up something so valuable, once he knew its worth, but he wanted to keep them off balance and second-guessing themselves. An enemy's doubts were always an opportunity.

Marius frowned. "You mean to say you would have parted with the last piece of our god willingly?"

"I didn't even realize I *had* the cursed thing!" Sanford thought for a moment, then nodded. "It came from that estate, didn't it, the Innsmouther in exile. I recall now, a jar with a bit of pebbled nastiness floating inside. My archivist catalogued it as 'a preserved sample of a sea monster, likely apocryphal', as I recall." Sanford shook his head. "Really, what a waste of time this has all been. Let's go to the Lodge, and I'll have someone fetch the jar for you. We can discuss a fair price on the way." He nodded toward his dead associate. "Plus restitution for poor Altman." Sanford wasn't about to make a deal with this monster, but it was worth a try to escape this slaughtering ground.

"You think I am a fool?" Marius said.

"You are *demonstrably* a fool," Sanford said. "But there is still time for you to change your ways."

"You will give us the body of our god," Marius said. "Freely, and without cost. Only, it won't be *you*, exactly." He laughed – but it was really more of a titter.

A suspicion in the back of Sanford's mind moved closer to certainty, but it was best to be sure. "Being cryptic? Tut-tut. How tiresome. Why can't you simply say what you *mean*, Mr Davenport?"

Marius moved faster than even Sanford's eyes could follow, until his nose was an inch from Sanford's own. The flesh of his face rippled, as if he was considering opening his secret maw again, and if he did that, Sanford would have to act quickly, and give up any hope of gathering more information. "You think you know me. But I am not Abel Davenport. He was my progenitor, but I am–"

"Cain," Sanford said. This must be the patron of the Berglunds, the monstrous duplicator of men. Sanford had allowed himself to be baited into a trap, but he had no intention of remaining in its jaws.

"Yes. I took a new name to signal devotion to my god, and became Cain Marius – Cain of the Deeps." Cain's breath was hot and stank of salt and rotten fish.

The world was full of fools, but most weren't as dangerous as this one. Sanford refused to show even a flicker of fear, and instead chose to display his contempt. "Marius is Latin and means 'of Mars' – manly, warlike – not 'of the deeps'. You're thinking of the word 'mare', I presume, for 'the sea'. But I suppose you didn't want to name yourself after a female horse–"

"You find all this amusing, Mr Sanford? We'll see how amused you are after I chop off your finger and drop it in that bathtub and grow a *copy* of you, one with all your memories and your clever mind intact, but loyal to our god, Asterias."

"Is *that* how it works, then?" Sanford whistled. He saw no reason to reveal his knowledge of the duplicated Berglunds… or his part in their deaths. "You were grown from a chopped off finger from the real Abel Davenport? That is a rather potent ability. I could be persuaded to pay a pretty penny for an amulet that makes duplicates of people, even if they do have webbed toes. It's unfortunate that these copies are loyal to a sea monster, but since said sea monster is dead, I don't suppose it matters in practical terms–"

"Asterias will live again!" Cain shouted. Zealots were so predictable. They were humorless, and they liked to sermonize. "We will recover the stolen body of our god, and take it to the temple, and restore it to life! Asterias will multiply, and fill the seas, and the *world* will become nothing but meat for the Ravening Deep!" Cain pulled the chain off his head and placed it and the amulet around Sanford's neck–

Visions exploded in Sanford's mind. He saw chanting

figures, a pool of brine and blood, torchlight, raking claws, a vast mouth that seemed to stretch for acres, the coral spire of a temple illuminated by moonlight, surrounded by stars–

Sanford decided he'd learned enough. He snapped his head back as hard as he could, driving his skull into Glenda's nose. She squawked and loosened her grip, and a hard stomp on her instep made her loosen it further – she was barefoot, too, fortunately.

Sanford ducked before Monty's axe swung through the air, and then Cain was yelling at his acolyte: "Be careful, fool, we need him *alive* to make a comet!"

Sanford snatched up his sword cane from the floor and swept Monty's legs out from under him, sending the man sprawling into Cain, axe flying. Sanford raced past them and flung open the door–

To a hallway filled with a dozen people, blocking the way. Some of them were people he *recognized*, prominent citizens of Arkham and members of his own Order, though none higher than the level of Initiate. These zealots had infiltrated the Lodge, just as he'd feared. Still, it was gratifying to know his instincts were correct, and further gratifying to see that none of these imposters were of sufficient rank to reach the basement where their dead god floated in preserving fluid. Their failure to turn anyone higher had doubtless led to their efforts to arrange this meeting, and capture him.

Sanford did not wish to be captured. He spun on his heel and ran back into the room, past a startled Cain and Monty, still disentangling themselves on the floor. Glenda, however, was alert enough to grab Sanford's ankle and send him sprawling forward himself. He kicked backward at her, but she climbed up his back, grabbed the chain of the amulet, and began choking him.

Fortunately, the chain was just a thin length of silver, and it snapped under pressure. Glenda was pulling it so hard she fell backward with a squawk. The medallion fell from his neck and bounced on the carpet and rolled under a chair. He considered trying to retrieve it, but time was of the essence. Sanford had hoped to escape *with* the medallion, but at this point, escaping with his life was more important.

He scrambled back to his feet and rushed for the largest window in the suite. When he got close, he swung his cane as hard as he could at the glass, shattering it. Without pause – to pause was to invite doubt – he launched himself through the opening, and proceeded to plummet toward the pavement several stories below. People on the street screamed and pointed. That was less than ideal.

He could not banish the specter of terror from his mind as he fell, even knowing he would not die – his *mind* knew, but his body did not, and his body was a panicked animal. He wore a ring, liberated from a temple in the desert dedicated to the Unspeakable One. He had used that ring to undertake certain rites, lengthy and complex ones, that required a willing and fully informed collaborator. One of those had been hard to find, but some people had so many debts that they would eagerly accept the *possibility* of ruin to avert the *certainty* of it, and in the end, Sanford had his volunteer, and his insurance policy.

Doubt crept in as the pavement approached. What if the rite hadn't worked? The problem was, with something like this, there was no way to *test* the effects beforehand. Worse, he realized that if he landed feet first, he might merely shatter his legs and pelvis – the ring's power would only activate if his wounds were *mortal*! Sanford flailed about, attempting to change his orientation, to make sure he'd hit headfirst, but it was damnably hard to do, and there was no time–

He closed his eyes in the moment before impact.

Sanford hit the pavement with his shoulder and rolled. It hurt no worse than falling out of bed. He got to his feet, brushing bits of glass off his lapels, and looked up. Cain and his adherents were gazing down at him from the broken window above. Sanford looked at his right hand, where the delicate ivory ring had nestled, and watched it crumble to dust and sift away on the breeze. Sanford knew that at that moment, most likely in a little bungalow on the coast of Vermont, a man was lying dead, and when the authorities found him, they would be baffled: why did he have injuries consistent with a fall from a great height, when he was in his own living room?

Sanford had no other immediate safeguards against certain death, which meant he'd better be going. The keys to the car were on Altman's corpse upstairs, so he'd have to walk. He hurried away, avoiding the wide-eyed onlookers and their exclamations of shock and disbelief. Would any of them recognize him? Well, if so, he'd simply deny all knowledge of such an event, and let the sighting add to the general air of mystique that surrounded him.

He hurried along for a few blocks, until he was satisfied he wasn't being followed, then found a pay phone and dialed the Lodge. His latest Initiate assistant answered, sounding distracted, and he snapped, "Put Van Shaw on."

"She, ah, yes, right away." The phone clattered down, and after too long a wait, the warden picked up.

Before Sanford could say anything, she spoke: "We have Ruby Standish."

That gave him a moment's pause. The thief was supposed to meet with Berglund, which meant she might have been compromised by Cain's cult, and they might well have sent her in to steal the artifact while he was distracted by the meeting with Cain. That premise didn't ring entirely true in his mind – that business at the hotel had been more than a mere distraction – but it was still too strange for him to chalk it up to coincidence. Standish might, at the very least, know *something* about this cult. "Is she secured?"

"We've got her locked up tight and waiting for your tender attentions."

"Good. Come and pick me up." He told her the closest intersection. He'd have to hide in an alleyway like a common mugger until she arrived. The indignity!

Van Shaw said, "I can send the girl, or–"

"No," Sanford said. Van Shaw almost never left the Lodge, and that meant the odds of her being compromised and replaced with a duplicate were low. "You, personally, and come right away."

"Right away, master."

Sanford hung up. His mind wanted to plan, to strategize, and to plot his next moves, but he simply didn't know enough.

He would soon. Acquiring knowledge was what he *did*.

CHAPTER SEVENTEEN
Reunions

Abel hid behind shrubs across the street and watched in secret as the Van Shaw woman hurried down the Lodge's path, through the gate, down the block, and out of sight. He'd led her on a merry chase nearly all the way around the perimeter of the fence earlier, shouting obscenities and taunting the dogs, but eventually she'd started hurling rocks at him with terrifying precision, and he'd been forced to retreat. After that she'd gone back inside and… well, something had gone wrong; that much was obvious. Even from all the way on the other side of the gate, Abel had seen the anguish on Ruby's face as she realized she couldn't get past those huge mastiffs. Abel hadn't been able to come up with any way to help. Diana was still in the Lodge, too, at least. Would she be able to help Ruby? Or did she need help herself?

He crouched in the bushes across the street in an agony of indecision. Whatever he was going to do, he should do it dressed in something other than rags. He had better clothes stashed in a pillowcase in the same bushes, and he switched out his shirt and pants. Then he shoved the big, battered hat he'd used to hide his face down in the pillowcase with his dirty clothes. He rose, checked to see if he was unobserved, brushed off the stray leaves, and walked toward the Lodge again. He pretended to saunter past, hoping to catch a glimpse of anything useful. But the old house just offered him a view of blank windows and solid doors–

A tingle troubled his mind, and he whipped his head around, looking north. The comets were moving. They were moving *this* way. Lots of them… and those were just the ones he could sense – the comets made from Cain. There could be others with them, too. Were they coming *here*? Had they finally gathered sufficient forces, or turned enough powerful Lodge members, to risk trying to breach the house directly?

The reason for their approach didn't matter. They were on the move, and that meant *Abel* needed to move. He took a deep breath and pushed open the gate. The Van Shaw woman was gone, and he understood from Diana that she was the chief guardian of this place, the "warden", making sure that no outsiders could enter. There were still the dogs to worry about, but surely they didn't savage *everyone* who walked down this path – people must knock on the door occasionally. But what if the dogs had his scent, and recognized him as a target from before?

He had to try. Abel stepped through the gate… and no dogs emerged from the long grass. That was good. He wasn't likely to do well in a fight against those beasts. Maybe they were off somewhere sleeping, or taking advantage of their mistress's absence to gnaw bones and rest. He moved slowly at first, in case the dogs were just lying in wait, then hurried up the walk and tried the front door. Locked. He didn't have any of Ruby's skill at housebreaking, so he did the only thing he could think of: he lifted the heavy brass knocker and pounded on the door.

When it opened, Abel wore his most impatient scowl, copied from the faces of any number of bankers and port authorities he'd encountered over the years. "I come with an urgent message for the master," he said into the startled face of the young blonde woman who answered. "Stand aside."

"I, ah, that is…"

"You would keep me waiting? A Guardian of the Black Stone?" Abel put all the offended hauteur he could manage into his voice.

Her eyes popped, and she squeaked, "I didn't, I, are you really?"

Abel made a complicated series of passes with his hands, all crooked fingers and hooked thumbs, and then raised an eyebrow at her. He huffed at her blank stare. "You're not even a Seeker yet, are you?"

"I am an Initiate, sir."

"Then move aside for your betters." Without waiting to see if she'd obey, he stepped forward. If she was the suspicious sort, he was in trouble, because his bluff didn't have anything behind it, but the Lodge had impressed the importance of hierarchy upon her, and she stepped aside. He strode across the foyer like he'd been there a thousand times before, the blonde following at his heels.

"The master and the warden are both out, but you can wait here–"

He stopped so short she bumped into his back, then spun on his heel, looking down on her with every inch of his height advantage. "*You* are telling *me* where *I* may *go*?" He felt bad for bullying the young woman – she probably didn't even realize what a den of vileness this place was, if she was a mere Initiate – and was a bit dismayed that doing so came this easily. This felt more like something Cain would do.

Cain did come from you, a treacherous voice whispered in his mind.

She found a little steel and glared up at him. "I keep the master's appointments. And *you* are not in his *book*."

Abel smiled. "Your loyalty speaks well of you, Initiate. Fine. When the master returns, tell him Brother" – he thought quickly, but his brain would only supply one alias – "Chesterfield is waiting beyond the Threshold of Salt. I have business downstairs anyway."

Her eyes widened, and he saw the wheels turning in her mind. If he knew about the Threshold of Salt, and knew how to find it, something even *she* didn't know as a lowly Initiate, then he obviously belonged here. Abel was grateful that Diana had offered up so many details about this place. Even so, he wouldn't have gotten past the front gate if the warden hadn't left. Come to think of it, *why* had she left?

Well, no matter. The comets were nearly at the bridge now – they seemed to be coming on foot, rather than by car, moving in ones and twos and spread out, but Arkham wasn't that big, and they'd reach the Lodge before long. Abel resumed walking, through the door and into some sort of conference room, trying to remember the map Diana and Ruby had drawn together when they planned their heist.

"Tell me, Initiate, have you seen Sister Stanley? She assisted me in an… errand… recently, and I wanted to give her some advice about how to better acquit herself in the future."

"I didn't know Sister Stanley ever *made* mistakes," she muttered, and then, in a rather sunnier voice: "She came in earlier, but I'm afraid I'm not sure where she is now. If I see her I'll be sure to let her know you asked after her."

"Oh, no need. I find that criticism works best when it comes without warning." He patted the Initiate on the shoulder and said, "I'll let you get back to your work now."

She took the hint and sat down in a chair by a pile of papers on the conference table, and Abel strode across the room like he knew exactly where he was going.

Once he'd gotten deeper into the house, he leaned against a baby grand piano, closed his eyes, and exhaled. There was a bar cart against one wall, crystal decanters glimmering with dark brown and deep red liquid oblivion, and he was tempted… but no. Maybe he'd have a drink after this was all done. For now, he needed his wits and speed. His priorities were to find Ruby and Diana and get them out of here before the warden returned, or Sanford himself did, or the approaching comets arrived.

But there was something else tickling at the edge of his consciousness, like a feather brushing his cheek, but in his mind. It was a different mental sensation than the sense he had of his comets – they felt more like pieces of him, moving off on their own. He'd heard men maimed in war talk about the feeling that their missing arms or legs were *still there* – some even said they could close their phantom fists and wiggle their phantom toes. The comets felt a bit like that, he imagined – they were his lost fingers, still tingling, still connected.

This new sensation was something else. It felt more like something looming, but not *above* him; like something looming from *below*, if that made sense. As if he were looking down, only to discover he was suspended over an abyss… or an open mouth, big enough to swallow him.

"Asterias," he murmured. What else could it be? The piece of his god was here, nearby, and he could sense it. If he closed his eyes and concentrated… yes, he could sense a direction. The piece of Asterias was off to his right, under his feet. What did it mean, that he could still sense the Ravening Deep, even without the amulet around his neck? Was he forever polluted and corrupted by their prior association? Abel was the chosen one – did that mean he was chosen forever, whether he liked it or not? Maybe that's why Cain wanted to feed Abel to their god. As long as Abel lived, *he* was the true high priest of Asterias, apostate or not.

Abel shook off those brooding thoughts and focused on the matter at hand. He had to help his friends and destroy Asterias – the god's true death would free him at last. If he had a pickaxe and infinite strength, he could hack his way straight down through the floor, following his senses to the god, but in the absence of those advantages, he'd have to find a more mundane way down. Abel envisioned the map Ruby and Diana had drawn together, and proceeded carefully through rooms and corridors. Once he found the old servant's quarters, the path was easier, and his fear of discovery began to diminish. When he reached the pantry, the shelf was already lifted, the secret door already open, and the lights beyond the Threshold of Salt lit.

Abel stepped over the threshold, hesitant, wishing he'd held onto his gun instead of giving it to Diana. Who knew what horrors lurked around the next corner?

The only thing lurking around the next corner turned out to be Diana herself, crouching before a closed door, shoving something under the crack and whispering, "I'm *sorry*, it's all I have, and you're lucky I have that! I don't usually even carry bobby pins – I hardly ever use them."

"Hello, Diana," Abel said, and she looked up at him, wide-eyed. He could sense that his god was in her bag, hanging off her shoulder. Its proximity throbbed in his mind like a rotten tooth in a jaw. He had a sudden urge to snatch the bag, flee the house, find a boat, reach the temple… He steeled himself against the god's psychic whispers, focusing instead on Diana, his friend, his ally, his savior. There was dust in her hair and a smudge of something sooty on her cheek, and she looked fierce and intrepid.

She rose to her feet. "What are you doing in here?"

"Is that Abel?" Ruby's voice came muffled from the other side of the locked door. "How did you even get in here?"

"I came to rescue you both, but you seem to be doing fine," Abel said. "I got in because Van Shaw left–"

"She's *gone*?" Diana said. "She… I heard she *never* leaves, that she's always here – they say she doesn't even sleep. There are rumors that she's under a magical compulsion to guard the Lodge above all else."

"I can't explain it, but we should take advantage of her absence, and get out of here," he said.

"I'm picking these locks as fast as I can," Ruby said. "I don't have proper tools, so it's like trying to build a house with nothing but an ice cream knife and a tennis racket."

Abel chewed his lip, but there was nothing he could do to speed things up. He turned to Diana and nodded to the bag. "It's in there, isn't it? The piece of Asterias. I can *feel* it."

"That's not disturbing at all," Ruby offered. Something clicked, and there was a little clatter, like a hairpin dropping on a stone floor, and she swore.

"Yes, it's here." Diana patted her bag. "I was expecting some immense container, but the jar is small, like something you'd keep pickles in. After Ruby lured the shoggoth away, I didn't have any trouble finding it." She turned toward the door. "Ruby, I am so sorry. I wanted to chase after you, to use my immunity to shepherd you to safety, but I knew it was our only chance to get the jar, and I feel terrible."

"If you'd chased after me, I would have kicked you," Ruby said. "I ran away so you *could* finish the mission."

"Even so. I helped summon that thing into existence. I was there at the ceremony, and if it hurt you–"

"Oh, stop that," Ruby said. "You didn't even know what the ritual was for. Don't take the blame for things that aren't your fault. I hardly ever even take the blame for things that *are*."

"I'm sorry," Abel said. "I'm feeling a bit lost. What's a… shoggoth?"

"A monster," Diana said. "It was guarding the vault, and, by coincidence, the room full of junk where your – sorry, the cult's – god was kept."

A monster? He'd had some experience with those. He looked around. "Did you kill it?"

"I don't know if it can be killed, but it seems to have been... dismissed," Diana said. "Sent back to its lair."

The door swung open, and Ruby stepped out, rubbing her wrists. "The manacles were harder to open than the lock. You didn't send us anywhere, Abel – we sent *ourselves*. The two of you just love taking responsibility where you shouldn't. It's like an illness. Right. Mission accomplished, then?"

Diana nodded.

"Good," Abel said. He could tell most of the comets were on this side of the river now, and their relative proximity made his teeth ache. "We have to go. They're coming. They're almost here."

"Who's almost here?" Sanford said, stepping around the corner with Sarah Van Shaw at his side. She looked furious enough to spit nails, but he was his usual self, urbane, with an expression of mild curiosity. His usual self except for his suit, anyway, which was ripped in several places.

Abel stepped forward, putting himself between the newcomers and Ruby and Diana, but Diana shoved him against the wall. "Master and warden," she said. "I caught this man trying to help Standish escape–"

"Please, don't bother," Sanford said. "We were around the corner listening for a few moments. We will discuss your actions soon, Seeker, and as for you, Ruby Standish, we'll do more than talk. But for now." Sanford turned, giving Abel a long, intense look. "What is your name, sir?"

He straightened. This was bad, but he would face the situation with dignity, at least. Working with Diana and Ruby had restored that much to him. "I am Abel Davenport."

Sanford pinched the bridge of his nose, then nodded. "Yes, I was rather afraid you'd say that. The resemblance is hard to miss. Are you the *original* Abel Davenport, at least?"

"The–" Abel stared. "You've met Cain, then?"

"It seems you and I should talk too," Sanford said. "But first – *who* do you say is coming?"

"Cain," Abel said. "And his comets – the duplicates he made from himself. I can sense them because, in a sense, they came from me. But there may be others–"

"Yes, I daresay there *are* – they filled three floors of the Independence Hotel, and several of my Initiates were among them." He turned. "Warden, we may have unwelcome visitors soon. Make sure they find it difficult to get inside."

"None shall enter this place without my leave," Van Shaw said.

Sanford sighed. "That's a nice sentiment, but they might enter anyway, you know. I gather these cultists are harder to kill than most people – isn't that right, Davenport?"

Abel nodded. He didn't have any love for Carl Sanford, but he had a lot less for Cain. "All the comets are tough, and strong, and they heal fast. As for Cain, while he's wearing the amulet, I'm not sure anything could stop him. If you cut off his head, he might just grow a new one."

Sanford nodded. "Then do your best, warden, but don't sacrifice your own life to keep them at bay. If they make it past you, so be it. We have other options. The Lodge will survive this insult, and we'll need you alive to keep protecting it."

"I'll get more dogs," the warden said, and hurried around the corner.

"I'd say let's talk in my office," Sanford said. "But Initiates know where my office is, and it's likely to be overrun by zealots soon. So... let's talk in my vault instead."

He walked past them, down the hall. Abel looked at Ruby and Diana. The latter shrugged. The former looked longingly toward the exit, then sighed. Then they all three fell into step behind their enemy.

Abel noted Ruby and Diana's tension as they approached a doorway shrouded in shadows. "Is this where the shoggoth was?"

"Yes, I heard you met my guardian," Sanford called over his shoulder. "I thought it best to install precautions after Miss Standish last visited the Lodge. I was unprepared for the possibility of, what do they call it – an 'inside job?' I'm curious to hear how you came to be involved with this thief, Diana, and even more curious to know why you chose to *help* her."

"I did it to save the world from Cain's cult," Diana said.

Sanford grunted. "Are things so dire as all that?"

"If your scholar from Yith is to be believed, yes," Ruby said.

From where? Abel shook his head. You'd think he'd be used to confusion by now, but there was always some new shoal of ignorance to run aground on. Someone would tell him if it was important.

The master of the Order turned, looked at Ruby for a long moment, and then nodded. "I see. You did make the most of your time in my basements, didn't you? Come along." He proceeded down a hall, and to another door.

"The shoggoth is just ahead," Diana said. "It's... horrible."

"I don't much like looking at it myself," Sanford said. "I once had cause to see the lungs of a man who'd spent his life working in a coal mine – until he encountered something far below the earth that *wasn't* coal, to his misfortune – and the shoggoth reminds me of those black and tumorous organs. I prefer not to see the beast at all when I come down here." He reached into his pocket and took out a little tin whistle, blowing a single, shrill note. "It's not the thin, monotonous piping favored by the attendants of Azathoth, but it gets the job done." He put the whistle away and opened the door.

No monster appeared, apparently made quiescent by Sanford's signal. The floor was stained, though. "It does leave a filthy residue behind, and of course no one below the level of a Knight is allowed here, and *they* have more important things to do than swirl a mop around. Perhaps you can keep this corridor clean as part of your penance, Diana."

"As you wish, master," Diana said.

Abel was impressed. She was trying to pretend she'd only joined Ruby and Abel because of the dire threat of Cain's cult, and not because she was looking for any opportunity at all to damage the Lodge.

Sanford paused by the storage room on the left, glancing inside. Abel looked in, too. It was full of shelves, built into the wall and freestanding, crammed with the refuse of what looked like a dozen attics and church rummage sales.

"All this time, there was a piece of an elder thing here, under my nose." Sanford clucked his tongue. "I must revise our inventory protocols. I assume you have the jar, Diana? The warden assured me she'd checked Ruby and found nothing of interest but lockpicks, but of course, she believed your story that the thief had overpowered you and escaped. She didn't suspect you of collusion. I would have scarcely suspected you myself." He favored the three of them with a charming smile. "Of course, I would have checked your bag anyway."

"I do have it," Diana said.

"I'll take a look once we're in the vault. If you'd all avert your eyes now, please."

Ruby snorted. "I know how to open it."

"You *knew* how to open it," he said. "And I'd very much like to know who told you that much. It's a short list of possibilities, and I considered punishing them all to be sure of hurting your source, but all of them are too valuable to waste that way. Only Knights and above come down here, as I said. Alas, the kind of interrogations that get definite answers don't leave much of use behind afterward."

They all turned away, drifting together into a huddle. Ruby and Diana kept looking through the open doorway on the right, which did seem unnaturally dark, and emitted a pungent, strangely chemical odor. "The shoggoth's room?" Abel asked.

"Den," Diana said. "Lair." She shuddered. "Just looking at that creature... I felt the tethers on my mind loosen."

"Try having it chase you through this haunted basement," Ruby said.

"All right," Sanford said. "Come inside." They turned to find the vault door standing open, revealing a lushly carpeted space within, gleaming and glinting with wealth. He ushered them in. "Hands where I can see them, please, Ruby."

Once they were all inside the spacious vault, he shut the door, securing a heavy lever with a clunk and spinning a combination dial on the inside. Once they were sealed inside, he walked around them and pressed a section of polished wood wall. A panel swung open, revealing a rack of suit coats and trousers. Sanford removed his tattered and torn jacket, put on a new one, and made a contented sound. "There. That's better." A small bar cart stood against the wall, and he poured himself a glass of brandy. The vault held only a single chair, facing an object on the wall covered with black cloth – a painting or mirror, Abel supposed. He looked at the strange objects surrounding them, but couldn't muster much curiosity. He'd had quite enough involvement with magical artifacts, and nothing here tempted or interested him.

Sanford turned the chair around to face them instead and sat down. "Do make yourselves comfortable."

Ruby leaned against the vault door, as far from Sanford as she could get, and crossed her arms. Diana sat on the floor at Sanford's feet, beside a pedestal that held an onyx egg as big as a melon. Abel opted to join Ruby by the door.

"So what's all this about saving the world?" Sanford said.

CHAPTER EIGHTEEN
In the Mirror and Out of the Vault

Diana craned her head to look at Ruby, who nodded in reply to Sanford's question, but turned to address Abel instead of speaking to the old man. "I already told Diana, but I should fill you in, too. I talked to a… very knowledgeable woman Sanford has locked up down here, his personal Oracle at Delphi, I suppose. She told me that if Asterias is restored to life, it will feed and eventually split in two, making a copy of itself. Then those two will split, and then those four, and so on, making more and more hungry monsters until they eat everything under the sea and out of it."

Abel frowned. "Surely that's not something that can happen quickly?"

"Perhaps not," Sanford said. "But even if it's slow at first, it will rapidly accelerate." He tapped a forefinger thoughtfully on his chin. "There is a story about a king of India who enjoyed chatrang, a sort of early version of chess, played on the same board of sixty-four squares. He would challenge visitors to a game, inevitably defeating them, until one day a traveling wise man visited. He was renowned as an expert in the game, but was reluctant to play, so the king offered him his choice of rewards, should he win. The wise man said he wanted only a little rice, but since they were playing on the game board anyway, why not use that to measure out the rice? If he won, the king would put a single grain of rice on the first square, then double it for the second, and double that on the third, and so on. The king readily agreed." Sanford cocked his head. "Well? Did none of you learn arithmetic?"

"My mother read me this story," Abel remembered. "The king lost the game. He called for a sack of rice. Then he put one grain on the first square, two on the second, four on the third, eight on the fourth, and so on... by the twentieth square, they'd reached a million grains of rice, and were not even halfway done."

"To finish would require enough rice to cover the entire territory of India, in a layer three feet deep," Sanford said. "*That's* where we'd get, with your Asterias – so many monsters that some of them would be dividing every day. They'd overrun the world sooner than you might think."

"Three centuries, the scholar said," Ruby supplied. "Before the world is covered in the spawn of Asterias."

Abel closed his eyes for a moment. "No wonder the Ravening Deep didn't show me *that* in my vision. I would hardly have agreed to restore it to life, if I'd known it would end all life as a consequence."

"I didn't see those details in my visions, either," Sanford said. "Just instructions, and directions, and promises of glory."

"*You* saw a vision of Asterias, master?" Diana made her

voice captivated and fawning. If there was ever a time to ingratiate herself with the old man…

"Indeed. None of you had the basic courtesy to ask why I look so battered, so I'll tell you: Cain lured me to his rooms under false pretenses. He intended to cut off a piece of me and make a copy, to lead the cult here. He put the amulet on me, to start the process, and I saw… a great many things." He did not elaborate.

Just like him to hold onto his secrets, even when their best hope was pooling their knowledge. Diana hated him, but just now, she also needed him. "How did you escape him?" she asked.

Sanford chuckled. "I am the leader of the Silver Twilight Lodge. Cain was born, what, a few months ago? As if *he* could best *me*. Though I admit, it was more difficult for me to escape than I'd have liked. The cult has been patient so far, gathering power, trying to infiltrate the Lodge, gathering enough information to trick me into a meeting… but when Cain thought I was captured, he let hubris get the best of him, and told me his plans."

"That's why they're rushing here," Abel said. "To stop you from moving the sample of Asterias, or destroying it."

"Master," Diana said, opting to play the loyal Seeker as hard as she could. He might still believe it, after all, or at least, be open to believing it. "Perhaps it would be best to destroy the specimen now?"

Sanford looked down at her. "You betrayed me, Diana."

"I was afraid, master," she said, truthfully enough; the truth was always best, if the lie of her life would allow it. "Abel told me about the god, and about the cult, and then

I met Ruby – the Berglunds had her held captive, and she agreed to help us get the jar. I was just trying to do the right thing."

Sanford seemed unconvinced. "Why didn't you come to *me*, child, and tell me about the threat?"

"I… I couldn't be sure *you* were still really you…"

He snorted. "Nonsense. If the cult had turned me, they would have run off with their bit of god-flesh already. No, Seeker, you had your own ambitions, and saw an opportunity to further them, though I'm not sure exactly what your plans were. Well, I knew you had fire in you – that's how you became a Seeker in only two years, after all. I just thought I could use that fire to fuel my own goals. Hmm." He waved a hand. "Your future in the Lodge is a debate for another time. For now, show me this god."

Diana didn't argue or protest or claim loyalty. She thought the best way to make Sanford believe she was still his meek subject was to act like one, so she reached into her bag and withdrew the jar. It was full of murky fluid, and a bobbing purplish-black lump of flesh smaller than Diana's fist. She held the jar out to Sanford, who plucked it from her grasp and held it up to the light.

"It doesn't *seem* to be alive. Funny if this is all for nothing – oh." Sanford turned the jar toward them. The purple lump was pressed against the side of the glass, and three eyes, smaller than a human's but not by much, stared out at them. The eyes had purple irises, and vertical slit pupils, and they shifted back and forth, as if memorizing all their faces. Ruby gasped, and Abel moaned, and Sanford said, "Very interesting."

Diana felt only a deep, primal horror. This thing *should not be*. If it had come from this world, it was an abomination; if it hailed from elsewhere, it was an invader. "We should destroy it now, master," Diana said. "Fire might work–"

"Fire doesn't work in *here*," Sanford said. "There are too many valuables, including delicate papyri. I have protective spells in place – I couldn't even light a pipe in here." He set the jar on a shelf. "There's no need to be rash, anyway. I gather there's a whole ritual required to restore the god. You have to take this sad remnant to a temple in the sea, yes? Then Asterias is harmless in this jar. We'll just have to keep it out of the cult's hands... and kill this Cain... and take the amulet... and lock everything away." Sanford shrugged. "This is a problem, yes, but not an insurmountable one. Hardly worth all the skullduggery you lot have engaged in." He put the jar on a shelf, those alien eyes still darting around. After a moment, he turned the jar so the eyes faced the wall instead. "A bit unsettling, isn't it? I wonder why it woke up now."

"Because I am here," Abel said, with simple certainty. "And because its followers are close. *Very* close. They're coming up the hill now."

"Let's see how the warden gets on with them." Sanford tugged the silk cloth from the hanging on the wall, revealing an ornate mirror three feet high and two feet wide, with a frame designed to look like twisted tentacles. The edges of the mirror were smudged with uneven darkness, but the center was still clear but, oddly, reflected nothing, just showed a silver expanse.

Diana gave a little shiver. They were in the presence

of the uncanny, and Sanford was so matter-of-fact about it all. What must it be like, to spend so long immersed in the unseen world that you could become inured to it? She thought it was sad.

"This is a charming little artifact," Sanford said. "It requires some attunement to use, but I've had it for a long time. It can see through *other* mirrors, you see, if they're prepared properly, and I've linked it to mirrors throughout the Lodge... and elsewhere, of course, where I think eyes might be useful."

He waved a hand across the face of the mirror, and the silver rippled like a pool of mercury with a stone dropped into the middle. Sanford stepped aside so they could all get a clearer view. Then the silver solidified and softened into a view of the front path and the iron gates. "There's a mirror on the porch?" Diana asked. Even knowing the Lodge contained items of great magic, it was astonishing to see one in action, and wonder supplanted her fear.

"Every window can be a mirror, when the light is right."

"This is amazing," Ruby said. "Better than a moving picture show – it's in *color*. And real."

"Thinking of stealing it?" Sanford said. "Selling it for enough to retire?"

"I don't know. This one I might keep for myself."

Sanford swirled his drink and took a sip. "Here come the cultists now. Comets, you called them? How poetic."

Diana had expected a mob, dozens of figures ready to storm the gates, but it was only a few people – two of them looked like Abel, though one was bearded and another wore a hat pulled low on his face. The third was an unknown woman. "There's Cain," Abel said, pointing to the one with the hat.

"I wondered if he'd come himself," Sanford said. "Leading from the front? Foolish bravado."

"He wants to be the first to see his god," Abel said.

"Gods," Sanford scoffed. "They're always more trouble than they're worth."

More people drifted in to join Cain, some dressed in the rough garb of dock workers, others in clothes Diana might have sold in her shop. Once eight of them had gathered, Cain yanked at the gate. It didn't move, and Sanford chuckled. "When the warden locks the gate, it *stays* locked."

A few other comets grabbed at the gate, too, pulling on the bars, and then wrenched it free, throwing it aside into the street. "No sound though," Ruby muttered. "This would be better with sound. I have to *imagine* the clang."

Sanford sniffed. "Property damage. So crass. So *physical*."

Cain didn't keep the lead – he sent his comets down the path first as even more comets strolled in from various directions to join them, pouring through the gap and onto the Lodge grounds.

"And now the hounds," Sanford murmured. Black dogs appeared on the path, six of them, stepping forward in formation like trained soldiers, hackles up and tails low.

"I thought there were only two?" Diana said.

"That's because two are usually enough." Sanford leaned forward and watched as the dogs leapt.

The comets fought, and though the dogs were vicious, the animals were outnumbered, with at least two comets for every one. The cultists were undeterred by bites and scratches, either impervious to pain or so desperate to reach their god that they were able to fight through it. They carried the thrashing dogs off into the long grass, out of the mirror's view. Four more cultists marched down the now-cleared steps, with Cain somewhere behind them.

"And now comes the warden," Sanford said.

Van Shaw appeared, and she was carrying a shotgun. She didn't pause to banter, just put the stock to her shoulder and fired. One of the cultists flew backward, hit square in the chest, and then another spun and fell, struck in the shoulder. Van Shaw then drew a pistol and shot the third, a blossom of blood appearing in her throat. Diana gasped. It was horrible, the blood so bright and vivid, but the silence and flatness of the image making it eerie.

The fourth cultist was able to slap Van Shaw's arm away, and then two more surged forward. She swung with her now-empty shotgun, cracking one across the jaw with the stock. Another reached for her, grabbing her arm, and she kicked him away. She looked back, toward the door, and there was real distress on her face, mingled with fury.

The warden was as ferocious as her hounds, but Cain still had reinforcements joining him. Three of the cultists managed to drag Van Shaw away, off to the side... and then Cain was walking forward, as if directly toward them. He was smiling, the lines on his face so dark they looked drawn on with charcoal.

The blonde Initiate stepped onto the porch, and Diana said, "No!"

"If she lives, I suppose I'll have to promote her," Sanford said. "She's Brother Altman's sister-in-law's daughter. I didn't think she was so brave. She wouldn't be, if she knew what that creature had done to her uncle."

Diana had met Altman a few times, and found him off-putting – the smile on his face never did much to dispel the distance in his eyes. "Wait – Cain killed Altman?"

"Just like he's about to kill Rebecca, it appears," Sanford said.

Rebecca. Diana had never learned the girl's name.

As Cain approached the mirror, his face unfolded. "No, no, *no thank you*," Ruby said. Abel grunted as if he'd been punched in the stomach. Diana could only stare. She'd thought the shoggoth was bad, but at least the shoggoth didn't *look human* at first. The fleshy petals of Cain's face folded back, exposing a horrible round mouth full of teeth that seemed to scintillate, the maw surrounded by little squirming tendrils like worms. Rebecca turned to run away, her expression of terror visible in the mirror, and then Cain seized her by the hair and jerked her head back. He spun her around to face him, then lowered his horrible face to hers.

Diana looked away. From the corner of her eye, she could see that Sanford watched with interest.

"Why don't the neighbors come running?" Ruby said. "Surely they must have heard the gunshots? Why isn't anyone *helping*?"

"The Lodge discourages outside attention," Sanford said. "All sorts of horrible things have happened on that lawn, unnoticed by those who live on the street, though never before *this* variety of horrible, I'll grant you."

"That's the way the Ravening Deep feeds," Abel said. "I've seen it, in my visions, but the god's mouth is so much larger. It can swallow a person whole. They go down slowly, though, inch by inch. The lucky ones go down headfirst, and die quicker."

Diana returned her attention to the mirror. It was better to know, even if the knowledge was horrible. Cain let the young woman fall, her head a ruin, then stepped over her, into the Lodge, and out of view.

"Hmm," Sanford said. "Right. Only a matter of time now, I'd say."

"You think they'll find their way down here?" Diana was keenly aware of their position, in a locked room at the end of a hall. If the comets came down here… She felt like a mouse listening to the approach of a cat.

"I think they'll check *everywhere*, in time," Sanford said. "And I can't rule out the possibility that they turned someone at your level, Diana, who knows the location of the Threshold of Salt. I don't want to wait around for them to ransack their way down here."

"They'll find us quickly." Abel nodded toward the jar. "I can sense the presence of Asterias – I could sense it as soon as I came inside. I'm sure Cain and the comets can, too."

"Won't the vault guardian be able to stop them?" Diana said.

Sanford shook his head. "Some of them, certainly. But I don't get the sense Cain values the lives of his underlings much, and if he throws enough of them at the shoggoth, some of them will make it past to the vault. My shoggoth is also young, and not very bright, and capable of being lured away, as I gather Ruby succeeded in doing. On balance, I think we'd better be going."

"Going where?" Ruby said. "Back upstairs? Good luck. You fight them, distract them, and we'll escape with the god in a jar—"

"Did you really think I'd only have one exit out of the Lodge?" Sanford said. "I have several, in fact, and some of them lead right out of this world... but the Plateau isn't hospitable this time of year, and I'm not taking an aquatic creature anywhere near the misty Lake – who knows how this fragment of Asterias might quicken in a place like that? No, we'll take one of my mundane escape routes, which is located... right here." He knelt by an ornate chest, banded with iron and inlaid with obsidian and silver, a trunk big enough to hide a body inside. He pressed the sides of the trunk, and the lid sprang open. Diana tensed up, half expecting something to leap from the chest, or for Sanford to draw out Excalibur, or Poseidon's trident, or a flamethrower. He didn't reach inside, though. Instead he said, "Take the jar for me, would you, Diana?"

I'll take it for *us*, Diana thought. She wasn't going to let Asterias end up in Sanford's hands any more than she'd leave it with Cain and his comets. "Of course, master." She put the jar back in her bag and secured it on her shoulder.

Sanford gestured to the trunk. "Abel first, I think, since he can sense the presence of at least some of the cult's members."

Abel looked into the trunk, grunted, and then stepped inside – and began to descend, apparently climbing down a concealed ladder. Seeing his head drop below the level of the trunk was like watching a magician do a trick. Ha! The trunk must have a false bottom concealing an escape route. Sanford did love his trickery.

"Do you think there are comets in the tunnels?" Ruby asked.

"Unlikely," Sanford said. "Only a handful of my most trusted associates know about this route, and the cult hasn't turned any of them – if they had, they wouldn't have needed to lure me to Cain's hotel room. They could have taken me unawares at another time. But I didn't get to be where I am today by taking unnecessary risks, so I don't intend to take the lead." He nodded to Ruby. "Down you go. I can't very well leave you in the vault unattended."

Ruby rolled her eyes and stepped into the trunk, descending faster than Abel had. "It smells down here," her voice wafted up.

"It gets worse," Sanford assured her. Then he gave Diana a little bow. "You next, my dear. I'll bring up the rear, since I know a trick to seal this entrance so no one can follow."

It was Diana's turn to look into the trunk. Sanford had lifted up a hinged false bottom to reveal a set of wooden rungs descending at a slight angle into a tunnel about ten feet down. Ruby and Abel were at the bottom, gazing up. "Part of an old cellar?" she asked.

"Indeed," Sanford said. "At least… the first part was. There are lanterns down there. They should have oil in them."

Ruby vanished into the dark as Diana made her way down, and by the time she'd descended to the tunnel floor, the thief had lit one lantern and was holding another out to Abel. The room smelled richly of dirt with an undercurrent of rot.

Sanford came down then, closing the hatch and then standing halfway up the ladder, muttering something. There was a clang, like someone had dropped a cast iron skillet into a galvanized steel tub. "Sealed," Sanford said with satisfaction. When he reached the bottom of the ladder, Diana saw him tuck a length of red chalk into an inner pocket of his jacket. What other mystical tools did he have secreted about his person? All she had was the pistol in her bag. And a god in a jar. Usually she just had a compact and a handkerchief or two!

A bubble of unhinged laughter built up in her belly, but she stifled it. How had her life come to *this*? She'd just wanted to run a shop and live in peace and plenty, and now she was trying to save the world. But there would be no peace for anyone if Cain succeeded. Sometimes the world made demands of you, and you had to answer.

They were in a rectangular stone room about five feet wide and ten feet long, with the ladder at one end and a metal door at the other. Beside the door there was a wooden crate that held the lanterns, oil, and a handful of crude spears – just lengths of wood with sharpened ends. "What are those for?" Ruby said.

"Protection," Sanford said. "French Hill is an interesting place. There's a whole complex of tunnels underneath here. We thought the caves were natural, at first, until we discovered… dens, you could say. Or lairs. They were full of human remains and gnawed bones. We located a number of passages that led to the graveyard and the mausoleums, and found coffins broken open… from below, their contents spirited away into the tunnels."

"What?" Diana said, horrified. "Spirited away by *what*?"

"We have a copy of Balfour's *Cultes des Goules* in the

Seeker's library," Sanford said. "You should have read it. This hill was once infested by the… shall we say, American cousins of the creatures that volume describes. There is considerable debate about their origins, whether they're a cannibalistic subspecies of human, or the result of humans mating with certain other entities, a sort of subterranean counterpart to the denizens of Innsmouth. I incline toward the latter notion. At any rate, ghouls are foul, scrambling things, all teeth and claws and filth, and they feast on corpses. We cleared the tunnels, but in time, the ghouls returned. Some of the passageways go very deep indeed, and not all have been explored. We've closed up most of the openings that lead to the surface to discourage them away from this area, and if a ghoul does creep in, it can usually be sent fleeing with a few jabs. I have my sword-stick. You're welcome to take spears. I wouldn't advise firing a gun down here." He looked straight at Diana. "The ghouls dug these tunnels, using their claws as far as we can tell, and as a result the passages aren't tremendously stable. I'd hate for you to trigger a cave-in."

Just what Diana needed: *another* horrible fate to worry about. She added it to the list and put the list aside. Worry would only slow her down and make her hesitate, and there was no time for hesitation now. "I understand," she said.

The other three took spears. "Wonderful," Sanford said. "Let's–"

A booming sound came from above, like metal slamming into metal, and dust sifted down from the ceiling like dry rain. "They've made it to the vault already." Abel stared above him. "God, Cain is *right there*."

"Then let's be elsewhere," Diana said, and opened the metal door.

CHAPTER NINETEEN
Reversal of Fortunes

Ghouls, Ruby thought. The more she learned about the secret world, the more she wished she'd been content with the known one. She followed Diana into the tunnel, holding her spear in one hand and a lantern in the other. She had to resist the urge to huddle up close to Diana – she'd end up poking the other woman with her spear if she got any closer.

The tunnel beyond the metal door wasn't finished at all – it was packed dirt, sometimes with roots poking down from above and in from the sides, and it smelled even more strongly of clay and rotten meat. The stink wasn't quite enough to make her gag, but it was getting close. The tunnel was round, like it had been created by the passage of an immense earthworm, and just tall enough for her to stand upright. Abel and Sanford would have to stoop.

"I just discovered that I'm claustrophobic," Abel said. "It's funny, I've spent plenty of time cramped belowdecks on boats, and that never bothered me much, but somehow having all this *earth* above me is different. I feel like the air is being crushed out of me."

"It's like a rehearsal for being dead and buried," Diana said. "Except at least the dead can't smell."

"Sure they can," Ruby said. "The dead smell terrible." Only Sanford laughed, which was worse than no one laughing at all.

The passage didn't have sharp turns, but it was full of meandering curves, and they passed side passages that had been blocked, some by natural cave-ins, others jammed with chunks of concrete and rocks shored up with lengths of metal – routes the Lodge had sealed, Ruby supposed. They walked, and walked, and walked, and a terrible certainty dawned on Ruby.

"Sanford, why are we going *down*?" Was this a trick? Was he luring them to some subterranean lair – to feed them to some horrible entity *he* owed fealty to?

"The Lodge is at the top of the hill, Miss Standish," Sanford said from the back. "We are heading for a point closer to the base on the eastern side, which lets out onto a little plot of undeveloped land I've owned for quite some time. We'll be there soon."

Ruby grunted, somewhat mollified.

A few moments later, Diana stopped. "There is… a foot. On the tunnel floor. A human foot. A… lady's foot, judging by the polish on the toenails." Her voice was strangely calm. Ruby moved a little closer to look, and there was indeed a dainty foot in the tunnel, with a shard of bone poking up out of the ankle. She shuddered all over. That used to belong to a *person*. A person who was *dead*. A person who was in *pieces*–

"Mmm," Sanford said. "The ghouls don't usually leave any

flesh behind, which means we probably startled one away from its meal. Let's step up our pace, shall we?"

"I'll go first," Abel said, squeezing by them and pointing his spear forward. Ruby and Diana exchanged a glance, and Ruby rolled her eyes. She didn't need a man to protect her, but then again, if Abel *wanted* to put himself in the path of a ghoul, who was she to argue?

The tunnel widened enough for Ruby and Diana to walk abreast, so they did. They kept their spears up and scanned the environment, side-to-side, but up above, too. Ruby had a particular horror at the idea of something dropping on her from the tunnel's ceiling.

When the ghoul appeared, though, it did so from below, squirming out of a crack in the ground. It wriggled out just after Abel passed the crack, its body pale and gangly, its proportions somehow doglike, its face more like a snout. It crouched, shoulder bones jutting out unevenly, its spine crooked and hunched, and leered at them.

Diana screamed, apparently forgetting all about her spear, because she smashed it across the face with the lantern. The ghoul howled, and Ruby stepped forward and jabbed it with her spear, scratching a bloody line across its pale chest as it twisted away. By then Abel had turned around and jabbed with *his* spear, and Sanford shouted, "Give it an escape route, you fools! If it can't run, it will *fight*!"

Ruby and Diana flattened themselves against either side of the tunnel, leaving an opening just wide enough for a terrified ghoul to flee from Abel's jabs.

And flee it did – straight toward Sanford, who was still taking up the rear. Ruby watched, partly horrified, and partly hopeful. If the ghoul fell upon Sanford… well, he'd already shown them the escape route, so did they really need him anymore? Ruby wasn't the bloodthirsty sort, but she was pragmatic, and she knew that Sanford would still want revenge on her for her theft. If he fell to the ghoul, it would solve one of Ruby's big problems.

But Diana shouted, "Master, look out!" Ruby wondered if the woman was just so caught up in playing the loyal acolyte that she warned Sanford instinctively, or if she simply placed a higher intrinsic value on human life than Ruby did. Probably the latter. In Diana's position, Ruby would have simply left town when she realized she was part of a monstrous cult, not stayed behind to try to dismantle the organization from the inside. That probably meant Diana was a better person than her. Ruby thought she could live with that.

"Yes, thank you, Seeker," Sanford said, and there was the rasp of drawn metal as he liberated his sword from the stick. "You'd best avert your eyes."

Ruby didn't look away – she always liked to *see* – and so she was blinded when the shaft of the sword lit up as bright as the sun and slashed out at the ghoul, separating its canine head from its body. The sword dulled to a faint glow for a moment and then went dark again, leaving them all to blink in the much deeper darkness.

"Apologies for the flash," Sanford said. "I've been through a lot today, and didn't relish the idea of anything like a fair fight in these tunnels. Ghouls aren't strong individually, but when cornered they can be ferocious, and their bites and scratches have a tendency to become infected. Doubtless because of all their scrabbling about in corpses and mud all day." Sanford's voice was calm.

"You have a *magic sword*," Ruby said, the dark blotches in her vision fading.

"I have magic, if you want to call it that, and a sword," Sanford replied. The stick rattled as he put it away. "Let's go before the commotion attracts the dead hound's relatives."

They set off again, Ruby trailing a hand along the side of the tunnel since her vision still wasn't entirely restored. The tunnel floor leveled out, and then her fingertips brushed what felt like brick.

"Is this the exit?" Abel called. "It's locked."

Sanford pushed his way past, pausing to cast a sardonic look at Ruby. "Of course it's locked. Only I can open it. It's good the ghoul didn't kill me, hmm? Because I sealed the other end of the tunnel in the same way. You would have had a terrible time down here without me... though not, it occurs to me, for very long."

Ruby crowded close to watch Sanford at the door, the twin of the metal hatch they'd entered at the other end of this journey. He pressed his hand against the metal, then drew a bit of chalk from his pocket and sketched a design on the door. After that, Sanford knocked a complicated series of raps, muttered to himself, and yanked the lever down. The door eased open a crack.

"How much of that was actually necessary to unlock the door, and how much was just misdirection to hide the real process?" Diana asked, and Ruby snorted in approval.

"Oh, about half and half." Sanford rubbed the chalk away. "Not that I expect any of you to come this way again, but security is a good habit." He pulled the door open the rest of the way, the metal creaking. "I keep a car in a garage a few blocks away. We'll head there, drive out of town, and then figure out what to do with Miss Stanley's jar. You can leave the lanterns here."

Sanford led the way out of the tunnel, and they followed. Beyond the door, the tunnel got smaller, forcing them all to hunch, and soon it became a drainpipe that was barely big enough to crawl through on all fours. Ruby told herself things were just getting worse before they got better. They *had* to be getting better, right?

She wondered if the comets were back there in the tunnels, coming after them, contending with ghouls, getting lost in side passages… or pursuing Abel unerringly. No use worrying about it. The only way out was through.

Sanford went into the narrow pipe first, his cane dragging beside him, but the rest of them discarded their spears along with the lanterns for easier movement. The drainpipe was short, and soon Ruby crawled out, following Diana. There were no streetlights nearby, but the moon was bright enough to outline their surroundings.

The pipe let them out in the back of an undeveloped lot backed against the hill, the ground fenced in on the three other sides. The lot was filled with weeds and flanked by derelict houses. Not a part of Arkham she'd had cause to visit before; not a part it looked like anyone would want to frequent. Ruby looked back at the short length of pipe protruding from the hillside. It looked for all the world like an ordinary drain. Now she knew it was a back entrance to the Lodge… but with the ghouls and the magical locks, probably not one worth using, even if she ever wanted to return.

Abel crawled out last, then rose and dusted off his pants. Sanford said, "Let's be on our way–"

"Is that you, master?" A figure stepped out of the shadows by the fence near the street and approached them. Diana had her pistol out in a flash, but Sanford stepped into her line of fire, making Ruby hiss in frustration.

"*Altman*?" Sanford said, astonished. "How did you survive?"

The man stepped closer, head lowered, face hidden in a broad-brimmed hat. Then he removed the hat and smiled, and though there was nothing alarming about his visage, Sanford gasped and took a step back.

"Well, that's an interesting question. *Your* Altman wasn't quite dead when you jumped through that window, so Cain put the amulet around his neck, cut off his finger, and dropped it into the tub of sea water they'd prepared for you." The man spread his arms wide, and one of his hands held a strange, curved dagger. "They made *me*. After I rose from the water and gasped my first breath, they asked me if I knew of any secret escape routes out of the Lodge, and oh, I know them *all*."

Oh, Ruby knew this sinking sensation well: when she found an unexpectedly good lock on a door between her and her escape route, or when a police officer made his rounds on the street below just as she was about to lower herself from a ledge, or when a door clicked open and one of her victims came home early. Except, all those other times, she'd managed to get away. This time, she didn't see a way out, and that sinking feeling just *kept* sinking, deeper and deeper.

Diana started to shuffle around, trying to get a clear shot at the comet. Ruby saw that and took courage. They weren't done yet, were they? They'd made it through those tunnels. They could make it through this.

"You know about two-thirds of my escape routes, anyway," Sanford said. "Just my luck that you happened to know the one I picked. Tell me, is *my* Altman–"

"Killing him was my first act, but it was a mercy, with his face gone. You'll be coming with us, now, sir, you and your friends–"

"Shoot him, Diana," Sanford said.

But before Diana could comply, someone jumped from the hillside and landed on her back, driving her to her knees and sending the gun spinning away. Ruby caught a glimpse of Abel being pinned by two men – comets, they were all comets, pouring down the hillside. She ran for the gun. Before she could reach it, someone slammed into her from behind, and ground her face into the dirt.

"Careful!" Altman shouted. "One of them has the jar. Don't break it, Cain will have our heads!"

"I thought you could *sense* them," Sanford said.

Abel said, "Only the ones that come from Cain!"

Altman chuckled. "Of course we knew that, and planned accordingly – Cain plans for *everything*."

Sanford laughed and said, "Nonsense. He's an amateur. You should *know* that, Altman, if this so-called god hasn't addled your brain."

Ruby couldn't stand listening to them banter and bicker

anymore and shouted, "Shut up, shut up, shut *up!*" Then
someone slammed her head hard into the ground, and
everything went swimmy. When the person on her back
yanked her head up and pressed a handkerchief reeking of
chemicals to her nose, everything simply went *away*.

Ruby woke, groaning from an ether headache. "No credit
for originality," she muttered. This was twice in two days
she'd been knocked unconscious with a drug-soaked bit of
cloth. That couldn't be good for her brain. She hoped any
deleterious effects weren't cumulative.

She was tied to a chair, this time, so it wasn't quite the same
as the Berglunds' basement. It was *somebody's* basement,
though, stacked with dusty boxes and lit only by a bulb at
the foot of a wooden staircase. As far as she could tell, there
was no one down here with her, unless they were hiding
behind her. They must be holding Diana and Abel and, ugh,
Sanford somewhere else. Unless… they weren't holding the
others at all. Unless they were already dead. Ruby shook off
the dark thought. She had to solve her own predicament.
Then she could worry about her allies.

The ropes bound her wrists to the chair arms, and her
ankles to the chair legs, and another looped around her
chest, pinning her upper arms to her sides and securing her
to the chair back. She tried to fling her body weight to tip
the chair over, hoping the impact would break the wood
and set her free, but the chair was immovable. Tied to a post
behind her, maybe? Clever.

Ruby tensed against the ropes, testing for slack, but they
didn't have much give in them. Whoever tied her up this

time was a lot better at knots than the Berglunds had been. Maybe Cain himself had done the honors – he was a sailor, sort of, and sailors knew their way around ropes.

She moved every part of her body she could as far as she could and discovered that she *could* generate some slack around her wrists, but only at the expense of tightening the ropes around her chest – the lengths were all connected in some fiendish way. She'd squeeze the air out of her lungs before she got a hand free. She stomped her feet in frustrated fury, then forced herself to calm down.

She considered all the available options. The post the chair was tied to was immovable and unbreakable. Her body was breakable, but she preferred not to break it – if she could get loose without dislocating any fingers, that would be preferable. The weakest point she was *willing* to break was still the chair, which as far as she could tell was old, wooden, and not sturdy. When she wiggled as hard as she could, she heard creaking in the joints and felt a certain looseness.

Okay. This was going to be unpleasant. She bent forward, pressed down with her toes, and lifted her butt, bringing the chair as far off the ground as she could – which was only a couple of inches, given the lack of play in the ropes and the complication of the post. Then she slammed herself down, jarring her tailbone in the process. At least the resulting bang of chair legs on concrete wasn't very loud… though if it had been louder, it would have also been more effective, so bit of a mixed result there.

She rose again, and slammed the chair down again, and then repeated the process, to no avail. The ropes burned around her chest as she rose higher and sat down as hard as she could, forcefully enough to make her teeth snap together – and she was rewarded with a faint *crack* somewhere under the chair, though the structure didn't collapse.

Emboldened, Ruby banged down the chair again, and again, and that last time, there was a louder crack, and one of the arms came loose from the back. Once the chair's structural integrity was compromised to that degree, it didn't take many more repetitions before one of the legs snapped underneath her and the whole chair canted over, increasing the stresses on its weak joints. And on her joints, too, but her freedom was worth a little discomfort.

With a lot of twisting and grunting, Ruby managed to stand up, and she was – not free, exactly, but close. There were chair arms tied to her wrists and chair legs tied to her ankles, but now she had enough freedom of movement to reach the razor blade she'd sewn into the cuff of her left sleeve. Once she had that in hand, she made quick work of cutting one hand free, then the other, and then her legs.

Good. Now to deal with her greater confinement. She cast around the basement looking for weapons, and settled on a rusty old screwdriver she found on a cluttered workbench. Thus armed, she crept up the stairs with glacial slowness to avoid making the risers creak, and then listened at the door.

Two voices, both male, spoke. "…see why we're even keeping them alive."

"Cain wants to make a comet of Sanford after he's finished at the temple – says the old man knows all sorts of secrets we could use to protect our god. As for the others, we'll feed them to the Ravening Deep so they can suffer being digested for all eternity."

"All *eternity*?" The first voice sounded aghast. "Is that what happens?"

"That's what Cain says. If you go willingly into the maw as a sacrifice, you experience an eternity of bliss, but if you're an enemy of the true god, you wallow in acid forever, conscious and in pain."

"I'm glad I'm on the good side of our god, then," the first said. "I had no idea. I only just joined up yesterday. Well, I say joined up, I mean, came out of the brine. This is all new to me."

"I've been with Cain for almost two weeks," the other voice boasted. "I've been inducted into all the innermost mysteries." Ruby heard a chair creak as one of them rose. "We should go check on the old man and the dressmaker, see if they're awake yet."

"How about the other girl?"

"She's tied up *and* locked in a basement," the second voice said.

"Sure, but I heard she got away from the Berglunds–"

"They were fools, and she had help. Anyway, we're being extra careful with her this time. Come on. I'll check the Stanley woman, and you look in on the old man."

"The old man is *creepy*," the first voice whined.

"I know. That's why you're checking on him and not me. Seniority has its privileges."

Two sets of footsteps tromped off. She listened a bit longer to make sure they wouldn't come back, and that there wasn't a third person loitering, and then felt assured she had privacy.

Ruby considered the door. The lock was nothing much, but she couldn't exactly pick it with her fingers. She went back downstairs and dug around on the messy workbench until she found a mallet. She nipped back up, pressed the tip of the screwdriver into the crack of the door, right where the tongue of the lock fit into the groove. Then she slammed the end of the screwdriver with the mallet. The screwdriver's end popped the tongue free, splintering the doorjamb in the process. The door swung open easily after that. Usually cat burglars left as little trace as possible, but she cared about escaping now, not covering her tracks.

It turned out everything was easier when you were willing to break things.

Ruby slipped into the kitchen – and, wonder of wonders, her bag and Diana's were both resting side-by-side on the counter. The jar was gone, of course, and the gun was too, damn it… but Sanford's cane was leaning against the counter. His *sword* cane. Either they hadn't realized it was a weapon, or they hadn't bothered to lock it away. It was good to remember these comets weren't professional criminals, or soldiers, or police. They were ordinary civilians, albeit with supernatural powers and zeal, but they didn't have street smarts or guile.

Ruby had done a little fencing in school, and she drew the blade and gave it a couple of experimental swishes. The stick was weighted differently than an epee, but she would manage, even if she didn't know how to make the blade blaze with light.

She moved to the kitchen door, peered through the crack, then went shadow-soft into a living room lit only by a single dim lamp. The furniture here was shabby, the whole place filled with an air of neglect. The door to the outside world was unguarded, and there was even a key protruding from the lock, but to her surprise she wasn't tempted to flee. She wanted to save Diana first. Sanford, on the other hand, could save himself. The two men hadn't mentioned Abel, and Ruby feared that meant he was beyond saving, at least right now.

A narrow set of stairs led to the second floor. Ruby moved up with her usual silent swiftness and reached the landing, where she had her choice of two bedroom doors, both ajar. Voices were coming from the room on the left – one of them was Sanford, bored, saying, "You will be richly rewarded if you set me free, young man."

She wanted the one on the right, then. She moved on light feet to the other bedroom door and peeked inside.

Diana was on the bed, spread-eagled, wrists and ankles lashed to the bedposts with rope. She appeared unconscious. A man in a blue shirt with immense sweat stains in the armpits stood over her, head bowed. He reached out and caressed her cheek.

Ruby scowled and slipped into the room without a sound. His back was to her, and she lifted the sword… and then hesitated. She'd never killed anyone. She was a criminal, but she wasn't a murderer.

But this wasn't really homicide, was it? These weren't *people*. The people they looked like were dead, wrapped in tarps in basements all over Arkham. These were the monstrous spawn of a monstrous god.

So Ruby stepped forward, and stabbed him through the back. The sword seemed to thrum in her hand, shifting of its own mysterious volition, in order to pass cleanly through his heart and out the front of his chest. He fell to his knees and then slumped forward, forehead resting on the edge of an end table. Ruby pulled the sword out and stared at its bloody length.

Then Diana's eyes popped open – she'd been feigning sleep, it seemed. "*Ruby*," she said, astonished.

"We have to get out of here." Ruby tugged at the ropes on Diana's wrists, unwilling to use the sword to cut them – what if it decided to plunge into *Diana's* heart?

"We need to rescue Sanford first," Diana said.

"What? Why? He's the head of the Lodge, and you want to bring down the Lodge – why not let the comets help you?"

"Because Cain *took Abel*," Diana said. "They're going to the temple. And I think Sanford knows the way."

CHAPTER TWENTY
Into the Sea

Sanford was a hard man to drug, but he feigned unconsciousness after they were assaulted in the empty lot, hoping to pick up some useful information in the process. Listening to Altman's voice, but knowing it wasn't *really* Altman, troubled him greatly. He'd have to kill the twisted copy soon. It was the least he could do to honor the memory of a longtime comrade.

"I got the jar!" Altman crowed after his enemies were subdued. The other comets – there must have been eight or ten of them – cheered.

"I can *feel* it," a woman's voice said. "Let's see, let's see!" Then a hush, and a man's voice, low and suffused with wonder. "Look at those eyes. Asterias sees us. Our lord *sees us*."

"We should get this to Cain," the alternate Altman said. His voice was choked with emotion in a way the original's never had been. *That* Altman's capacity for reverence had been burned out of him long before, in the tunnels beneath Kashmir. "He wants to go to the temple right away, and begin the ritual."

"What do we do with the heretics?" the woman asked. A boot nudged into Sanford's ribs.

"They're to be sacrificed," Altman said. "Possibly inducted into the order first. Cain wants them alive for now. Let's get them over to Sonia's house. It's closest to the dock where Cain's boat is moored."

Sanford permitted himself to be carried and loaded into the back of a truck, like *cargo*, next to the unmoving bodies of his allies. They weren't the allies he would have chosen – the fool who'd started this cult in the first place, the thief who'd robbed the Lodge, and the Seeker who'd betrayed his trust – but he'd had stranger bedfellows over the year. The point was *outcomes*, and his outcomes now were a bit uncertain.

Sanford had certain gifts and capabilities, but he wasn't capable of overcoming eight comets possessed of superhuman strength and resilience, especially when one of them possessed all of Altman's memories, and knew many of Sanford's nastier tricks. It was a good thing Sanford had never mentioned his resistance to chloroform and ether – in truth, he possessed a general immunity to noxious gases, a gift he'd first acquired in order to visit a certain miasmic demi-realm. He would have to wait for a better moment to free himself and turn the tables on his enemies.

The truck trundled down bumpy streets for a short time, only fifteen minutes or so, and then they stopped, and Sanford was unloaded again. He cracked one eye, just a little, enough to see a row of short piers with boats moored here and there. They were near one of the small marinas along the river, just across from a row of shabby little houses, most darkened at this late or, rather, early hour. One of those shabby little houses was their destination, and Sanford allowed himself to be conveyed upstairs along with Diana Stanley. Ruby was carried off elsewhere on the ground floor, and Abel... Abel wasn't being taken into the house at all. Curiouser and curiouser.

Sanford's captors dumped him on a lumpy mattress, and then tied his arms and legs to the bedframe. That was a problem, but not an insurmountable one – Pain exploded on the side of Sanford's face and his head snapped to one side, forcing an involuntary gasp out of him. "Thought you were awake," Altman's voice said. "You breathe differently when you're *really* asleep, old friend." Then Altman's hands were around his throat, squeezing. Sanford did *not* possess any particular resistance to having the blood supply to his brain cut off. His vision clouded, fuzzing black at the edges, and then he saw no more.

Sanford woke some time later when his door creaked open, the sound stirring him from groggy underwater dreams. He didn't think he'd been unconscious for long, but he was disoriented, his mind a cloud of associations and sensations and thoughts arrayed in no particular order.

"Wake up, oh great one," a man said, and chuckled.

Sanford looked into the face of a young man with a wolfish grin. "You're an Initiate," he said, the force of his will allowing him clarity. "Ronnie Shiflet, isn't it? You joined last year."

"My father was a member, is the only reason," Ronnie said. "I thought the Lodge was a bunch of fusty old nonsense.

I would have never believed you had a *god* locked up downstairs." He shook his head. "Anyway, I'm not Ronnie Shiflet, or not exactly, anymore. You know that, unless Altman choked you so long you got brain damage. He said that was a possibility, but not to worry about it, because your *comet's* brain would be just fine."

"How reassuring," Sanford said. "Mr Shiflet, you have been press-ganged into a doomsday cult, and no sensible person wishes for doomsday. A world consumed in scarlet fire, or inundated by rancid water, or overrun by crawling monstrosities, is not a pleasant world in which to exist. Whereas the world, in its current state, can be pleasant indeed for those who have the right friends and resources. I am an excellent friend to have, and I possess ample resources." Sanford didn't think this approach was likely to work, since zealots were difficult to bribe, but if nothing else, he was stalling for time and fishing for information. Both were always good to have. "Whatever you hope to achieve, I can get it for you. You will be rewarded if you set me free, young man."

"I am not young," the comet said, eyes faraway and dreamy. "I am not a man. I am as ancient as the sea. I am the spawn of the Ravening Deep. You are meat for my god's hunger. I will watch you slide into the maw of Asterias, and I will cheer."

"That's very short-sighted of you," Sanford said. "Do you know your god's ultimate goal? If it can even be called a goal. A tumor doesn't have *goals* – it just grows until its host is consumed, and the beast you call god is the same."

"Asterias will devour this world," Ronnie said. "And when

it's done, the Ravening Deep will set out for the stars, and find new worlds to conquer."

Ah. That answered Sanford's curiosity about whether Asterias was native to this world, or a visitor from somewhere else. The latter, it seemed. How many dead worlds had the Ravening Deep left behind, covered in copies of itself? Or did *every* copy on a given world launch out into the universe, seeking new planets to consume? The universe was mostly clouds of gas and barren stones floating in the void – Sanford had learned that much from his contact with beings from beyond Earth – and it was heartening to think that most of the monsters would starve in the emptiness.

Sanford wrapped his hands around the ropes binding his wrists to the bedposts. He hated to expend more of his resources on something so trivial as escaping his captors, but it wasn't as if anyone *else* was going to step in–

Ronnie cocked his head at the sound of a muffled thump. "Did you hear something?" he asked.

"I heard a great load of nonsense pouring out of the mouth of a spoiled brat of a boy who never learned to honor his elders," Sanford said.

Ronnie's focus turned back to Sanford. "My elders? Ha. You mean my father? You mean *you*? Self-righteous, self-important, self-centered, the lot of you. I *am* respecting my elders – but only the ones worthy of respect. I'm respecting an elder g–"

He didn't finish the sentence, because Diana Stanley hit him on the back of the head with a heavy stoneware vase, and he fell. "Miss Stanley, how lovely to see you." Sanford was a trifle surprised they'd come for him. Unless they were here to kill him while he was restrained? No, they would have simply left him to his fate in that case. They'd more likely made the wise decision that they could use his help. "Perhaps you might untie me?"

Diana undid one wrist, while Ruby Standish untied the other. Then they released his legs. "My sword?" He held out his hand, and after a moment's hesitation, Ruby handed the weapon over. "Some blood on the blade, I see." He wiped it on the bedspread. "You killed the rest of our captors?"

"It was just these two," Diana said. "The rest of them... they're gone, master. Ruby heard them talking and–"

"Cain has taken Abel to the temple, to make him the first sacrifice to the restored Asterias?" Sanford guessed.

"Your guard must have been talkative." Ruby looked down at the unconscious comet.

Sanford stood up and walked around to the foot of the bed. "Oh, he didn't divulge anything useful. I merely surmised. Cain has all the necessary elements to enact his plan, so why would he hesitate?"

Diana put a hand on his arm. "Master. Mr Sanford." She took a breath. "*Carl.* We have to stop them. You wore the amulet, however briefly, and you were granted visions... Do you know the location of the temple?"

He patted her hand. She was holding up well, considering it was her first time embroiled in supernatural escapades of this magnitude. "Of course I do. Asterias *wants* to be found, to be revered, and to be revived. I suspect that anyone who dons that amulet is given enough information to help achieve those goals. The island temple is several miles off the coast, north by northeast. Nowhere near any land mass or significant shipping or fishing route, just an unremarkable bit of ocean."

"Can we get there?" Ruby said.

"I don't see why not." Sanford looked at the comet on the floor, and then stabbed him neatly through the heart. "There. No use giving mercy to creatures like these. They'll all have to be hunted down and killed anyway." He strode out of the room, toward the stairs, then paused when he realized he wasn't being followed. How tiresome. He returned and stood outside the bedroom door. Diana and Ruby had their heads together in some ferocious consultation. "Is there a problem? I assumed the two of you would be eager to save your friend, and save the world, and so forth?"

"You just stand up and act like you're in charge!" Ruby said. "You're *not* in charge. You were chased out of your own Lodge tonight, and barely escaped with your life."

"My life was in no danger."

"You were tied to this bed until we came! *I'm* the one who got Diana loose, and Diana knocked out your guard. You stabbed an *unconscious* person. You didn't escape. We set you free!"

"Hmm," Sanford said. "I was in the process of setting myself free, but, it's true, you saved me the trouble, and I should have said thank you. May we go now?"

Ruby seethed. Diana put a hand on her shoulder, and then looked into Sanford's eyes. "I think what Ruby means is, you shouldn't act like you are our leader. We are not your followers. We have been tangling with this cult since before you realized it existed. Ruby especially has proven herself adept at dealing with them."

"And Diana has been impossibly courageous and clever," Ruby said. "She's also been level-headed in situations that should have made her sanity crumble."

Sanford considered, then nodded. "You have both acquitted yourselves well, though of course I disagree with your tactics, and wish you'd just come to me in the first place… but I can understand why you didn't. With the nature of this cult, it is impossible to know who to trust." Altman's comet was still out there somewhere, a vicious reminder of that fact. "We are all working together now, and I… apologize… for my tendency to take the lead, and to expect unquestioning obedience. It's the force of a long habit, but in this case, you are not my followers, but my allies and collaborators."

"He finally noticed," Ruby said.

"A team!" he said. "A partnership, even. Sanford, Standish, and Stanfield." He chuckled. "We sound like partners in a law firm."

For some reason, that made the thief glower. Diana laughed and then covered her mouth. "I'm sorry. Ruby made the same joke not long ago, about our two names."

"Who knew we had so much in common, Miss Standish?" Sanford asked.

"Stop it." Ruby shuddered. "Don't make jokes. It makes you seem almost human."

"Of course I'm human." Sanford was actually offended. "I'm the best of what humans can be. So. Colleagues. With the acknowledgment that time is of the essence, let us discuss our next course of action."

"Thank you–" Diana began, but Ruby cut in.

"We need a boat. There are lots of them around, and while I've never stolen a boat before, I've stolen cars, and the principle is probably the same–"

"I own a boat," Sanford said. "No stealing necessary."

"We could also use weapons," Diana said. "They took our gun with them."

Sanford nodded. "Then we are doubly fortunate, because I have numerous weapons *on* my boat."

"Why?" Diana said.

"Oh, we had a spot of bother on the little island in the river recently." Sanford shrugged. "Certain artifacts there sometimes attract unsavory attention, and interlopers have to be discouraged. The problem was taken care of, but we left the weapons and ammunition locked up on my vessel. As I recall, we have a shotgun, two pistols, and even a so-called Tommy gun. A socialite-thief and a shopkeeper, though… do either of you have proficiency with firearms?"

"We both know our way around," Ruby said. "Maybe we'll leave the machine gun to you. And don't stand behind me while you're holding it, if you please."

Sanford nodded. "A capital ideal. So. The plan?"

"We get your boat," Diana said.

"We get the guns," Ruby said.

"And we kill Cain and the other cultists?" Sanford nodded. "Elegant in its simplicity. Ladies, please do lead the way."

Diana and Ruby left the room, and Sanford followed. That had wasted a few minutes – they could have just followed him, and he would have taken him straight to his boat anyway – but he needed allies, and if some nods toward collaboration kept them happy, it was worth the time.

The women collected their bags from the kitchen, and Sanford picked up the sheath for his sword-stick, and then peered out the front windows in case Cain had left guards. They detected no watchers, and slipped out. Dawn was closer than dusk now, but it was still deep night, and they moved through the shadows, along the grassy shoulder of the street that followed the river southeast. "I have a private boathouse less than a mile from here. I hope you don't mind if I lead us *there*, at least?"

"Ass," Ruby muttered, and Sanford smiled in the dark, where no one could see.

They walked silently through the quiet streets for a while until Diana said, "Do you think we'll make it in time?"

"In time for what?" Sanford said. "To stop them from beginning the ritual? I doubt it. I don't think the process is all that complicated. Asterias was only defeated in the first place because its followers were all massacred, and it had no one to restore it to health. I'm sure as soon as Cain reaches the temple, he will immerse that stolen piece of sea slime in the sacred pool and do all the necessary chanting and so forth."

"I feel like 'and so forth' is probably hiding a lot of gruesome details," Ruby said.

"Very astute, Miss Standish. I think the cultists will have to cut off several of their own digits, or even limbs, and throw them into the pool, to provide blood and flesh to catalyze the rebirth. That's what my vision suggested, anyway. Willingly offering their own flesh is crucial to the ritual. Gods do love sacrifice. I don't think we'll reach them in time to stop that part, unless Cain took a very slow boat indeed. But after the opening ceremonies, as it were… Asterias will grow, and the first thing it will grow is a *mouth*. I doubt it will take long, perhaps half a day, for the Ravening Deep to gain sufficient mass to include a hideous maw. Once it does…"

"That's when the cult will sacrifice Abel," Diana said.

"Abel will be the *amuse-bouche*," Sanford agreed. "The god will grow larger after that, and faster, and then the cult will bring other victims, and so on, until the delightful doomsday scenario my scholar in the basement outlined, when one god becomes two."

"We can stop *that* from happening," Diana said. "And we can save Abel, too."

"We can certainly try our best," Sanford agreed. "And if we fail, well, we'll die screaming in the mouth of an immense starfish, and after that, our failure won't bother us anymore."

It had been some time since he'd faced danger so directly, and he found himself exhilarated. He barely even matched wits with anyone anymore; almost everyone he met, he easily outmatched. Sanford didn't believe Cain was smarter than him, but the priest had many more resources and the backing of something akin to an actual god, which made it a challenge. Sanford had never yet met a challenge he couldn't overcome.

"You're assuming we'll die if Asterias eat us," Ruby said. "What if we're digested for eternity without ever losing consciousness? That's what one of the cultists said would happen."

"Hmm," Sanford said. That was a disturbing notion, even by his standards. "In that case, let us try our *very* best."

They reached the boathouse, a large wooden structure behind an abandoned cottage, but it had a good lock, and more subtle defenses in the form of certain sigils drawn on the interior walls. "Sadly, I do not have my keys with me. Miss Standish? Demonstrate your skills?"

She crouched before the lock. "My picks are still in my bag, luckily. I couldn't open this thing with hairpins. You splurged on good security." Even so, she opened the lock with distressing speed. Sanford put his hand against the wall and murmured a few words, disabling the other wards.

He opened the door and stepped inside, flipping on the electric lights he'd recently installed. The interior of the boathouse was spacious and well appointed, with lockers and benches along one wall, but the eye was drawn instantly to the motorboat itself, one of his many prides and joys, a sleek four-seater of dark wood and gleaming steel.

"Ladies, this is the *Silver Key*. Eighteen feet long, handcrafted with a bonded wood hull, metal trim, and seats cushioned in marine leather. The inboard motor was built by an acquaintance of mine who makes his living designing engines for aircraft." He knelt and ran his hand along the shining black wood of the bow. "I usually take her out on the river – she's a close-shore vessel, not meant for the open sea – but there are various... augmentations... built into her structure to prevent her from capsizing or taking on water. Should make her suitable for a brief sea voyage."

"You have a magic boat," Ruby said.

Sanford sighed. "Must you be so reductive–"

Ruby held up her hands. "No! I am *excited* that you have a magic boat. Are the guns magic, too?"

Sanford climbed into the back of the boat and patted a locked panel behind the rear seats. "Gunpowder was first made by alchemists. So, in a sense. Do you think you could open this, too, Miss Standish?"

She retrieved her picks and obliged, and they looked down at the weapons stored neatly inside, with ample boxes of ammunition alongside them. And not *just* guns, either. "Wait," Ruby said. "Is that…?"

"Yes," Sanford said. "It could be useful, don't you think?"

"I daresay," Ruby murmured. "I do love a day out on the water."

"Let us hope we don't end the day *under* the water," Sanford said. "Miss Stanley, if you'll help me open the doors? We can prepare for departure."

CHAPTER TWENTY-ONE
The Temple

Abel woke in the dark with his nostrils full of fish stink. He tried to sit upright, and couldn't – he was tied in loops of rope, lying on his side, cheek pressed against wooden boards. The one arm pinned underneath him was numb, and he managed to roll over on his back to relieve the pressure. The floor was rocking slightly, and rumbling. He was on a boat, under engine power. From the stink, it was a working fishing boat, or had been before Cain commandeered it.

Metal hinges squealed as a hatch opened in the ceiling, though no light poured in, so it must still be night. A man – no, almost certainly a comet – climbed down the ladder, carrying a lantern that cast a weak and wavering light across the hold. He hung the lantern on a hook and turned to look down on Abel.

"Hello, son," Abel croaked. He was incredibly thirsty.

"I am not your child." Cain spat onto the floor beside Abel's head.

"More like a grandchild, it's true. Seth was your father. He was twice the man you are, even if he was only half the man I am." Abel laughed. He was going to die – quite soon, probably – but he wouldn't give this copy of a copy the satisfaction of seeing his fear. "What did you do with Ruby and Diana?"

Cain sat down cross-legged beside him, the amulet dangling around his neck on a golden chain; he'd upgraded his jewelry. Cain said, "I understand why you fled. You were usurped, after all. Bested by a younger man."

"*Much* younger," Abel said. "And not a man. If you were a human, you wouldn't even be old enough to eat solid food yet."

Cain ignored him. "You went groveling into the shadows, to lurk on the outskirts of Arkham, and that was appropriate, for someone in your position. But to actively work *against* us? That I cannot understand. You sought allies, you plotted, and you nearly succeeded in stealing Asterias from us. But why? You were the first prophet. You have seen the glory that is to come. Our god gave you strength. Saved your life. I remember all the things you do – the awe we felt, standing in the temple."

"You've never stood in the temple. You're a growth. A wart with legs."

Cain took no notice. "I remember the gratitude we felt, to be spared from death. Those feelings inspire nothing but devotion in me. Yet somehow, they fail to inspire the same thing in you. You turned against your savior. Why?"

"Because you're horrible monsters who want to feed the whole world to an even *more* horrible monster. And if you can't understand that, then I can't explain it to you any more clearly."

"Too human." Cain caressed Abel's cheek with one of his transformed hands, the fingers wriggling tentacles and crooked crab legs and rough starfish. Abel couldn't stop himself from trying to flinch away, and Cain gripped him firmly by the face. "You could have been the best of us. You know I hate you – you can see the hate, I'm sure – but I don't think you can see the sorrow. Making you the first sacrifice to the Ravening Deep is not a punishment. It is an honor, Abel. It is recognition for your role in bringing this to pass – in bringing *me* to pass. You will be the god's first meal in centuries, and you will give Asterias strength." Cain released him.

Abel took a ragged breath. "If I'm such an honored guest, give me a drink of water. Unless you want me to die of thirst before you kill me."

"We brought no fresh water. Why would we? We are creatures of the salt. But even a human can survive some time without water. You will not die before you serve your purpose. Here. Let me show you, so you can savor the anticipation of what awaits you."

Before he could object, Cain pressed the amulet against Abel's face. The cool metal touched his cheek, but then it seemed to *move*, like tiny tendrils were writhing against his skin. Abel tried to jerk away, but Cain held his head with a grip made inhumanly strong.

Abel whimpered as his vision went black, and then filled with new lights and colors. This vision was different from the ones before – those were memories, mainly, of the devotees and priests who'd come before him. This was hazy and blurred, and Abel understood that this was a vision of the *future*, or at least, a possible one – the future the Ravening Deep wished for.

Abel's point of view hovered somewhere near the ceiling, looking down on the scene.

Cain and six of his acolytes stood in a dark chamber of stone and coral, the walls lit by flickering torches. A rough oval pool filled most of the floor, its depths sparkling with eerie yellow-green light from glowing algae, like festering stars. Cain gently laid the fragment of Asterias atop a stone in the center of the pool, then stood with the rest of his kin. The comets drew blades – knives, shears, clippers – and methodically cut off the fingers of their left hands, scattering the blood droplets into the water. When the blood sank, the water *rippled*, the fragment of Asterias twitching, and extending tiny, threadlike tentacles to gather in the blood. Then the cultists cast their severed fingers into the pool, too, and more tendrils whipped out, curling around the bloody digits and pulling them inward as the acolytes began to chant.

The fragment of Asterias *swelled*, like a balloon being slowly inflated. It rippled, growing new appendages, first as stubby as thumbs, but lengthening, until finally it had turned the flesh of those severed fingers into seven arms, spotted with small eyes. The tentacles stretched out languidly, and all the eyes rolled.

"More," Cain cried, "our god needs more!" The acolytes exchanged glances, then knelt, helping one another saw off the fingers of their right hands as well, each in turn, until only one remained who could hold a knife. Cain drew a hatchet from his belt, impatient, and chopped the whole hand off the last one, throwing it spinning into the pool. The other acolytes pushed their fingers in as well, and let their bleeding hands drip over the water, feeding their god from themselves and continuing the chant.

Why don't they pass out? Abel wondered from his floating vantage, but he knew: they were not human. They were comets, and could take tremendous punishment. They would carve themselves down to nothing if that was what Asterias desired. He tried to move, to change his viewpoint, but he couldn't seem to alter anything, and even his desire to do so drained away after a moment. He was detached, disassociated, his true self with all its fears and worries and desires located some distance away at the end of a long, long tether.

The monstrosity in the pool grew larger, from several inches across to several feet, its seven arms thickening and rippling and reaching out for the edges of the pool. Asterias was purplish-black, its flesh warty and pebbled, and dotted all over with eyes. The eyes grew, too, as the body of the monster did, expanding from the size of shirt buttons to the size of human orbs, and then even larger. Some of the eyes had whites and pupils and irises in colors you might see in any person's face, but other eyes were red, or black, or yellow, and some had horizontal pupils, and some vertical, and some were shaped like barbells or S-curves. *It has the eyes of everything it's ever eaten,* Abel thought, and knew it was true: an insight granted him by the touch of the amulet. The eyes of devoured humans, and Deep Ones, and every sort of sea creature unlucky enough to stray close to the maw, or to be tossed into it.

That meant *Abel's* eyes would look out from that hideous pebbled hide, in time. The thought should have brought horror, but he considered it with the same detachment he did the rest of the vision. Asterias had etherized his fear. In its place there was only curiosity: would some part of Abel himself remain after he was devoured, his mind alive inside, seeing what Asterias saw? The amulet did not give him an answer to that, and Abel understood that Asterias wanted him to wonder about the possibility instead. He knew the idea would torment him later.

A slit formed in the center of the monster's mass, then opened into a ragged circle filled with teeth and waving tendrils that unfurled like a score of prehensile tongues to pull the last few floating bits of cultist-flesh into the Ravening Deep's maw. The mouth widened. It widened further. It widened... enough.

"It is time," Cain intoned, and suddenly Abel's vision went black. At the same time, all that detachment vanished, and the accumulated fear slammed into him like a breaking wave. Asterias had only held it back to toy with him. Abel would have screamed, if he'd had a mouth to scream with. He tried to swim back to consciousness, but it didn't work, because the vision wasn't *over* – his perspective shifted instead. Now, rather than being a bodiless observer, he felt like himself, kneeling on stone, arms bound roughly behind him, a sack of stinking canvas covering his head. The cloth was ripped away, and Abel blinked, seeing out of his own eyes now, looking up at Cain.

The priest of the Ravening Deep had given up his pretense of humanity, his face wide open, revealing his maw-in-miniature to match the larger one in the pool. His sliced-off fingers had already regrown, each one now a rope composed of dozens of intertwined tendrils. He reached down, seizing Abel under the armpits, and dragged him to his feet.

"No, no," Abel whimpered. In the past he'd hidden his terror of Cain behind a façade of courage and contempt, but now those bulwarks crumbled. He tried to tear himself away, but Cain was too strong, here in the heart of the temple, wearing the amulet – his power was growing *with* that of his god, and he could not be resisted.

Cain dragged Abel to the edge of the pool, the bleeding and maimed zealots moving aside to open a path. He shoved Abel forward, then grabbed onto his arms, still tied behind his back. Cain let Abel dangle, leaning over the pool, his arms screaming in their sockets from the agony of the position. Cain lowered him slowly, slowly, until Abel was looking directly down into the open maw. All of the Ravening Deep's dozens of eyes were fixed on his face. Abel imagined Asterias growing, spreading, expanding beyond the pool, covering yards, and acres, and everything.

"You could have been the one feeding the god," Cain said. "Instead, you are the food."

"No," Abel said again, and then a hundred tendrils burst forth from the revived god's maw and broke the surface of the water. The slimy appendages wrapped around Abel's body, his neck, his face – every tendril a burning line of acid – and yanked him out of Cain's grip, down into the waiting mouth of the Ravening Deep–

Abel screamed and rolled away, breaking contact with

the amulet. He thrashed in his ropes, bucking wildly on the floor of the hold, sobbing and whimpering.

Cain laughed. "You see? You *see*, Abel, apostate, heretic, blasphemer? Our god knows the future. He knows what will be. He knows what *you* will be." Cain crawled across the deck, his face opening up to reveal that horrible gaping gnashing hunger at the center. His voice still emerged, somehow unchanged. "And what you will be is *breakfast*." Cain stood up. "You asked about Diana and Ruby. They'll be lunch and dinner. Sanford will be dessert. We want to make copies of them first, though, so they'll have to wait. Being fed to the Ravening Deep by better versions of *themselves* will be particularly humiliating… as you'll soon experience yourself."

Abel closed his eyes and rolled away, shuddering. He could still feel every line of those burning tendrils. He could still feel the cold of the water when he was pulled in.

He could still feel the first bite.

Cain went back up the stairs, laughing all the way, leaving Abel to the darkness.

Eventually the phantom pains from the vision faded. Abel tried to wriggle out of his ropes, but they were too secure – he could tie knots well, and Cain could do anything he could do, and more.

His attempt to escape was more a salve to his pride than anything else. Even if he did get free, what would he do? He was on a boat, doubtless miles out to sea. The best he could do would be to leap over the side, and without the power of Asterias to lend him strength, he would drown. Of course, a death in the merciless sea would be preferable to a death in the guts of a monster, but either way, his death wouldn't do any *good*. Maybe he'd find a moment in the temple to make a move – in the vision only his arms had been tied, and he knew Cain would follow the dictates of that vision like scripture, sure he was fulfilling a prophecy. If he could run away... free his hands... get the amulet away from Cain... snatch the fragment of Asterias before it could be fed with blood and quickened... If, if, if.

At least Abel's friends were still alive – Cain had no reason to lie about that. But how long before Diana and Ruby found themselves in the same position he was in, tied up in the hold of a boat, heading for certain doom? Perhaps *they* could escape. They were resourceful and quick-thinking – both had proven that more than once. Sanford was with them, too, and there was no telling what secrets he had hidden up his well-tailored sleeves.

"There's still hope," he murmured. His friends might make it out. They might even help. He needed to believe they would.

And because he believed, he would do everything he could to distract and delay Cain, to give his friends more time to save him.

By the time the priest came back down into the hold, his face was folded up again, and Abel had wriggled up into a sitting position with his back against the wall. He regarded Cain placidly. "Come for another chat?" he said. "The first one was so enjoyable for both of us."

Two acolytes, both unknown to Abel, came down the ladder too, and dragged him to his feet. "We're almost there," Cain said. "We thought you'd like to see landfall."

The acolytes untied his legs and prodded him up the

ladder, which was hard going without his hands to help. Two more cultists waited at the top to drag him up onto the deck and march him to the railing. They were on a single-masted fishing boat, the boards gray and the metalwork scuffed and tarnished. "You couldn't get your hands on a yacht?" Abel said when Cain emerged from the hold. "This seems a bit beneath you."

Cain ignored him. "Bring him to the bow. I want him to see his fate approach."

It was after dawn, the sun low off the starboard side, and the sky was almost cloudless. Light blue above, darker blue below, and they were riding the line between. *I can't believe there was a time I truly loved the ocean,* Abel thought.

The acolytes led him up front and then stepped back, leaving him to stand beside Cain. Being so close to the priest made Abel's skin crawl. The temple was there on the horizon, an unlovely spire of rock like a crooked finger emerging from the waves. "The ledge and entrance to the temple proper are on the far side," Cain said to the comet manning the helm. "Take us around." The captain obliged, and the boat began a slow curve to loop around the spire.

"It's just a bit of rock covered in guano," Abel said. "To think there was a time it looked like salvation to me."

"It was your salvation, heretic. Soon it will be your doom." Cain leaned on the railing, radiating eagerness. Abel was surprised he didn't jump over the railing and start swimming toward the temple. The boat made its way around to the far side and Cain swore.

There was another boat, a small motorcraft not suited for oceangoing, bobbing nearby. He burst out laughing, his first thought that Diana and Ruby had somehow beaten him here, but that didn't make sense. Cain glared at him, then began shouting at his acolytes. "Prepare for landing! Someone got here before us, and we must–"

A gunshot cracked the air, and Cain spun around, blood flying from his left side. Abel dropped to the deck, flattening himself as best he could. Was it Ruby and Diana after all? No, they wouldn't have fired a gun while Abel was so close to their target. Sanford would, though, or people who worked for him, dispatched here to stand guard?

Cain sat up, clutching his left arm. "Who's *shooting* at us?" he shouted. "Start shooting back!"

The comet called Altman crawled toward them across the deck, expression more determined than afraid. Once he was close enough to speak to them, he said, "We don't have a clear shot, Cain. He's got the spire for cover. What I propose is, I'll slip into the water, swim over, climb up the side, and see if I can get the drop on him."

"Go, go!" Cain snarled.

Altman crawled to the side of the deck and slithered over the side, disappearing from view.

"Didn't see this in your visions, did you?" Abel said. "If he'd been a better shot, he'd have splattered your brains all over the deck. I don't think even Asterias could heal *that*. I guess Altman would take up the amulet, in that case, and continue the great work–"

"Shut *up*," Cain hissed, and then dropped to the deck as another shot fired.

"Go away!" a reedy voice shouted. "This is sacred land, and I claim sanctuary!" Another gunshot, this one wild.

"Who the hell is that?" Cain said.

Abel laughed. "You have all my memories, and you don't recognize that voice?"

Cain stared at him for a long moment. "No. The *professor*?"

"We thought he drowned himself," Abel said. "But I guess he just swam away, and found a boat, and made his own pilgrimage."

"He's defending the temple." Cain shouted, "Stillwater, you idiot, it's *us*!"

A moment later, there was another shot, and then Altman's voice, booming: "It's safe. Bring in the boat."

After an interminable period – for Cain; Abel relished every moment of delay – they moored their boat alongside Stillwater's smaller craft. They used his motorboat as a stepping stone to reach the temple, and soon the broad, flat ledge was crowded with acolytes, and Abel, still with his arms tied.

Professor Stillwater was sitting on the stony floor, blood running down his face, one arm hanging at a terrible angle. Altman stood over the comet, holding an old hunting rifle. "I came to pledge myself," Stillwater mumbled. "I made obeisances at the altar. I made sacrifices." He held up one hand, short a few fingers. "I have been *loyal*, I have been *devoted*, I am sorry, I did not know, I did not know you were also the faithful–"

"Stillwater," Cain said. "Look." He snapped his fingers, and one of his acolytes reached into a leather bag and drew out a familiar jar. "Look what we've brought."

He held up the jar, and Stillwater gasped. "You brought Asterias *home*!" He struggled upright, and Altman shifted the gun, but Cain shook his head, stepped forward, and embraced the professor.

"We should never have doubted your faith," the priest said. Stillwater sobbed tears of joy. "Let us make our way below, and restore our god."

Abel took advantage of everyone's distraction and kicked the nearest cultist in the knee, making him collapse – and slide right off the slimy rock into the sea. Altman lifted his rifle again, but Cain said, "No, we need him alive!"

"In that case," Abel said, and kicked another cultist, this one between the legs, causing him to clutch himself and howl. Before Abel could do any further damage, two other acolytes pushed him down to his knees.

Altman stepped before him, rifle in hands. "Should I smash him over the head, and let him nap until he's needed?"

"No," Cain said. "Just put the sack over his head. He won't be able to lash out if he can't see." A cultist handed Altman a canvas bag, and the comet grinned as he tugged it down over Abel's head, cutting off his vision.

"Let's get started," Cain said. "First we go up, and then we go down."

Abel was dragged to his feet and yanked roughly forward. He tried to resist, flopping his body and becoming dead weight, but the comets were too strong. He slowed them down, though – free-climbing up that tower of rock to the cave entrance while carrying an unwilling body was difficult even for the preternaturally strong. Abel thought he could prevent their ascent entirely, until Cain finally barked orders and the cultists rigged a rope harness they secured around Abel's chest and under his arms. They *dragged* him up the rocky spire, sharp edges of coral ripping into his flesh and making him bleed in two dozen places.

Death by a thousand scrapes, he thought, and almost giggled. When they paused in their pulling, probably to adjust their grips on the rope, he planted his feet on the wall and pushed off as hard as he could. Someone above shouted, and Abel dropped a few precipitous feet, then banged into the stone tower. He did laugh then. "Careful up there!" he yelled. "Precious cargo here!"

"Just get him up here!" Cain snarled.

Soon after – too soon – they hauled Abel over a ledge and dragged him into the little cave. His sack slipped and tore half off his head in the process, and he caught a glimpse again of the altar, the star on the wall, and the hole in the floor. The place, which had once been so eerie and grand, looked like nothing special to him now. It was a ruin, and one best left to its slow work of decay.

Then someone jammed the bag down on his head again, and the cultists manhandled him down a set of spiral stairs. The hole in the center of the chamber floor, the one he'd glanced into the first time, and only seen darkness – it was actually a passageway to the chambers below. Had there *always* been stairs in that hole? Surely he would have noticed them. Or had the stairs... grown, in response to the return of the temple's god?

Whatever their origin, the stairs went on and on, and Abel made the cultists fight for every step, and in return, they bashed him against the walls until his bones ached. Eventually the passage leveled out, and he heard the hiss of matches being lit. Someone forced him to his knees, down onto hard, damp stone. "You just wait here," Altman whispered in his ear.

It was the voice of hopelessness and despair.

There were murmurings, and shufflings, and gasps, and chanting. Abel couldn't see what was happening, but he didn't need to. He'd seen it already. He'd seen it all in his vision.

And he knew how it would end. Unless Ruby and Diana could somehow change his fate.

CHAPTER TWENTY-TWO
The Ravening Deep

Diana, Ruby, and Sanford crouched low as the *Silver Key* motored toward the temple spire and the two boats moored there. They were prepared for resistance. "My boat is bulletproof," Sanford said. "Among its many other fine qualities. Alas, the two of you are not. Stay behind the windscreen, and keep those guns ready."

Diana watched the temple grow larger, a pistol clutched in her hand. The rocky island was just as Abel had described it, only without even a hint of majesty – it was just a finger of stone and coral pointed at the sky, the whole isle no bigger than the gazebo in Independence Square. She was tensed for a gunshot, or at least a shout, but no one seemed to take notice of their coming but the crying gulls.

Sanford circled around the spire, approaching the side of the rock where the other boats were moored, one good-sized fishing vessel and one small motorboat. "You know, they might not have beaten us here by much, if that was their transport," Sanford mused. "We're a lot faster than they are. I will slightly revise my estimate of Abel's chances of survival."

"Don't ask him to put a number on that chance, Diana," Ruby said. "I'm afraid it will still be depressing." She rose a little, peering at the bobbing boats and the flat shelf of rock beyond. "Why isn't anyone trying to kill us? Didn't they leave any sentries?"

"Perhaps not. Imagine that the god you adore above all else, even above the value of your own life, is about to be reborn downstairs. Would *you* agree to stay above on guard duty, and miss the blessed event? Cain could have insisted, and I'm sure his acolytes would have obeyed, however reluctantly, but…" He shook his head. "These priests of… eldritch faiths… have a tendency toward overconfidence."

"Because they believe their god is on their side," Diana said.

"Exactly," Sanford said. "I know you can't trust gods at all, and they're best avoided entirely, unless you have considerable leverage over them."

"I love hubris." Ruby checked her shotgun's load. There was a pistol tucked into her purse, too, which she wore across her chest like a bandolier. "It always makes my job so much easier. What's the plan?"

Sanford smiled. He might have been discussing a garden party. "We will descend into the lower chamber, and kill everyone we see." He guided the *Silver Key* alongside the smaller of the cult's crafts, then picked up a pistol. "The tommy gun would have been useful for a fight up here, if the comets had been waiting to drive us away, but I'd rather not take a machine gun into an undersea temple."

"You're leaving your sword-stick?" Diana asked. It was hard not to view the weapon as a sort of lucky charm, since it had dispatched multiple comets and a ghoul as well. She was reluctant to give up any advantage available. They were going into a dark place populated by unknown terrors, and the only thing that kept her from hyperventilating with fright was the fact that she'd seen how competent and cool her companions could be under fire.

"The sword would be unwieldy in confined quarters, which we're about to find ourselves in. I have a dagger, if close work becomes necessary." Sanford rose and stepped to the edge of the *Silver Key*.

"Don't we need to tie up your boat?" Ruby said. "Or do you usually have people to do that for you?"

"This vessel won't go anywhere without my leave," Sanford said. "You must understand, I don't have the same little worries that other people do." He used the smaller craft as a stepping stone to reach the flattish ledge on the island, and waited there impatiently.

Diana was about to follow when Ruby touched her arm, then swept her into a hug – awkwardly, as they were both holding weaponry. "Hey," she said. "Are you all right?"

"I don't know," Diana admitted. "Sanford is a sorcerer, and you're a cat burglar. Both of you are *good* at things like this. But I'm just a shopkeeper who has bad dreams."

Ruby leaned away from her, looked at her for a moment, then laughed in disbelief. "Are you serious? Diana. You tricked our way into the Lodge. You faced down a shoggoth. Before any of that, you decided to take on Sanford and his cult yourself, without allies, without help, without any idea where to begin. You're *so* much more than just a shopkeeper. You astonish me."

Tears welled in Diana's eyes. Had anyone ever believed in her the way Ruby did? "Thank you."

"You're welcome. I need that fearless, dedicated Diana now." Ruby clutched her close. "How does that speech go? We few, we happy few, we band of – well, sisters, this time, if two can make a band." She stepped back. "You dragged me into all this, and I don't even hate you for it. It's been good to work with someone, and toward something important, for once."

Diana was touched. "I'm glad you stuck with us. I'll watch your back, and you'll watch mine, and we will win through. We *have* to."

"We'd better go before Sanford kills them all without us." Ruby followed Sanford, and Diana came after, picking her way with care. Apart from the odd fishing trip in a rowboat, she didn't have much experience with watercraft, and after this week, she was in no hurry to change that. Finally all three of them stood on the rocky island, looking at the tide pool in its center, bereft of life.

Ruby said, "Where's the *door*?"

Sanford gestured to the tower of rock. "We have to climb. It looks simple enough – though someone found it more difficult, judging by the smears of blood."

"I bet it's Abel's," Diana said. "He wouldn't have gone up that tower willingly."

"Could be," Sanford allowed. "I'll go up first, Ruby, and then you can come halfway, and Diana can hand the shotgun up to you, and then to me–"

Someone hauled himself over the ledge, dripping sea water and gasping, startling all of them, even Sanford, to back up a step. Ruby even plunged one boot into the tidepool. A man none of them recognized sprawled, sputtering and coughing, facedown on the rock.

"That fool broke my knee," he growled, eyes squeezed shut. "I could hardly swim, the pain is terrible, and I thought I was going to drown, but praise the Deep, water cannot kill me now–" He tilted his head and opened one eye and stared up at them, then froze.

Sanford knelt and his hand lashed down and back up again, sprouting a dagger somewhere in the process. The man gurgled from a hole in his neck. "Still vulnerable to death by dagger, it seems." Sanford placed a foot against the comet's side and shoved, rolling the cultist back into the sea. "I suppose the fool who broke his knee was Abel," Sanford said. Diana stared at the blood on the rocks, stunned by the sudden ferocity of the violence. "I didn't have the chance to get the measure of Mr Davenport, but it seems he has a bit of steel in him. Good." He wiped his dagger on the leg of his trousers and tucked it away. "Shall we?"

Several difficult minutes of climbing later, Diana pulled herself over a ledge and into a small tunnel, which led into a large chamber. Too large. "Remarkable," Sanford murmured. "Even in death, the power of Asterias persisted in these profane geometries, twisting space to suit its needs."

There was no guard present in the upper chamber, either, but a rifle leaned against the altar, testament to the presence of violent people. The three of them spent a moment looking around in wonder at the luminous growths on the walls, the chipped effigy of Asterias carved on the wall, the altar with its briny font, and the almost perfectly circular hole in the chamber floor. A narrow stairway spiraled down, with no guardrail to protect those descending from a long tumble if they should lose their footing. When Diana listened hard, she thought she heard snatches of rhythmic voices – chanting?

"I have a fair bit of dynamite on the boat," Sanford said, with the air of one making dinner-party conversation.

Diana frowned. "Really?"

"Several sticks," Ruby said. "I saw them, tucked in with the guns and ammunition. Neat little cylinders, just like in the movies."

"I didn't notice those," Diana said. "You explained why you had guns, Sanford, but why on earth did you need dynamite?" When she thought of Sanford, she thought of manipulation and finesse, not blowing things up.

"That trouble I mentioned, on the island in the river. There are standing stones there. I thought it might be necessary to remove a few of the stones – or at least alter their specific spatial relationships. Fortunately, we were able to address the problem with less violence. Here, though we could simply toss a few sticks down this shaft, flee to the boat, and collapse the temple on top of the cultists. Problem solved, don't you think? And without a bullet wasted."

"Abel is down there," Diana said. "We have to save him."

Sanford shrugged. "Very well. It's possible the cultists and some piece of Asterias would survive the cave-in anyway, so I suppose it's for the best. You should go down first, I think, Ruby."

Ruby nodded, and Diana said, "Why?"

"I have the shotgun," Ruby said. "A gun like that, it's better to have up front."

"And I refuse to stand in front of Miss Standish while she holds *any* gun," Sanford said. "I don't trust her to hold her fire if I'm standing between her and her target."

Ruby rolled her eyes. "I'm not going to kill you, Sanford. We're working together now. You have to trust the people in your crew."

"Trust?" he said. "I've heard that word before. I believe it was... yes, in the nursery, where I learned the moon was made of green cheese, and Father Christmas brings gifts to good little children, and the monster under the bed isn't real, and other pretty lies."

"We have to trust one another," Diana said, so firmly that Sanford's eyebrows shot up. "If we don't stand together, Cain will pick us off separately."

After a moment, he nodded. "I apologize again. I am not used to collaborating. To partners. But... very well. Trust. At least until all this is finished. I'll take the middle, then, as a show of faith that Diana won't shoot me in the back."

"I won't, Carl," she said. *At least until all this is finished.* Sanford was helping them save the world now, but it was hardly altruism, just a different flavor of self-interest. She meant what she said, though: they had to work together for the moment. That was Abel's only hope; it was the world's only hope.

Ruby went down the stairs, moving silently, shotgun at the ready. If she was nervous about slipping and falling, she didn't show it. Sanford went next, just as light on his feet. They were different people, but they were both at home dancing on the edge of the abyss. All Diana had ever wanted was peace and comfort, safety and security… but the world demanded more, and she would meet the challenge.

She straightened her spine, steeled herself, and followed her allies down, into the dark.

They descended in silence for long minutes, the air growing cool and damp. They had to be far below the surface of the waves, now, and the walls began to shimmer with condensation, the stone steps growing slick and treacherous. Sanford was just a dark shape ahead of her, and Ruby was entirely out of sight. Diana kept one hand on the wall and followed the regularity of the spiral down, down, down – And finally detected a hint of light, flickering and irregular, and a whiff of smoke. Torches? She almost bumped into Sanford, who whispered, "We're at the bottom. Careful now. Spread out."

He was leading again, but she let it pass, because it was good advice. Her eyes adjusted to the gloom. They'd reached a new chamber, connected to a wide passageway lit by a torch in a stone niche on the wall. That passage led in turn to a rough archway that doubtless gave access to the ritual chamber. Lights flickered beyond, and a droning chant rumbled–

Interrupted by Abel bellowing, at full volume and off-key: "And when we came to Greenland where the bitter winds did blow, we tacked about all in the north among the frost and snow! Our fingertips were frozen off, and likewise our toenails!"

"Is he *singing*?" Ruby whispered as Diana stifled a laugh. It was the same tune he'd been singing the night she found him.

"An old whaling song, I believe," Sanford said.

"Will someone shut him *up*!" Cain's voice shouted, which only made Abel sing louder. There was a loud slap, and the singing cut off. "Begin again!" Cain demanded. "And if he starts caterwauling again, just ignore him. Don't let him distract you from the rites!"

"Didn't see any of *this* in your visions, did you?" Abel bellowed.

"Good old Abel," Ruby said, and lifted her shotgun. "Let's get this done." Before Diana could object, she marched off toward the arch, and Sanford flowed after her, like a quicksilver shadow. Was he actually harder to *see* than he had been a moment ago? More magic? She couldn't quite focus on him.

Diana came last, gun up, telling herself she was ready. She stepped through the arch and…

Oh, Lord. The stone room; the figures in robes; the torches on the walls. It was different, but all too familiar. For a moment, she was *back there*, in the summoning chamber beneath the Lodge, a blade in her hand, and the past was more real than the present.

Then Abel cried out again, and she snapped back to reality, and there was no knife in her hand; there was a gun. She looked around the chamber and counted targets. There were seven cultists arrayed in a semicircle, facing away from them: Cain in the center, with three on either side. They were dressed in hooded garments, but not the black silks and velvets favored by the higher levels of the Order of the Silver Twilight – these robes were made of sailcloth and canvas and netting.

Ruby wasted no time. She walked up to the chanting line of cultists and fired at short range, catching two of them in the backs with the blast. One went spinning into the wall, and the other dropped into the wide pool in the center of the cavern. The gunshot was so loud in the confined space that it physically staggered Diana.

Then she saw a man kneeling on the stones with a bag over his head, a cultist standing beside him, holding an axe. It was Cornelius Berglund – *one* of the Berglunds, anyway – and Diana shouted "No!" as he lifted his axe high, about to split Abel's head like a log.

She raised her pistol and fired, missing his chest but catching him in the right shoulder, making him drop the axe and bellow. Abel flung himself to one side, trying to roll away, the bag over his head slipping partway off in the process. One of his blue eyes gazed at her with wonder.

Berglund lurched toward the axe, reaching with his good arm. Diana forced herself to stop, set herself, and lift the pistol in the two-handed grip her father had taught her so long ago, plinking away at bottles and cans in the back field. Back then, she could hit what she aimed at more often than not, at least when she set her mind to it. She took a breath, let it out, and squeezed the trigger.

The top of the comet's head came off, and he fell into the wall. A cool, calm part of Diana's mind thought, *A little high, but good enough.* Then she rushed to Abel, ignoring the shouting behind her. She had a pocketknife in her bag, and she flipped it open and sawed through the ropes. "You came," Abel said, shaking out of the ropes.

She smiled, even as mayhem unfolded at her back. "We couldn't very well let the world end, could we?"

"I suppose not." He stood, glanced past her at the chaos, and then picked up Berglund's axe. "I want to get a few licks in before Ruby finishes them off."

Diana rose and looked at the fray. Two cultists were coming their way, armed with long knives, and Abel went to fend them off with wild swings of the axe. Ruby was backing away from one cultist while reloading her pistol – with her blood-streaked face, in the flickering torchlight, she looked like a warrior queen.

Sanford, predictably, had gone for the glory. He stepped over the body of a dead cultist and advanced on Cain. The magus was still blurry and hard to focus on in the low light. The priest stood before the pool, a long knife in each hand, his face unfolded and hideous, mouthparts pulsating. "Your blood will feed my god," Cain said. "You think you can kill me with a gun? Your flesh will quicken–"

Sanford shot the priest in the center of his hideous face, and Cain fell backward, into the pool.

Diana cheered, and then focused on her own problems, notably the cultists spreading out to try to flank them. One was a woman, her pretty face twisted in a snarl, and Diana thought, *I sold you a cloche hat two months ago, didn't I?* and then shot her in the chest. Abel sank his axe into the neck of another, and while he tried to wrench it loose, Diana finished the job with another shot to the comet's chest.

She looked around, breathing hard, streaked with sweat, thrumming with fear and exhilaration. Were all the comets dead? Ruby had dispatched the one closing in on her by the wall. Diana quickly counted the corpses she could see, and added one for Cain in the water. That was seven, and there were only seven–

No, there were seven chanting by the *pool* – plus Berglund, watching over Abel. There was still one cultist unaccounted for.

Diana turned in time to see the last cultist rush from the deepest shadows in the cavern, where he'd been waiting for his moment. It was Altman's comet, and he held a strangely curved blade in his hand. He rushed straight for Sanford, ready to plunge the knife into his back–

Altman jerked back, struck by gunfire in the chest. Sanford spun around, narrowed his eyes, and drew his own gun, but didn't have time to fire before Ruby aimed her pistol a second time, putting a hole in the center of Altman's face and sending him to the cavern floor. The thief walked across the chamber and stood beside Sanford, who looked at her for a moment, and then gave a slow nod. "Consider us even," he said.

Ruby rolled her eyes. "I stole from you, but then I saved your life. Isn't life worth more than property?"

"It depends on the property," Sanford began, and then Cain *leapt* from the pool, like a flying fish, and landed with a crouch on the cavern floor.

His body had changed, transformed perhaps by his proximity to the god in the water. His shoulders were twisted, his arms elongated and jointless, and tendrils as thick as fingers extended from the maw in his monstrous face. Diana choked back her scream, but she couldn't hold back a whimper, and her legs threatened to fold up underneath her. Cain rose up behind Sanford, a foot taller than before, torchlight shining off the viscous ooze that dripped along his extremities. The amulet glittered on the monster's chest.

"Meat," Cain said, voice slushy and broken. "You are all meat for our god." He seized Sanford by the shoulders and lowered his mouth toward the man's head.

Ruby stepped behind Cain, but she didn't shoot him, or club him, or anything of the sort. Instead, she unclasped the necklace that held the amulet, quick as a pickpocket, and spun away, taking the amulet with her. Cain roared, turned, and chased after her – but he moved more slowly, lurching now, as if his altered form suddenly pained him.

"Kill it!" Ruby shouted, dodging away from one of the priest's lashing tentacle-arms.

Without the amulet, Cain was vulnerable… but still formidable. Diana tried to shoot him, but Abel was in the way, stepping forward with the axe.

"Cain!" he shouted. "I was your beginning, and I will be your end!"

Cain hesitated, and then dodged, avoiding the axe blow. One tentacular arm slapped the axe away, and another lashed out, wrapping around Abel's neck like a hangman's noose. The priest got behind Abel and pulled him close in a bear hug. Cain backed up against the wall, holding Abel in front of him like a human shield.

"Drop your weapons," the priest said as Ruby, Diana,

and Sanford slowly approached him. "Or I'll feast on this pathetic human's–"

"Tedious," Sanford said, and fired three times in rapid succession.

CHAPTER TWENTY-THREE
Ebbs and Flows

"No!" Diana screamed, but it was too late – one of Sanford's bullets buried itself in Abel's shoulder, a second took off his ear in passing as it slammed into Cain's face, and another tore through the side of Abel's neck before striking Cain in the throat. Blood gushed from both of them, spraying across the chamber, and Cain slowly slid down the wall, monstrous arms now limp. Two of Sanford's bullets had struck the priest, either one of them mortal wounds for a normal man, and without the miraculous healing powers of the amulet, it didn't look like Cain was going to get up again.

Abel fell to the floor, clutching at his neck and gagging. Ruby stared in horror, while Sanford just walked over to the pool.

Diana darted to Ruby, jerking the amulet out of her hands, and then sprinted to Abel. She pressed the medallion against the wound, closing her eyes, wishing, hoping, and praying almost incoherently. "Please, please, please," she said. She didn't like to think about what she was praying *to*.

A moment later Ruby was kneeling at her side, with the jar that had once held a piece of Asterias. "I got sea water, from the pool," she explained, and poured the water over the wound, then went back to get more. The brine made an immediate difference, though: the wound stopped pumping blood and began to crust over before Diana's eyes.

Abel squeezed his eyes shut, moaning "No, no, no." He thrashed around, and she had to press her body against his to hold him still and keep the amulet in place. She had no doubt he was beset by horrible visions… but the amulet was saving his life, and though the power was born of a foul source, Diana didn't care. She wanted him to live; she *needed* him to live. After everything she'd gone through, everything she'd lost or given up already in her life, she couldn't lose more. They had become siblings in the struggle, and if she could save her brother's life, she would, no matter what the cost. Besides, he'd worn the amulet for months. If it had poisoned him, he was already poisoned.

Ruby ferried over a few more jars full of salt water, and the scab fell away, leaving an ugly scar on Abel's throat. His shoulder and ear stopped bleeding, too, and the latter even began to grow back, though the flesh had a strange and nacreous luster. Diana took the amulet away, watching to make sure Abel would keep breathing without it. He did, though he didn't regain consciousness. Diana was envious. She wanted sleep, too.

She looked up at Ruby. "Are there still shells for that shotgun?"

Ruby nodded. "In my pocket. I didn't have time to reload, is all."

"Do so now, please."

Ruby went to pick up the gun.

Sanford turned from his place by the pool. "Ah, you used the amulet to save his life, did you?"

"You *shot* him," Diana snarled, rising. "He was your ally, and you *shot* him!"

"I shot Cain," Sanford replied mildly. "Abel was simply in the way. Anyway, no harm done – he's healed now." He glanced at Ruby. "What do you plan to do with the shotgun? I don't think it will be sufficient to kill Asterias. You should come look into the pool. It's really remarkable, how much it's already grown."

Diana stood and took the shotgun from Ruby.

Sanford raised his eyebrows. "Is that meant for me? Our alliance has come to an end? Dear me. Are you not as loyal to the Lodge as you led me to believe, Seeker?"

"I'm not going to shoot you," Diana said. "I'm not *like* you." She tossed the amulet onto the ground a few feet away from her, pointed the shotgun at it, and fired. The amulet shattered, bits of stone and metal flying, destroyed beyond any hope of piecing together or repair.

Sanford groaned. "I almost wish you'd shot at me instead. I might have survived. That amulet could have done a lot of good in the world, you know, Miss Stanley."

"It could have done a great deal more evil." She put the shotgun down on the cave floor, happy the necessity for violence had passed. If she never touched another firearm, it would be too soon. Her spirits had lifted considerably now that the unholy symbol and source of the comets was reduced to fragments. They were nearly finished here. "Now the only thing left to do is destroy Asterias and get rid of the comets."

"They're gone," Abel murmured, opening his eyes. Diana rushed to him, cradling his head in her lap. "I can't feel any of them anymore. None of the ones that came from me, that is, from Cain, anyway. I don't know about the rest."

"Interesting." Sanford stroked his chin. Diana suddenly noticed that he was the only one of them who wasn't covered in blood – how had he managed that? "But not without precedent," he went on. "Sometimes when an artifact of such power is destroyed, its effects immediately cease. Every comet was made from the touch of that medallion, and now that it's been destroyed… we'll have to see what awaits us in Arkham, but perhaps I won't have as much cleanup to do as I thought."

"What do we do about… that?" Ruby stood by the pool, looking down into the water.

Abel struggled upright, waving off Diana's attempts to restrain him. "I want to see," he said.

Abel gazed down into the water, where parts of a dead cultist still floated. Asterias was much larger now, having fed on the blood of that corpse – and stripped some of its flesh, too, by the look of things. The Ravening Deep was only as wide across as a manhole cover, though, and its mouth was a pitiful thing, a writhing slit with small tendrils reaching out ineffectually, not the horrible abyss of hunger from Abel's visions.

The Ravening Deep's dozens of eyes fixed on Abel, boring into him, and the visions that filled his mind when the amulet touched the wound on his neck suddenly flared back, vivid: Abel wearing a crown of coral and pearls, standing on the prow of a giant ship, riding a tidal wave toward a shining terrestrial city. Abel shrugging off bullets and striding forward, laughing, a trident in hand, slashing at a crowd of policemen. Abel standing over a dozen humans, Carl Sanford among them, all on their knees, wearing iron collars and chains, awaiting his judgment–

Abel spat into the pool. "No, thank you." He looked at Diana, who was spattered with blood, but serene, and at Ruby, who had regained some of her impish insouciance in victory, and finally at Sanford, who mostly looked bored. "How do we kill this thing? Drain the pool and set it on fire? There's gasoline on the boat. I wish we had white phosphorous grenades like the Brits used in the Great War. I've heard those will burn even under water."

"Alas, we possess nothing so exotic… but we do have dynamite." Sanford smiled.

Abel blinked. "That should do it."

They trudged back to the surface together, none eager to remain below with Asterias, and Abel noticed that he was the most sprightly of the bunch – the healing effects of the amulet were miraculous, even if it was the miracle of an evil god. He wondered if he would ever shake off the lingering effects of his relationship with the Ravening Deep and his long exposure to its holy relic. When he saw this horrible temple again in his dreams, which seemed inevitable, he would always wonder if it was just the torment of memory, or a message from the god he'd betrayed.

Ruby made her way across to Sanford's boat and fetched the munitions, and then they all went down again.

They found Asterias moving, albeit slowly. The small

god had crawled out of the pool onto the stone, and was dragging itself along with its seven limbs, toward the stairs, leaving trails of ichor behind. Abel shuddered. He'd known the Ravening Deep was capable of locomotion, but seeing it was something else.

"Did you think we'd abandoned you?" Ruby said. "Don't worry. We were just fetching your going-away present." She glanced around. "So, who knows how to use this stuff?"

"I have some experience." Sanford took the satchel from Ruby and removed a few sticks of dynamite and a spool of fuse wire. He made a wide berth around the creature on the chamber floor, still pathetically trying to reach freedom, and set the dynamite against the walls, connecting their fuses together. Then he said, "Wish me luck," and darted forward.

Sanford jammed one cylinder into the center of the Ravening Deep's maw, like an oversized candle in a grotesque birthday cake. A tendril whipped around his wrist, and he hissed, jerking away. "That's the only taste of me you'll get," he said. "You couldn't ask for a better last meal."

Sanford unspooled the fuse wire, backing toward the stairs, and the others went up with him as he unrolled the wire, until they'd made it about halfway to the top. He gave a decisive nod, then cut the wire free from the spool and withdrew a box of matches from inside his suit coat.

"You can't just conjure fire by force of will?" Ruby asked.

"Seems a waste of energy when we have matches." Sanford struck a light and touched it to the fuse, which fizzed and sparkled and sent fire racing away down the stairs. "We should go, *now*."

They raced up the stairs, miraculously without anyone

losing their footing and falling to the chamber below. They reached the small cave at the top, and then hurried down the face of the tower, Ruby and Sanford in the lead, both adept at climbing. Abel was less adroit, but still, the descent was much easier than the ascent had been – he could see now, for one thing, and he wasn't being dragged across sharp stones. Abel reached the plateau at the bottom and helped Diana down, and then they all clambered and leapt back to Sanford's boat, which was one of the nicest craft Abel had ever seen.

"You traveled here in style," he said to Diana as they leaned together in the back seat. "I came tied up in the hold of a fishing boat."

"I think I want to stay off the water entirely for a while," Diana murmured.

"I can see the appeal of a more landlocked life myself," Abel said.

Sanford turned on the boat and guided it away from the temple, until they reached what he deemed a safe distance. Then they watched the spire.

"The temple is not exploding," Ruby said. "Are you sure you know how to use dynamite?"

"I wanted to give us ample time to reach safety," Sanford said, and then there was a deep rumble, and smoke and stones burst forth from the tower like a volcanic eruption. A wave struck the *Silver Key*, rocking the vessel hard, and then the stone spire slowly collapsed into the water. After a few moments, nothing was left of the tower and the temple but a small spur of coral and stone that barely broke the surface.

Abel groaned, slumping against the side of the boat,

and clutched his head. Diana rushed to him, touching his shoulders. "What is it? Are you all right?" Abel only shook his head and groaned. Tears streamed from the corners of his eyes.

"Those touched by such powers naturally feel something when those powers die," Sanford said, as if passing a comment about the weather.

"So Asterias is really gone?" Ruby said.

"It seems," Sanford began, but then Abel lowered his hands and interrupted him.

"I... don't think so," Abel said. "Or, not entirely. When the dynamite exploded, there was this wave of... *red* in my mind. Asterias is hurt, it's diminished, but I think there are still a few scraps of living flesh down there."

Sanford sniffed. "Even if that's true, those scraps are buried by a ton of rock. No one can reach them, the temple is gone, and the amulet was destroyed. If Asterias can't find acolytes, and it can't feed, it doesn't pose much of a threat. Let it languish in eternal hunger and darkness." Sanford pushed a lever, and the boat began to motor away from the smoking water. "Well done, all of you. But Miss Stanley, I'm afraid with everything that's happened, with your insubordination and your secret-keeping, I have no choice but to strip you of your rank and expel you from the Silver Twilight Lodge."

"You've saved me the trouble of resigning," Diana said.

Two weeks later, Ruby sat in a back booth at one of the finest French restaurants in Arkham, which meant it was as good as a mediocre place in Boston. The restaurant sold champagne, at least – you just had to ask for "something sparkling" – so she was content. Sanford arrived, a little late, because of course he did; every play he made was a power play.

"You look lovely, my dear," he said a few moments later, sipping from his glass.

She raised her own in an ironic toast. "You look sleek and well fed and smug, yourself. Why did you want to meet me?"

"Various reasons. I thought you might like to know that, as far as I can determine, all of the comets are dead."

"I read about the rash of mysterious deaths in the *Arkham Advertiser*. Medical experts are baffled, simultaneous heart failure, tainted caviar, mysterious mold, unknown identical siblings... it all sounded a bit far-fetched, if you ask me. Yellow journalism at its worst."

"The sheriff and the chief of police are both accustomed to unusual happenings, though these were more unusual than most. No one is dying anymore, though, and there's no evidence of foul play or obvious connections among the victims, so." Sanford shrugged. "This will be a nine days' wonder, marveled over and then forgotten. Such is the way of the world." He cocked his head. "How are Abel and Diana getting on?"

"I don't think they'd want you to know details." Ruby had received a letter from Diana the day before. She and Abel were going to travel together for a while, maybe find one of those towns where rich people liked to vacation, so she could set up a new shop – someplace far from the sea. "Diana did ask me to pass on her thanks for your generosity, though. You paid quite a bit more for her shop than it was worth."

He nodded. "I can be generous when it's called for. And I prefer them out of my city. Those two are troublemakers, and they know too many of my secrets."

"I'm surprised you didn't have them killed. I didn't take you for the sentimental type."

Sanford sipped his champagne. "I am not sentimental. Leaving them alive is just good business. If you murder people who save your life, word could get around, and then other people might be reluctant to save your life in the future. Tell me – was Diana working against the Lodge all along, or was she really just swept up in that business with the Ravening Deep, like she claimed?"

"I have no idea," Ruby tilted her glass back and forth, watching the liquid slosh. She wasn't about to share confidences with this man, especially about Diana and Abel. She knew well that Sanford could hold grudges, and hold them well. "Also, I'm bored, because we aren't talking about me. Why did you *really* want to meet? So far everything you've said could have fit on a postcard."

He ran his fingertip around the rim of the champagne glass. "I told you we're even. You saved my life, so your past transgressions against me are forgiven."

"I got the short end of that deal, but sure."

"I worry that you'll be tempted to transgress against me in the *future*, however," he said. "I don't believe your experiences have changed you in any fundamental way – you are, in certain respects, unchangeable. I respect that. I may even be similar. You have an even more intimate knowledge of the Lodge and my own potential weaknesses than before, and you may want to exploit them."

"I get it – if I steal from you again, you try to kill me again. I know what a clean slate means. I didn't expect permanent immunity."

"You misunderstand. I think the best way to make sure we're never at odds again is to... continue our alliance. You are skilled, Miss Standish. You can acquire valuable items discreetly and with minimal bloodshed. I could use someone with your abilities."

"You want to hire me? To steal what?" She'd anticipated a lot of ways this night could go, but a job offer hadn't featured in any of her speculations.

"Nothing, right now. What I propose is to keep you on retainer, the same way I do with my attorneys. I will pay you monthly, and in exchange, you will make yourself available to me as needed." He leaned forward. "And just like those attorneys I keep on retainer, you will be forbidden to work *against* me."

Ruby thought about it. "I don't much like being on a leash, Sanford."

"It would be a long leash, and it would furthermore be a leash made of gold. I don't anticipate calling on your services more than once or twice a year. We can craft a contract that addresses your concerns. I am a reasonable man. What do you say?"

Ruby knew Diana would disapprove. Working for Sanford meant furthering his interests and those of the Silver Twilight Lodge. But it would be *much* better to have him as a friend than an enemy, wouldn't it? Besides, a girl had to eat, and dance, and otherwise keep herself entertained.

Ruby nodded. "All right. Assuming we can work out the details, I'm game."

"Let's drink to our partnership." Sanford raised his glass, eyes twinkling. He could be almost charming when he bothered to make the effort. Ruby just had to remember he was actually as sentimental as a crocodile.

After she sipped, she said, "Does this mean I get to be a Keeper of the Crimson Veil or a Master of the Final Abyss or something?"

"We'll have to come up with a special title just for you," Sanford said. "I'm glad Cain never managed to duplicate you. You're much better as one-of-a-kind."

"I'm happy there's only one of you, too, old man."

Carl Sanford relaxed in the red leather armchair in his innermost office, safe in the comfort of the Silver Twilight Lodge. His warden had just briefed him on the improvements made to security. They wouldn't suffer from a breach like Cain's again.

He flipped through his membership roster, noting the rows of red slashes. Cain had coopted nearly fifty citizens of Arkham in all, and far too many of them had been connected to the Lodge in one way or another. Sanford had lost a great many Initiates, and a few Seekers, but no one of higher ranks, apart from poor Altman. Any greater adept who'd allowed themselves to be captured and killed by Cain's cult would have been stricken from the rolls retroactively anyway, for incompetence.

The damage to the Lodge had mostly been cosmetic, with some regrettable exceptions. His vault had been breached, and some of the precious objects inside irreparably damaged. The shoggoth had managed to kill a number of invading cultists, but had been almost destroyed itself in the process; the comets had simply torn it to pieces. The creature would take a while to regenerate enough to be of use again. In all, Cain's pride had cost Sanford a great deal in terms of people and materiel, but at least the attack had revealed weaknesses that could now be fortified. The Lodge would recover.

Sanford hadn't emerged from the ordeal entirely empty-handed. He'd given Diana and Abel money and encouraged them to move away for a good reason: as the last surviving priest of Asterias, Abel still had a connection to the creature… and if he'd stayed in Arkham, he might have realized that part of the Ravening Deep had returned to shore with them.

While Ruby and Diana were fussing over Abel's gunshot wounds, Sanford had quietly sliced off a tip of one of the god's arms and wrapped the fragment in a handkerchief. Abel had naturally sensed the tiny piece of god-flesh, but he'd assumed he was feeling the fragments in the ruins of the temple at first, and later that he was suffering residual effects from the violence of his final visions when Diana healed him with the amulet. Sanford made a point of putting physical space between himself and Abel as soon as he reached the shore, racing off to check on the state of the Lodge, and he'd gotten away with the gambit.

Now Sanford opened his desk and removed a small crystal bottle, its stopper sealed with red wax. A thumb-sized piece of pebbled flesh floated inside. A single eye blinked at him.

"You're never going to live again, not properly," Sanford said. "But I can still put you to work." He put the fragment of Asterias close to his lips and whispered, "I am *your* god, now." He pocketed the vial, then left his office, and took one of his personal secret passages into the basement. He turned down corridors that smelled strongly of disinfectant – they'd had to clean up a lot of corpses, and his anatomists were exploring the remains of the comets even now.

Sanford made his way to a corridor marked with eye-twisting sigils in red and yellow, until he stood before a door festooned with chains. "Hello, scholar," he said. "I've come with a query." He held up the vial. "How would I go about using a small piece of *this* to create an amulet capable of healing, regeneration... and duplication?"

The scholar from Yith stirred inside the cell, chains rattling. "That... is an interesting question. I believe I could devise a successful process." The scholar paused. "I do not, however, see why I should help you, when you keep me prisoner here."

The magus smiled. This part was easy. This was just *negotiating*, and no one could negotiate better than Carl Sanford. "Perhaps you'd like a few books to help you pass the time?"

ACKNOWLEDGMENTS

Writing is a mostly solitary endeavor, but even so, it takes a lot of help to make a book. I am grateful to my spouse Heather and our kid (no, our teenager!) River for making my home life so wonderful, and also for my other nearest and dearests, Aislinn, Amanda, Emily, Katrina, and Sarah, for their support and kindness, and the fact that they always listen, even when I mostly want to talk about horrible starfish monsters. Thanks also to my friend and fellow writer Molly Tanzer for a thousand conversations about horror and the Mythos over the years. I appreciate the good people at Aconyte, especially my editor Charlotte Llewelyn-Wells, for letting me do such weird things, and also the *Arkham Horror* team for inviting me to play in their sandbox, and to my agent Ginger Clark for handling all the business stuff so I can focus on, well, horrible starfish monsters.

And thanks to you, dear readers, for coming along with me to Arkham! I hope we can visit again sometime.

ABOUT THE AUTHOR

TIM PRATT is a Hugo Award-winning SF and fantasy author, and finalist for the World Fantasy, Sturgeon, Stoker, Mythopoeic, and Nebula Awards, among others. He is the author of over twenty novels, and scores of short stories. Since 2001 he has worked for *Locus*, the magazine of the science fiction and fantasy field, where he currently serves as senior editor.

timpratt.org
twitter.com/timpratt